## PRAISE FOR

"A tense, taut thrill ride through a gritty murder case where guilt and innocence are much more complicated than they seem. Dharma Kelleher is a top-notch storyteller."

KRISTEN LEPIONKA, AUTHOR OF THE ROXANE WEARY MYSTERY SERIES

"Dharma Kelleher delivers bad-ass blue collar crime fiction with a snappy sense of humor and a lot of heart."

THOMAS PLUCK, AUTHOR OF THE JAY DESMARTEAUX THRILLER SERIES

"Dharma Kelleher takes snarky badassery to a whole new level."

TRACY CLARK, AUTHOR OF THE HARRIET FOSTER MYSTERY SERIES

# A CONSPIRACY OF RAVENS

# A CONSPIRACY OF RAVENS

AN AVERY BYRNE THRILLER

DHARMA KELLEHER

A CONSPIRACY OF RAVENS:

AN AVERY BYRNE CRIME THRILLER



Published by Dark Pariah Press, Phoenix, Arizona.

Cover design: Dharma Kelleher



Ebook ISBN: 978-1-952128-21-9

Paperback ISBN: 978-1-952128-22-6

Hardcover ISBN: 978-1-952128-23-3

*To my wife, Eileen*
*who has given me the greatest adventure of my life.*

# CHAPTER 1
# SECOND CHANCES

SAM FERGUSON GLANCED at her partner, Julio Cuervo. She knew what was coming. And for the first time since being hired by Mr. Bramwell, it bothered her.

Still, she couldn't let on. There was no room in the Desert Mafia for weakness.

"Look, you guys," Whitmore pleaded as they hustled him down the hallway. The muffled bass beat from Club Elektronik, the dance club downstairs, vibrated through the floor. "You don't have to do this. Just take the money and say you couldn't find me. Mr. Bramwell doesn't need to know."

"You believe this guy, Cuervo?" Sam snickered, hoping to hide her mixed feelings. "First, he skims forty large from the boss. Follows that up by making a deal with the cops. Now he's offering us a bribe."

"No! I didn't tell the cops nothing. I swear."

Cuervo smacked the side of the whining man's head. "You think we're stupid? We know they picked you up while making your protection rounds. But did they charge you with anything? No. They let you go. Tells me you cut a deal."

"It's a setup. They're pressuring me to talk by making it look like I already did when I didn't."

"Tell that to the boss." Sam opened the heavy wooden door to the office.

Theodore Bramwell was a squat man wearing a bespoke double-breasted suit with gold-plated buttons. He sat behind a hardwood desk that looked easily a century old. Above him was mounted a Rembrandt painting of a ship in a storm. Rumor was that Bramwell had stolen it from a gallery up in Boston thirty years earlier.

Next to the painting was an autographed photograph of the former president. Bramwell idolized the corrupt politician so much, it made Sam ill every time she stepped into the office and saw the photo.

"Mr. Whitmore." Bramwell's tone was warm and consoling as he put a hand on the other man's shoulder, but his eyes held an arctic chill. He stood as they approached the desk.

"I was concerned for your safety when you didn't show up at your usual time. Little bird says you ran into a little trouble with the police."

"I didn't tell them anything, Mr. Bramwell. I promise. I'd never betray you. You know that."

Cuervo tossed a small canvas bag on the desk. "Found him at his apartment with this and a couple of packed suitcases. Looks to be about forty-two thousand dollars and change. Someone's been skimming."

"That's a lie. I won it in Laughlin two weeks ago. I swear to God."

"Sit," Bramwell commanded. "Let us discuss this situation like gentlemen."

Sam and Cuervo stood nearby, waiting. She didn't want to be here for this.

Since she'd started dating Avery six months earlier, Sam had felt something she hadn't in a long time—hope. Hope for a better life. Hope to become a better person. Hope for a future that didn't involve violence and the ever-looming threat of prison.

Whitmore sat hunched in the guest chair like a whipped dog. "I haven't been skimming, Mr. Bramwell. Honest. I'd never double-cross you. Not in a million years."

"Of course not." Bramwell sat on the corner of his desk, arms folded, staring down at the man. "But the police did arrest you, did they not?"

"Yes, sir."

"And where did this occur?"

"Bennett's Liquors, McDowell and Third Street."

"I see. And how did they catch you?"

"The old man's kid was on the phone when I walked in for my usual pickup. Hung up right away, looking smug. Must've called 9-1-1 when I pulled up. Always gave me queer looks whenever I saw him. Cops blocked me in just as I was leaving."

"That's very helpful, Mr. Whitmore. What's this kid's name?"

"Don't remember. Darnell or Dante or something like that. He and I never really talked, you know?"

"It's Corey," Cuervo offered. "Corey Bennett."

"Corey Bennett. Yes, we might have to chat with Mr. Bennett and his son, Corey. But first, I want to know more about what happened after you were arrested. Did you call Ms. Olsen, my attorney?"

"Uh, no."

"Why not? Her services are at the disposal of all of my employees. And at no cost to you. Not many jobs offer such a perk."

"I… I didn't want to trouble her. Or you," Whitmore sputtered. "I know she don't work for free. Plus, I was afraid calling her might make me look guilty."

"Very considerate of you. You're correct. She charges a

considerable amount for her services in situations such as this. But I assure you, it is small change compared to the cost of putting the future of the organization in peril. I've worked hard to provide solid employment for so many individuals, such as yourself. You would hate to see that go away, would you not?"

"Uh, yeah. I… I'll keep that in mind for the future."

"Excellent. So, who in the police station questioned you?"

"Two men. One white, one Hispanic. I'm trying to remember their names."

"Such a momentous experience, and you can't remember their names? Mr. Whitmore. Benny. Do try to remember their names. Try as if your very life depends on it."

Bramwell's tone shifted from friendly to hostile. The temperature in the room dropped ten degrees. Even the rhythmic beat from the nightclub below went deathly quiet.

"Brooks," Whitmore managed to say. "And… and Dom… Dom… Dominguez. That's it. Detectives Brooks and Dominguez. Don't think they gave me their first names, but they're from the Organized Crime Bureau. But like I said, I kept my mouth shut. I ain't no a rat."

"Of course not. And I want to believe you. But Detective Martin Brooks is an associate of mine. We go way back. And he says you were quite loquacious."

Whitmore's gasp was so intense that Sam felt it in her chest. The man's eyes widened in horror. "No, no, I just made up lies to throw them off the scent."

"Mr. Whitmore, you know me for an understanding man. I believe in giving people second chances." He walked over to Sam and cupped her cheek.

His smile reminded her of the Grinch. A thrill of fear and uncertainty raced up her spine. What was he going to do?

"Before Miss Ferguson came to work for me, she started a fight in this very club . Put one of my bouncers in the hospital. But did I press charges? No, I saw potential in her. A fire all too rare for members of her fair sex. And now she is one of my most trusted employees."

Sam responded with an appreciative smile. *Does he know I want out? Is this one of his games? Is he testing me?*

"Thank you, Mr. Bramwell," Whitmore said. "You won't regret giving me a second chance. I promise you."

Whitmore's blustering was rattling Sam's nerves. She knew it was bullshit. And Bramwell clearly knew it was bullshit. This was just foreplay. A cat toying with its prey before the inevitable.

"Of course, Mr. Whitmore. I don't like to see potential wasted. I am a businessman, after all. Second chances are an investment."

"Thank you, thank you, thank you."

"Although..." The word hung in the air like the countdown to an explosion. The music in the club below resumed. "As I recall, I gave you a second chance not two years ago. Did I not?"

"What?"

"You forced yourself onto one of my girls."

Again, Whitmore sputtered, his mind no doubt scrambling for excuses. "But... but she was just a whore."

"Indeed, she was, Mr. Whitmore. She was my whore. And you did not pay for the privilege. I didn't say anything to you then because I believed you had potential. I had invested in you. But one of the unfortunate aspects of business is that not all investments yield a positive return. And when that happens..."

"No, no, no."

"You did not pay then. But you will pay now. Because while I do indeed believe in second chances, I do not believe in third chances. And here you sit, having compromised my business, putting all of our futures in jeopardy."

He picked up the bag of cash and held it in Whitmore's face.

"And all this time, you've been stealing from me. Stealing! You had your bags all packed. Ready to run. Third chance, fourth chance, fifth chance! Wasted. I detest waste, Mr. Whitmore."

With the fluidity of a cat, he whipped out the Walther P38 Sam knew he usually kept in his desk drawer.

"Please no, Mr. Bram—"

Sam's ears rang from the thunder of the gunshot. Whitmore collapsed onto the floor, blood pooling from the gaping hole in the back of his head where the bullet had exited before embedding itself in the hardwood floor.

She watched Bramwell punch the combination into his large wall safe and toss in the bag of money. From where she stood, she could see dozens of kilos of smack. Something big was in the works. The devil on her shoulder began whispering in her ear.

Bramwell closed the safe and faced Sam and Cuervo. "I have guests coming from Las Vegas tomorrow. An enormous business opportunity. That means no more disruptions like this. Are we clear?"

"Yes, sir," Sam and Cuervo replied in unison.

"And, Cuervo, you will entertain Alma while I'm meeting with my guests tomorrow evening."

"Yes, sir."

"Excellent. Now clean up this mess. I don't want my office looking like a slaughterhouse." Bramwell spat at Whitmore's body with a look of disgust.

# CHAPTER 2
# LURKERS IN THE LOT

IT WAS a quarter after nine in the evening when Avery Byrne set the alarm at the Seoul Fire tattoo studio and stepped out the back door into the dark parking lot alone.

Normally, she and at least one of the other tattoo artists would walk out together. But Frisco was visiting family in Colorado. Butcher had finished his last client at eight. And Bobby Jeong, her foster dad and the owner of the shop, had left early to go on a date.

Avery's 1959 black Cadillac Coupe DeVille, which she'd nicknamed the Gothmobile, sat under the glow of a security light at the far end of the lot. Between her and the car stood two boys in their late teens, smoking and leaning against the brick wall that separated the lot from the one next door.

Avery tensed.

Occasionally, homeless people hung out there. She never minded them, since she'd been homeless herself when she was a teenager.

But these two weren't homeless. More like high school athletes, judging by their physiques.

She kept them in her peripheral vision as she strolled toward her car, willing herself to be invisible. But the taller of the two guys stepped into her path.

"Check you out, Elvira. Don't you know Halloween's still six months away?"

"Pardon me." She tried to maneuver around him, but his buddy blocked her way.

"What's the rush, honeybunch? Don't ya wanna party with us? Always wanted to do it with a freaky chick."

She glared at him, the full force of her will in her gaze. "Move out of my way, please."

"Aw, don't be a bitch. I got some E. We could have a real good time." The tall one cupped her crotch with one hand and squeezed her left breast with the other.

A mixture of fury and panic exploded in her. She pushed him away and bared her teeth.

She'd been born without lateral incisors, which emphasized her canines and gave her glower a vampiric look.

"Leave me the fuck alone!" she hissed.

To her surprise and relief, they backed off. "Fine. Jesus Christ. Probably all crudded up with the herp or some freaky shit."

She dove into her car, locked the door, and roared out of the parking lot.

Avery was still shaking when she arrived home and tried inserting her key into the dead bolt. But it wouldn't fit.

"Dammit, get in there."

By the time she realized she was using the wrong key, she was in tears and shaking. The door opened.

Sam stood there, a concerned look on her face. "Oh, my god! Avery? What's wrong, babe?"

Avery tried to speak, but emotion choked off her words. Before she knew it, she was sitting on their couch. Sam's arm around her, comforting her.

"Sweetie, whatever's wrong, just tell me. I'll fix it." Sam handed her a box of tissues.

"I…" Avery dabbed at her face and took a deep breath. Air filled her body. Energy flowed, allowing her to reclaim her power. "I was locking up. Alone."

"Okay."

"Two guys were hanging out in the parking lot. I…" Avery's body shuddered as old traumas buffeted her spirit. "They started saying the usual shit. I tried to ignore them…"

"Did they hurt you?"

"No," She took another long breath, using the relaxation techniques Bobby J. had taught her. "They blocked me from getting to my car. One of them put his hands on me."

"Fucking assholes. They clock you as trans?"

"No. Least, I don't think so. Just a couple of good ol' boys thinking they could have a little fun with the goth chick. It triggered some old shit from when I was on the streets. I pushed past them and got the hell out of there before anything happened."She swallowed hard. "Ran a red light at Camelback and Nineteenth Avenue. Probably gonna get a ticket."

"Important thing's you're safe, babe. And if the City of Phoenix sends you a red-light-camera love letter, give it to me. I know a guy who can take care of it."

"Really? How?"

Sam shrugged and hugged her. "Friend of a friend. That kinda thing. I got your back, girl. So sorry that happened. It must've been scary for you."

"Not so much scared as pissed off." It was partly true. "Just so sick of living in a city full of small-minded dickwads. So what if I'm trans or into gothabilly? I'm not hurting anyone. One of these days I'm gonna say 'fuck it' and move some place more progressive, like San Francisco or Seattle." She pulled a compact mirror out of her purse. "Shit, my makeup looks a mess."

"Yeah, but even with streaked eyeliner, you look fucking hot." Sam kissed her cheek.

"Thanks, I think." Avery pressed her forehead against Sam's and kissed her on the lips. "Why do you smell like bleach?"

"Uh, had to clean up a mess at work. I can take a shower now if you want."

"What kind of mess? I thought you worked as a bouncer."

A shadow cross Sam's face, but she didn't answer.

"Sam, what's wrong?"

"It was no big deal. Just a crazy day at work."

"You wanna talk about it?"

"No. It's boring. Fight broke out around six o'clock. There was some blood. You don't want to hear about it."

"You never want to talk about your work. I don't even know *where* you work other than some downtown club. I shared about my day. Now it's your turn. Spill."

"Technically, I'm not a bouncer. I work security. Most of the time, I'm just standing around, trying to look menacing. If you'd like to see where I work, I can take you to the club tomorrow night. Introduce you to one of my coworkers. In the meantime, I just want to fuck your brains out."

They kissed some more. The anger and fear began blowing away like the seeds of a dandelion. Avery had never been in love until she fell for Sam. She was a woman of mystery. Of secrets. But also of tenderness and passion.

Everything had happened so fast. One minute, Avery was inking a new tat on this sexy woman, the next, Sam was asking her out. Two weeks later, Sam invited her to move in.

Granted, Avery had been complaining that her lease was up, and her landlord was jacking up her rent by thirty percent. Jokes about U-Hauls and second dates ensued.

But in the six months they'd been together, Avery had no regrets.

Sam didn't care that Avery was transgender or that she dressed like a cross between a vampire and a '50s housewife. Sam treated her with respect, kindness, and love. Real love. It was something Avery had never dared to hope for until it happened.

"You make me want to be a better person, you know that?" Sam whispered.

"A better person? What's wrong with the person you are?"

"You're sick of living in this close-minded town. I'm sick of working security. Maybe we both need a new start."

"Wouldn't that be nice?"

Sam stood up and pulled on Avery's arm. "Come on. Let's have some fun."

Avery followed her into the bedroom.

# CHAPTER 3
# MORNING REVELATIONS

THE NEXT MORNING, Bobby Jeong's Toyota was already in the lot when Avery pulled in. No sign of the guys who'd harassed her the night before. But the memory of the guy's hands grabbing her and the threat of violence they'd implied were still palpable.

"Morning, Appa," she said, using the Korean word for father, something she had started calling him a year after he'd become her foster father.

Bobby was in his midfifties and stocky, standing four inches shorter than her. His arms bore two sleeves of ink that were a mix of traditional Korean art and contemporary design. A Buddha sat serenely on one arm against a background of stylized lotus flowers. Yobi, an anime five-tailed fox, lay curled at the Buddha's feet.

On the other arm, Princess Leia held a blaster with the word *Rebel* underneath.

Bobby kissed her on the cheek when she set her wicker purse on the cabinet of her workstation. "Good morning, kiddo."

Six years earlier, Avery had been a sixteen-year-old living on the streets of downtown Phoenix after her father kicked her out of the house for being transgender. To survive, she had panhandled, created homemade tattoos for friends, and when necessary, committed the occasional burglary. When desperate, she'd resorted to sex work but hated it with a passion.

She had broken into Bobby J.'s old studio, Artoo Tattoo, looking for things to pawn, when he caught her. But rather than turn her in to the cops, he'd offered her a place to live and later became her foster father.

"How was your date?" she asked.

He shrugged. "Dana's nice, but she's an investment banker. Very straitlaced. Maybe too straitlaced to date a Star Wars–obsessed tattoo artist like me."

"And she's not Melissa," Avery said, filling in what she suspected he was feeling.

"No, she's not. I'm trying hard not to compare. No one can replace Melissa. But still…"

"You know, a lot of corporate business types are getting tattoos these days. And you are an entrepreneur. Maybe there's hope yet."

"Perhaps. The litmus test will be when she sees my action figure collection."

Avery chuckled. "Sounds like a high bar."

"How did it go last night, closing up by yourself?"

"Okay, I guess."

"Were those boys in the parking lot again?"

"You've seen them before?"

"Couple of neighborhood kids. Seemed harmless, but I shooed them out of the lot a few nights ago. I gather they were back last night. Did they bother you?"

"It was fine." She didn't want to worry him.

The concern on his face told her he knew there was more to it. "I can make sure no one closes alone anymore. I don't want anything to happen to any of you."

Butcher walked in. He was a white guy of indeterminate age. Could've been in his thirties or even late forties. He had perpetually mussed brown hair and an unreadable expression. Almost never spoke.

When Avery first met him, she'd assumed he disliked her for some reason. Frisco had assured her he was just wary of new hires. Then she wondered if he had some physical or mental impairment that prevented him from speaking.

"No," Bobby had explained. "He just doesn't have a lot to say."

"Morning, Butcher!" Avery and Bobby said.

Butcher waved in response.

"By the way, I'm cutting out early tonight myself," Avery said. "Sam's taking me to a club."

Bobby mumbled something under his breath.

"Why you don't like her, Appa? She's nice."

"Something about her. Can't put my finger on it. Just feel a disturbance in the Force when she's around."

"Okay, Obi-Kwon Kenobi, but she's my girlfriend. You'd find fault with whoever I brought home with me."

"Are you saying I'm overprotective of my only daughter?"

Avery crossed her arms and stared at him.

"Okay, maybe I've been a little over-suspicious. But that's only because I care. After all that you endured with your biological parents, you deserve a father who looks out for you. So, what club is she taking you to? The Rebel Lounge? Tailfins?"

"Not a rockabilly or goth club. The one where she works security. I think they play electronic house music."

Bobby held her gaze. "Did she tell you the name of this club, or is it still a big mystery?"

"Club Elektronik. Downtown."

Bobby's face fell. He shook his head in dismay. "I knew there was something not right about that girl."

"Why? What's wrong with where she works?"

"Do you know who owns Club Elektronik?"

Avery shrugged. "Should I?"

"Theodore Bramwell."

"The real estate mogul?"

"And head of the Desert Mafia. If it's illegal, he's involved with it—extortion, murder for hire, arson, drug trafficking. Remember when I owned Artoo Tattoo downtown? Bramwell would send his toadies around each week to collect protection money."

Avery's heart sank. He'd never told her about this. "He was extorting you? Did you call the police?"

"Wouldn't have done any good. The man's got cops in his pocket. Probably people in the county attorney's office too. One week, I was short. Real short. It was the middle of summer, and business was slow. They put me in the hospital."

Avery tried to remember. "You told Melissa and me that you surprised a burglar."

"I didn't want to worry you. But that's why I closed the old shop and opened Seoul Fire several miles away. Fortunately, Bramwell hasn't sent his guys after me here."

"But Sam's not like that, Appa. She's kind and funny and sweet. She treats me with such respect. So what if her boss is a thug? She just works security at a club he owns. It's not like she's a criminal herself."

"You sure about that?"

Avery remembered Sam saying that Avery inspired her to be a better person. Was that what she was talking about? Was Sam involved in Theodore Bramwell's criminal activities?

"All I know is that she's been nothing but nice to me. Never lost her temper. Never tried to control me. Never made me feel less than."

"Perhaps I've misjudged her," Bobby said with a shrug. "Just be careful. If she's only now telling you where she works after you've been living together for several months, what else might she be hiding?"

"Can't be anything worse than what I'd done before you caught me breaking into Artoo Tattoo." She began setting up her station for her first client.

"I am not saying the things you did back then were okay. Much less legal. But you did what you had to in order to survive and protect your friends. And now you live an honest life."

"And so does she. Working security is an honest living."

"Generally, I would say yes. But why the secrecy? What do you really know about her?"

"Maybe she didn't want to be judged for working for Bramwell. And she's the first person to love me for me, at least romantically. She doesn't care that I'm trans or that I'm into the gothabilly scene."

"My dear, if the only requirement is that they're not transphobic, that's a low bar. I dated several women before Melissa. At the time, I didn't think I was much of a catch either. I was overweight, tattooed sci-fi nerd.

"My only requirement for a girlfriend was that she like me. But after a few disastrous, short-lived romances, I realized I deserved more. I wanted a woman who was smart, who had a great sense of humor, and who could be geeky and silly like me."

"That was Melissa all right." Avery recalled the woman's ever-present smile, her nurturing personality, and her passion for anime and cosplay.

"We had twenty wonderful years together before she died. I encourage you to do the same. Don't settle for the lowest common denominator. There are plenty of kind, funny lesbians who *don't* work for violent criminals and who would love to date someone as beautiful and unique as you."

"Maybe."

"Please understand. I want nothing more than for you to be as happy as Melissa and I were."

"I am happy, Appa. Sam makes me happy."

He sighed, cupped her face in his hands, and gave her a fatherly kiss. "I hope she continues to do so, kiddo. I truly do."

## CHAPTER 4
# A FISH OUT OF WATER

AVERY STARED out the passenger window of Sam's Audi at the back entrance of Club Elektronik, the throbbing bass of a techno tune filtering through the parking lot.

She would rather have been at one of the Valley's goth or rockabilly clubs. Or at the studio, inking a biker. Even getting a root canal seemed preferable. Anywhere but here at Club Elektronik.

"Okay, I've seen where you work. We can go home now."

"I realize it's not your usual scene." Sam's strawberry-blond pixie cut fluttered in the cool air from the AC vents. "But you've been wanting to know where I work for months. And here we are. Might as well get the ten-cent tour and a free drink."

Avery didn't respond. Nor did she make any move to get out of the car.

"Come on, babe. We'll have a private table away from the crowds. Besides, I want you to meet Cuervo."

"Cuervo? Like the tequila?"

"No relation to the tequila empire, far as I know, but that's his last name. His first is Julio."

"I don't know."

"He's dying to meet you."

A jolt of alarm added to her existing bad vibes about the club and its owner. "Why? What did you tell him about me?"

"Nothing about the T, if that's what you're worried about. Just told him you're a damn good tattoo artist and into the goth-rockabilly scene. He's been thinking about getting a new tat. Could be another client for you."

"I have plenty of clients."

"Come on, Ave. It'll be fun."

"I don't know, Sam." Avery turned to meet her girlfriend's pleading expression. Big mistake. Sam's handsome face melted Avery's resistance like ice cream on a hundred-and-ten-degree day.

"Babe, just have one drink with us. Next weekend, I promise we can go to one of the clubs that play music you prefer. Tailfins, Fast Jerry's, the Rebel Lounge, wherever you like."

"Music's not the problem, Sam."

"Then what is?"

"It's your boss."

"What's my boss got to do with it?"

"You mean, aside from Theodore Bramwell being the head of the Desert Mafia? Extortion, drugs, arson, murder. How can you work for a guy like him?"

"Don't believe everything you hear. Most of what people say about Mr. Bramwell is bullshit. Not saying he's a saint. But who is? He gave me a job when he could've had my ass thrown back in the can. Even pulled some strings and got my rights restored after my time down in Florence."

"You served time?" How did she not know this before?

Sam stared down at the floorboards. "Spent a few years in juvie for dealing when I was a teenager. Then on my eighteenth birthday, some loud-mouth asshole called me a fucking rug muncher. So I kicked his ass. Got sent down to

Florence for seventeen months. Assault and underage drinking."

The similarity in their stories struck a chord with Avery. "Yeah, I done some shit too. But what happens when your boss gets busted? What's to keep him from dragging you down with him? There are lots of clubs in the Valley. Why not quit and work security somewhere else? "

"I'm a convicted felon, babe. No one else would hire me, certainly not for what Mr. Bramwell pays."

"Sam, his enforcers put Bobby J. in the hospital when he had his shop down on Roosevelt Row." Had Sam been one of them?

"They did? It wasn't me, I swear. I never handled collections."

"Still, you work for this man. And you could end up back in prison because of him. I don't want anything bad to happen to you."

"Ave, sweetie." Sammy kissed her gently on the lips. "I swear on everything I hold sacred, nothing bad is going to happen to me. Or us. I work as a bodyguard. Nothing illegal, I swear. Even if the cops busted Mr. Bramwell, I'm in the clear. Come inside and meet Cuervo. It'll be fun. I promise."

"Fine, I guess we can go in. But only for one drink. Then tomorrow night, we hit the Rebel Lounge, okay? Damaged Souls is playing."

"Sorry. No can do. Mr. Bramwell's got some bigwig business associates coming in from Vegas. Cuervo and me are working the security detail. But the night after, I promise."

"They're going on tour in a couple of days. Tomorrow's the last chance I'll get to see Kimi for a while."

"Wish I could, babe. Duty calls."

"Yeah. Guess I'll go solo. Again."

"Come on. You'll see Kimi and the gang when they get back, and I'll be happy to join you. But tonight, let's hang out with Cuervo, have a drink or two, maybe dance a little.

Then afterwards, we can go home, and I can make it all up to you."

"Damn, I can never say no to you." Avery kissed her, feeling a warmth down below.

"It's my butch charm," Sammy teased. "It's irresistible."

They stepped out into the late-April evening. Even at nine o'clock at night, the Phoenix heat remained in the nineties. Avery felt sweat trickle between her breasts as they rushed for the door.

Sam led her through the employee entrance, saying hi to coworkers along the way. Avery caught more than a few double takes over her lacy goth dress and raven-black fifties-style Bettie bangs. She was used to the gawking stares and the snickers, but it still made her feel like a fish out of water.

The steady synth beat rose to near deafening levels when they stepped into the main room and climbed a spiral staircase to a balcony overlooking the dance floor. The warm air was pungent with the scents of sweat and alcohol.

Sam pointed to a table where a bald man with a goatee sat next to a woman in a revealing outfit.

"Cuervo, this is my girlfriend, Avery!" Sam shouted over the music when they sat.

Cuervo smiled warmly, which helped settle the butterflies in Avery's stomach. "Mucho gusto, Avery. This is Alma." He leaned over to the woman seated next to him. "Sammy and I work together."

Alma nodded, raised her glass in salute, and said something Avery couldn't make out over the noise.

For the next half hour, Avery sipped a Moscow mule, catching bits of conversation between Sam and Cuervo but not enough to understand what they were talking about.

Eventually, she leaned over to Sam and said, "Where's the ladies' room?"

"Downstairs, to the right. You okay?"

"Fine."

"Sorry for talking shop. Maybe we can dance when you get back."

Avery shot her a halfhearted smile. "Okay."

When she stood, Alma put a hand on her arm and mouthed the words, "I'll go with you."

On the main floor, Alma gave a "follow me" gesture, and Avery tailed her down a hallway and into the women's restroom. The sudden quiet was profound, though the steady thud of the bass beat still penetrated the walls.

"I like your dress," Alma said from the stall next door.

"Thanks." Avery felt too out of her element to be chatty.

"Where'd you get it?"

"Yester Threads in Downtown Glendale. They specialize in vintage clothing." She mustered up the courage to add to the conversation. "How long have and Cuervo been going out?"

"Julio? Oh no, we're not a couple. He's just keeping me company while Theodore is meeting with his business friends from LA."

"Theodore? You're dating Theodore Bramwell?"

"I know. He's old enough to be my dad, but he's so charming. Have you met him?"

"Uh, no." Avery flushed and walked out of the stall toward the sinks. Alma appeared next to her. Even in the restroom's unflattering fluorescent lights, Alma was strikingly beautiful.

"Wow, I didn't notice your tattoos before." Alma touched the goth anime version of Peter Pan and Wendy that ran the length of her right forearm. "They're so distinctive."

"Thanks. I did most of them myself."

"You're a tattooer?"

"Tattoo artist, yes."

"How creative. My mother was an artist before she married my dad. Your Peter Pan looks very feminine. Almost like a girl. Was that intentional?"

"Yes. Pan has often been portrayed by women in film and onstage. I just took the next logical step and made her Petra Pan."

"Wow. Very sexy and creative."

"What about you?" Avery asked, feeling a little more comfortable. "What do you do?"

"I've done some modeling, a little acting. Low-budget stuff mostly. Hoping to move to LA. Theodore said he might make some introductions."

"That's cool."

On the way back to their table, a couple of drunk guys giving off a frat boy vibe started chatting up Alma, boxing her in and ignoring Avery.

When it became obvious from Alma's body language that she was uncomfortable, Avery pushed her way in and took Alma's arm. "Hey, guys, she's not interested."

"Brandon, check this chick out," said the one with a beard. "Didn't know the circus freaks were in town."

Brandon, the clean-shaven one, added, "Yeah, the casting call for Morticia Addams was last week, freak."

She ignored the taunts and tried to help Alma back toward the stairs. Unfortunately, the guys weren't having it. Brandon took hold of Alma's other arm and jerked her back.

"We aren't done talking yet, sweetheart."

Avery stepped between them, breaking Brandon's grip on her arm. "Guys, you're making a big mistake. Just let her go."

"Back off, Vampira!" The Beard shoved her hard into a group of people.

She stumbled into a group of people. Her purse fell to the floor and popped open. Fury exploded inside her. She shot to her feet and nailed the Beard from behind with a kidney punch.

He whirled around, catching her in the cheek with an elbow. Before she knew what was happening, she found herself on the floor, cradling her head while enduring a series of kicks and punches.

The blows stopped as suddenly as they began. A hand pulled her to her feet. Cuervo's face appeared, though the room pitched awkwardly for a moment.

"You okay, sweetie?" Cuervo asked, concern evident on his face.

"Fine." Everything hurt. She could feel her face swelling and tasted blood. "Where's Sam?"

"Escorting those two assholes out of here. She'll be back shortly." He offered Avery her purse, and guided her and Alma back upstairs to the table.

She realized the music had stopped, and the silence was a blessed relief.

"I'll grab you some ice for your face."

"No need," she tried to say, but he hustled away toward the upstairs bar before she could stop him.

"Thank you for stepping in, Avery," Alma said. "I'm so sorry you got hurt. I feel bad."

Avery shrugged. "Not your fault. Glad you're okay."

Sam appeared just as Cuervo approached up with some ice wrapped in a damp bar towel. Sam took it from him and placed it on the side of Avery's face.

"Ow!" Avery jerked away. The cold and pressure felt like knives stabbing into her already tender cheek.

"Oh, Ave! Maybe we should take you to the ER."

"No. Just want to go home."

"You sure? I can—"

"Home."

"Okay, baby. You got it. See you tomorrow, Cuervo."

Hours later, Avery's mind felt like it was floating while her pulse gradually slowed from its climax.

The sex, with the help of a two-year-old, leftover pain pill, had helped, though kissing was still painful with a busted lip. So Sam had focused on other areas.

Avery gazed absently at the perspiration on Sam's face glistening in the faint bedroom light.

"Ms. Ferguson, you are so good at that."

Sam chuckled. "Happy to be of service, ma'am."

Avery slapped her playfully. "Can I do anything for you?"

"Naw, I'm good. Figured I owed you after what happened earlier."

"I've survived worse. Cuervo and Alma seemed nice, at least."

"I was thinking in the morning we could grab brunch at the Fleur de Lis Café." Sam kissed her gently. "I know how you love their macarons."

"Like edible rainbows."

A cloud passed over her girlfriend's face. "Then I was thinking we could do a little target practice at Shooter's World before you head off to the tattoo studio."

Avery's excitement faded. "Not really how I wanted to spend a Saturday. You know how I feel about guns."

"It's important you know how to defend yourself, babe."

"Oh, not this again. I know how to defend myself. Not my fault I was outnumbered two to one earlier. And having a gun would have made the situation a hundred times worse."

"I'm glad you can kick ass when you need to. Just thought you should know how to use firearms as well. Especially since I keep them in the house."

"Sam, please. I know how to shoot a gun. My bio dad taught me when I was nine. I just don't like them. I get you need them for work and have to stay in practice. Just leave me out of it. Okay?"

Sam rested her head against her hand. "Okay. Just think about it."

Drowsiness swept over Avery like a heavy blanket. "One day maybe we'll move someplace like Seattle, and I won't have to worry about getting murdered by transphobic bigots. We can just be ourselves and live our lives."

"One day, I promise." Sam leaned over and kissed her. "Good night, sweetie."

"Night, night." Avery rolled over and spied the plushie unicorn barely visible on the bookshelf across the room. "Night, Melissa," she whispered to it.

# CHAPTER 5
# A MYSTERIOUS INVITATION

AVERY NODDED to the driving bass of the Golem Grinders on the tattoo studio's sound system. She could still taste the macarons they'd had at Fleur de Lis Café that morning.

Her wrist ached from their outing at Shooter's World after giving in to Sam's pleading.

The little .380 she'd shot had quite a kick for such a little gun. She hated to admit enjoying the sense of power it gave her. But even the minor thrill wasn't enough to make her want to carry one in her purse, despite Sam's urging.

When she'd arrived at Seoul Fire, Bobby J. took one look at her bruised face and grimaced.

"Don't say it," Avery spouted before he could speak. "I know I look like I went ten rounds with Mike Tyson. But in case you're wondering, this wasn't Sam's fault."

"I didn't say anything, kiddo. Merely concerned."

"I'm fine. Just a little sore."

He didn't press the matter, and she had gotten to work.

The half-naked man now lying on the table next to her squirmed and made mewling noises. She'd finished outlining the design after an hour and had moved on to coloring and shading.

"Don't fidget, Hatchet. You'll ruin the art." She wiped away the blood from the guy's torso and continued filling in the design. The tattoo machine buzzed happily in rhythm with the music.

The guy let loose a whimpering growl. "Hurts."

"Geez, dude. Didn't know you were such a wimp. You always talk so tough when you and your rat rodder buddies are street racing down Sun Valley Parkway."

"My other tats didn't hurt this much."

"Well, duh. You're getting it just below your left nipple. Lotta bone and nerve endings, not a lotta muscle. Why'd you want it there, anyways? Afraid the other guys will see you with a fairy tat?"

"No. Well, not completely. It's just personal, you know? To honor my kid sister's memory."

"I'm so sorry. What happened to her?" She felt bad for taunting him.

"Leukemia. She was twenty-six. It'll be a year in May since she died. Figured it was past time to honor her."

"That fucking sucks."

"Fuck cancer," he grumbled.

"Yeah. Fuck cancer. Now sit still. Shouldn't take more than a few more hours."

"A few hours? Shit." Hatchet let out a sigh. "Maybe I should have a little something to drink. You know, to help me relax."

"No booze," Bobby said sternly from his workstation. He was working on the shoulder of a female client. "You'll bleed more, and the ink won't stay. It'll look like a muddled mess when it heals. This studio has a reputation to uphold."

"Listen to the man," Avery added. "Just toughen up, buttercup."

"I'll try."

"Do or do not—" Bobby started to say before Avery cut him off.

"Enough with the *Star Wars* quotes, Appa."

"Very well. I will not Force the issue."

Avery groaned. Dad jokes.

She wiped away more blood and studied the emo goth girl pixie tattoo she was inking. The pixie held aloft a giant battle-ax, swinging it toward the word *cancer* in a bold Courier font. "It's looking good, though."

"Can I see?" Hatchet raised his head, and his eyes went wide.

Avery had the feeling he was staring at her chest peeking out above her low-cut polka-dot blouse. She pushed his head back down. "When I'm done."

Her cell phone rang. Avery turned off the machine and pulled off her gloves. "Break time. Grab some water from the cooler in the corner."

"Thanks."

Avery's heart skipped a beat when she saw Sam's name and photo on her phone. "Hey, sexy, what's up?"

"I've got a surprise for you." Sam's husky voice was rich as honey.

"A surprise? Color me intrigued. What is it?"

"Meet me tonight at the Ocotillo Inn on the corner of Glendale and Forty-Third Avenue."

"Ocotillo Inn? Aren't you playing bodyguard for the boss man tonight? Bigwigs coming in from out of town and all that."

"I kinda switched with somebody."

"Kinda switched?" Something in Sam's tone unsettled Avery. "Is everything all right?"

"It's great. Really. What time you get off?"

"Whatever time you want to get me off, baby," Avery replied in a teasing voice. She was excited about getting to see Kimi and the boys before they started their tour.

"When do you get off work, my dear?"

"Oh, that. Around eight."

"Good. I'm in room 171."

"You got a room at that dump?" When her question was met with silence, she added, "Sorry, sweetie. I'm tired and cranky and sore. I'm sure whatever you've got planned is very romantic. Afterward, though, can we go see Damage Souls play at the Rebel Lounge?"

"Sure. I'll see you when you get here."

Avery hung up, trying to make sense of the conversation.

"That your boyfriend?" Hatchet asked as he sauntered back over to her workstation with a cup of water in hand.

"Girlfriend."

He raised an eyebrow. "You're a lesbo?"

All eyes in the studio turned to him.

"That a problem?" Avery asked, letting a hint of a threat into her tone. "Don't forget, I'm the one stabbing you a gazillion times with needles. Trust me, I can make this hurt a whole lot more."

"I… uh… no. No problem. When Mikey recommended you, he never mentioned… you know."

She snapped on a fresh pair of gloves and restarted the machine. "I'm also transgender. Got a problem with that?"

"Nah, it's cool, man. Er, ma'am."

"Good. Now sit your ass down and let's finish this. And no more whining."

"Yes, ma'am."

She caught Bobby J. staring at her. "What?"

"Everything okay with Sam?"

"It's fine. More than fine."

He just nodded. "Okay."

# CHAPTER 6
# AN UNEXPECTED PARTY

AVERY PARKED the Gothmobile under a flickering security light in the crowded Ocotillo Inn parking lot. The place had always been a joke when she was in school, a location for clandestine rendezvous and sex by the hour. The joke became less funny when she was living on the streets.

The paint was peeling on the motel room door. The lights along the walkway were yellowed with age. A few flickered. The few people she'd seen in the parking lot looked like they were hustling. Why the hell did Sam want to meet her here? Did she think this place was romantic?

She knocked on the door of the room.

"Just a minute!" came an immediate reply.

A moment later, Sam opened the door with a big grin on her face. "Hello, sexy! Come on in and have a drink!" Sam offered her a plastic champagne flute full of bubbly.

Avery stepped into the room. Streamers hung on the walls along with a banner that read "Happy Independence Day." Near the bed, a bottle of champagne sat in a bucket of ice. The Vampire Beach Babes' "Gothmobile" played on a Bluetooth speaker next to Sam's phone.

"Uh, Sam, what's going on? And why'd you want to meet in this… place?"

"Wanted to surprise you." Judging from her lidded eyes and the way she slurred her words, Sam had already had a few.

"Well, mission accomplished. I'm definitely surprised. But dare I ask, what's the occasion? Fourth of July's not for a couple months yet."

"We're celebrating our independence! Cheers!" Sam clinked Avery's plastic glass with her own and took a gulp of champagne.

"Independence from what?"

Sam starred bleary-eyed for a moment. "Sit. Lemme explain."

Avery sat next to her on the floral polyester bedspread. "Okay."

"Last night, you didn't want to go into the club because of who I worked for. So, I done did a lot of thinking about that." Sam's celebratory expression sobered. "You're right. I shouldn't be working for him. He's not a nice man. And I… I've done some… bad things."

An awkward silence fell over the room before she continued.

"However much Mr. Bramwell helped me out way back when, I decided my debt to him's been paid. I even saved his life a few times. I ever tell you about that?"

Avery shook her head.

"Anywho, after you left for work, I looked at myself in the mirror and took a good long look. And you know what I saw?"

"A beautiful butch woman?" Avery answered.

"A loser."

"Sam, you're not a loser."

"No, no, I am. I work for a mobster. I've always known it. Sure, he acts like he's some real estate mogul or some shit. A Trump wannabe. But I knew the truth. He hurts people. He hurt your foster dad."

Sam rubbed her face. "So I asked myself, who works for an asshole like that? Losers. That's who. So I decided that's it. I'm not gonna work for that piece of shit any longer."

Avery gave her a quick kiss, still feeling there was something Sam wasn't saying. "Good for you. You said you wanted to be a better person. And tonight, you've taken a big step in that direction. What'd he say when you told him?"

Sam's expression got all squirmy. "Well, that's the thing. I didn't exactly tell him. But he'll figure it out. Which brings me to the second surprise. We're moving to Seattle."

"We're what?"

"You said you wanted to live there. Now we are. We can stay with my friends Erin and Jackie until we can get jobs and find a place of our own. But yeah. Seattle. Can you believe it?"

Avery took a breath. "But why now?"

"Because I want to give you your dream. You said you were sick of this town and all the narrow-minded people. Seattle's one city you wanted to move to, so I figured I'd seize the opportunity."

"I... I... I don't know what to say." Avery's mind whirled. They were moving to Seattle. It didn't seem real. And now she wondered if that was what she really wanted. "When are we going?"

"Right away. Well, not like right this minute. I'm a little drunk. A lot drunk. But tomorrow morning."

Avery gasped. "Tomorrow?"

"I packed us some suitcases for till we get settled. Even packed your laptop and accessories in your computer bag. And my friends Jamie, David, and Bruce put the rest of our belongings into your storage rental. I hope you don't mind."

"But, Sam, I have clients scheduled for the next month. Why does it have to be tomorrow?"

Sam got that wounded-puppy look. "Because Mr. Bramwell won't exactly be happy that I left."

Avery studied her girlfriend's face. "Because you know too much? Because he's afraid you might snitch to the cops?"

"Something like that."

"Can we at least stop by Seoul Fire in the morning so I can say goodbye to everyone?"

"Yeah, I suppose."

Avery let it all sink in. They were getting the hell out of Dodge because Sam quit working for Bramwell. And what would happen if Bramwell tracked them down? She didn't want to think about it.

"And the house. You were renting it, right?" Avery asked. "When's the lease up?"

"The house belongs to Bramwell. As does most of the furniture. We can come back and get your furniture from the storage unit once we get a place of our own. And anything we're missing, we'll buy."

"What are we going to live on? I don't want to be mooching off your friends for however long it takes to get new jobs."

At that, Sam beamed with pride. "Don't worry. I got money. I'll take care of us."

"You've got money? Just last week, you were asking me for three hundred bucks to get your car fixed."

Sam squirmed some more. "I got a bonus recently. I can pay you back now."

Clearly, there was more that Sam wasn't saying, but Avery wasn't sure she wanted to know.

She took a deep breath and imagined living in Seattle.

How would she cope with all that rain and the cold, dreary winters?

She'd lived in the Phoenix area her entire life. And while she kept out of the direct sun as much as possible, she knew that the endless sunny days filled her with happiness. How would she adjust?

And would she make new friends in Seattle? Would she find a new job? Would she be able to visit Bobby and the others at the shop? Or would that put them at risk?

"Well, I guess we're moving to Seattle," Avery said at last.

Sam hugged and kissed her. "I'm so happy. This is an exciting new adventure. Let's party!"

Avery considered asking if they could stop by the Rebel Lounge to hear Damaged Souls play a set or two. But Sam was already three sheets to the wind. Best if they stayed put.

A few hours later, they were both a little drunk. They had talked and danced and made out. By the time they climbed into the lumpy motel bed, they were both too exhausted for sex.

"Night, babe," Sam said as she turned off the light.

"Wait, where's Rainbow?" Panic sent Avery's pulse racing.

"Rainbow? Who's Rainbow?"

"The stuffed unicorn that Melissa gave me when I was seven."

"Um, I don't know. Where was it?"

"On the bookshelf in our bedroom."

"Oh." Sam turned the light back on and sat up, obviously concentrating. "I'm not sure."

"Did you pack it in one of our suitcases? Or did your friends put it in the storage rental?"

"I remember Jamie asking me if she should pack up the books on the shelf. I told her no, because the books belonged to Bramwell."

"And Rainbow?"

"Probably still on the shelf. Look, I can buy you a new one."

"No! I need Rainbow. It's the only thing I have left of my

foster mom." Tears sprang to her eyes. She knew she was acting ridiculous over a stuffed toy.

Sam put her arms around her. "Okay, okay. Don't cry. Please don't cry."

"I'm sorry. It's just…"

"Hey, I get it. It's special to you. I know how much you miss her. My mother didn't give two shits about me. I'm glad you had one that did."

"My birth mother didn't care much about me either. Not even when my father kicked me out of the house. Just a frightened little mouse. But Melissa loved and accepted me as my true self. I like to think she's been watching out since she died."

"I get it. Tell you what. I'm gonna get dressed. Go back to the house and bring back Rainbow. Because you are the most precious person in my life. And I want nothing more than for you to be happy."

"You okay to drive?"

"I'm fine."

Avery studied her eyes. She looked tired but sober. She wasn't slurring her words like she had been. "Thank you, baby."

Sam kissed her hard. "Anything for you."

"Hurry back."

# CHAPTER 7
# WAITING

AVERY LAY IN THE BED, staring at the walls and waiting for Sam to return. Despite the exhaustion and the alcohol, her mind wouldn't stop thinking about moving to Seattle.

Was she really doing this? Despite the suddenness, she couldn't think of a reason why not. She would miss Bobby J., Butcher, and Frisco. Not to mention Kimi and the band.

What would she tell Bobby? That he was right about her getting involved with Sam? Was this all a mistake? Should she stay here and let Sam go without her?

She glanced at the digital clock on the nightstand. It was nearly one o'clock. How long had Sam been gone? Almost an hour? It shouldn't have taken her that long to run by the house, pick up Rainbow, and get back. Maybe she had found some other things they'd forgotten to pack. Or Sam's friends had packed it up in a box, and Sam had to run to the storage unit.

A tremor of fear rippled through her mind. Or maybe Sam had been involved in an accident. Maybe she was still drunk. Or maybe she got pulled over for a DUI. Or maybe, maybe...

No. Sam was fine. She had to be. No reason to panic.

Avery called her. It rang five times before rolling over to voicemail. "Hey, Sammy. Just wondering where you are. Call me if you're going to be much longer."

She turned on the TV, but the only programs on were infomercials and porn. She had no interest in either. Not while sitting here alone waiting for Sam.

At one thirty, the panic settled in deep. Something had gone wrong. Car trouble. Accident. DUI. She remembered the horror when she found the Lost Kids dead in the house they'd been squatting when she was sixteen. And then losing Melissa to a terrorist bomb a few years later, it was impossible not to go to those dark places.

She called again and got Sam's voicemail. "Sam, please call me now. I'm worried about you."

At two, Avery was pacing around the room. Should she call the police? Hospitals? She had met some of Sam's friends but didn't know any of their numbers.

Finally, she decided to drive by the house. That was the first place to start.

Once dressed, she threw their bags in the trunk of the Gothmobile and drove into the night. Her body shook with fear despite using all of the relaxation techniques Bobby J. had taught her.

*Everything is fine,* she tried to assure herself. There had to be a perfectly rational explanation. And even if Sam was in an accident or got a DUI, it would all work out. At worst, it would cost them some money and delay their move. And that wasn't necessarily a bad thing.

Avery turned onto their street and spotted Sam's Audi in their driveway. The lights in the house were dark. A voice inside her told her to park a few houses down. Her pulse was now screaming. She turned off the ignition and hustled back to the house.

The dome light in Sam's car was on; the passenger door and trunk were ajar. But no sign of Sam. Avery reached under the driver's seat and found a Glock Sam kept there. It felt heavy in her hand. But she wasn't sure what she'd find inside the house.

She crept to the front door. It was shut but unlocked.

"Sam?" she whispered when she stepped into the pitch black living room. "Sam?"

The air had an all too familiar smell—the same one she remembered when she'd found her housemates dead years earlier. *It's just a memory. Not real. Just my PTSD.*

"Sam, are you here?"

She listened in the dark for what felt like forever, but the only sound was the AC kicking on. Finally, she gathered enough courage to flick on the overhead light.

The room looked like a monsoon had blown through. The furniture was overturned. Cushions had been slashed. AC vents had been removed from the walls. Panic gripped her hard now. She struggled to breathe. The gun in her hand shook.

"Sam? You here?" she said a little louder.

She followed the hallway to their bedroom and flicked on the bedroom light.

The bed and walls had been stripped bare. The mattress turned over and slashed. The lamp from the nightstand lay on the floor. The drawers from the nightstand had been ripped from their tracks and overturned. A reddish-brown smudge on the wall looked like blood. But still no sign of Sam.

She found Rainbow the Unicorn under a pile of books on the floor next to the smashed bookshelf. She clutched it to her chest.

"Where are you, Sam?"

She wandered back down the hall, checking bathrooms,

finding them empty with drawers and cabinets open. At last, she came to the kitchen. A sledgehammer crushed her soul. Her knees buckled, and she clung to the refrigerator for support. “Nooooo…”

# CHAPTER 8
# A STONE-COLD DYKE

"DID YOU FIND MY MONEY?" Mr. Bramwell sat dressed in golden silk pajamas in the middle of a huge four-poster bed. A laptop lay open before him, bathing him in an eerie blue glow.

The bedroom itself was an obscenity of gaudy nouveau riche design with gold-and-imperial-red curtains that matched the wallpaper a bit too perfectly. A crystal chandelier the size of a VW Beetle hung from the ceiling, illuminating dark-walnut furnishings with wrought iron accents.

Picassos shared wall space with the works of Edvard Munch and Francis Goya. Whether they were originals, forgeries, or some other kind of reproduction, Cuervo had never dared ask.

He stood in the doorway, his heart heavy. Beside him stood a short wiry man named Luther Jackson. Something about the guy always reminded him of a spider.

Cuervo still didn't want to believe Sam could be so stupid. Robbing Mr. Bramwell? Surely not after what had happened to Whitmore.

But he'd watched the security footage of Sam opening the safe and dumping the money into a blue gym bag. More than two million bucks. She had then sat down at Mr.

Bramwell's desk, apparently searching for something on his computer. *But what was she looking for?*

By sheer luck, they'd caught her at the house, which had been emptied of personal possessions. Nothing but the furniture and appliances left. *How could she be so stupid? Did she think they wouldn't catch her?*

When Sam refused to say where she'd hidden the money or explain what she'd been doing on Mr. Bramwell's computer, Luther had taken a sadistic delight in trying to torture the information out of her.

"Please, Sammy. Just tell us where you put it," Cuervo had begged. "I'll make it right with Mr. Bramwell and let you go. You're obviously planning on skipping town. Just give us the money, and you can live a new life somewhere else in peace."

Sam had opened one bloodied eye and spat a mixture of blood and mucus into his face. "Fuck. You."

Despite her screams, the cops never showed. He knew they wouldn't in this neighborhood at this time of night. Not for screaming.

But no matter what that evil little spider did to her, she refused to say where the money was.

It wasn't even Bramwell's money. At least not all of it. A little more than a million belonged to the Sinaloa cartel for the fifty kilos of heroin they had fronted the Desert Mafia.

"Bitch wouldn't talk." Luther told Mr. Bramwell. "Gotta say, she was one stone-cold dyke. Wouldn't even admit she took it. Stupid cunt."

Cuervo wanted to punch him for talking that way about his partner, even if she had brought this world of hurt on herself.

"You search the house?"

"Top to bottom," Cuervo said glumly. "Not much left there but the furniture. All her personal stuff was gone. Like she'd packed up to move. Searched her car too. Nothing."

"I need that money, gentlemen. Do I need to spell out what the Mexicans will do to each and every one of us if we don't have their money when they come to collect?"

"No, sir." Cuervo and Luther replied in unison.

"What about the girlfriend?" Mr. Bramwell asked.

"Girlfriend? What girlfriend?" Luther fixed Cuervo with a penetrating gaze.

Cuervo cursed silently. He suspected Avery might have it but didn't want to bring her into this mess. She seemed like a decent kid.

"Alma mentioned Sam was with a girl the other night," Mr. Bramwell continued. "Amy, Aubrey, something like that. Cuervo, you were Sam's partner. What's the girl's name?"

"Avery." Cuervo hoped it wouldn't get her killed too. He could still hear Sam's cries of agony echoing in his mind. "Don't know her last name."

"Go back to the house and wait for her," Bramwell said. "Bitch is bound to turn up, looking for Sam. When she does, grab her and find my money. Our very lives depend on getting it back and paying the Mexicans for the dope."

Cuervo followed Luther out of the office. He wanted to be doing anything but hunting down Sam's girlfriend.

# CHAPTER 9
# WORST FEARS REALIZED

AVERY FORCED herself to her feet and and stumbled to where Sam sat at the kitchen table.

She'd been stripped down to her underwear. Her body was so bruised and bloody, she was almost unrecognizable aside from her red hair. Her head lolled to one side, eyes half lidded and lifeless. A strip of duct tape covered her mouth. Zip ties secured her wrists to the chair's arms.

"No, no, no, no. Sam, wake up. Wake up. Wake up. Sammy, please wake up. Please."

Sam's blood-slick skin was still warm to the touch. Avery pulled off the duct tape and cupped her head in her hands, hoping against hope. "Wake up, baby. It's me, Avery. Come on, just wake up for me."

To her surprise, Sam muttered something inaudible.

"What'd you say?"

"Love. You."

Avery laughed and cried so hard, she nearly choked. "I love you, too, baby. Let me call an ambulance. We'll get you fixed up."

She was reaching for her phone when the front door creaked open.

"Run," Sam croaked.

"No! I'm not leaving you."

Avery turned toward the intruders and raised the pistol. The instant she saw Cuervo and another man, she pulled the trigger, flinching at the gunshot. A barrage of return fire sent her ducking behind the fridge.

She glanced at Sam. A dark-red halo of blood now stretched across the wall next to what was left of her head.

"Nooooo!"

More gunshots shook the house. Avery emptied her gun at the intruders then fumbled open the back door and fled into the yard.

She vaulted over the cinder-block wall on the far side, drawing on muscle memory from the years of gymnastics before her bio dad made her quit.

Like a bat out of hell, she flew through her neighbor's yard and out the gate. She ran flat out until her lungs were burning and she was dizzy.

With her chest heaving, she collapsed behind an SUV. The gun was gone. Probably dropped somewhere along the way. But she still clutched Rainbow with a death grip in her left hand.

"Fuck, fuck, fuck, fuck." She choked on her sobs, the horror of the situation crushing down on her with the weight of a dump truck.

Sam was gone. Those fuckers had murdered her. But why? Just because she quit working for Bramwell? Why did Bobby have to be right about this? Why had she not believed him?

"What do I do? What do I do? What do I do?" Her first instinct was to call 911 and report the murder.

And then she remembered Bobby had told her that Bramwell had cops on his payroll. Possibly people in the county attorney's office too. Like an idiot, she'd left behind a gun with her fingerprints on it. How easy would it be for some corrupt homicide cop to pin this on her?

She had to run, just like Sam wanted. But where? And how? She didn't know Sam's friends in Seattle. She had a little money in the bank but probably not enough to live on up there while trying to find a job.

Maybe Bobby could hide her until this all blew over. But how long would that take? Would it ever blow over? Sam was dead. And the last thing she wanted to do was put Bobby or anyone else at Seoul Fire at risk.

"Oh fuck. What am I gonna do?"

Kimi. She and the band, Damaged Souls, were going on tour. Maybe she could tag along. Maybe she could even do some tattoo work on the side. Kimi was always saying how much the band members admired her work, sharing pics on social media. It would get her out of town until she could come up with a better plan.

"Hello?" Kimi answered a tired voice after Avery dialed her number.

"Hey, it's Avery. Did I wake you?"

"No, I was just about to hit the sack. What's up, girl?"

"I… I don't know where to start. But… I was wondering if somehow, maybe…"

"Girl, just spit it out."

"I was hoping to come with you on your tour. I can pay my way. It's just… I need to get outta town. Like, fast."

"Avery, are you okay? What's happened?"

"I just… Sam. She's dead. Someone killed her."

"Oh God. Avery, I'm so sorry."

"No, I'm the one who's sorry. I shouldn't be imposing on you—"

"No, no, no. Babe, if you're in some kind of trouble, come on over. We'll talk about it. And if you want to tag along with us on the tour, we'll make room. Okay?"

"I feel like such a bother."

"Sweetie, you're not a bother. You're my sister from

another mister. I love you. Do you have a way to get here? Or do you need me to pick you up?"

"I…" She needed to get back to the Gothmobile without being spotted. "I can get there."

"Come on over then. I'll wait up for you."

"Okay, okay. Thank you." Avery took another deep breath. "I need to pick up some stuff from the shop. Is an hour too long?"

"Take however long you need, babe. I got your back."

"Thanks, girl."

She struggled to her feet. Her muscles had stiffened, as if she'd run a marathon.

She circled the block, keeping to the shadows as much as possible and listening and watching for approaching cars. The only sound she heard was a dog's bark echoing through the dark neighborhood.

When she turned onto her street, she froze. Their house was midway up the block. A streetlamp lit up their yard, revealing Sam's car still in the driveway. Another car sat parked in front at the curb. A sleek sports car of some kind. Maybe a Tesla or Corvette. Hard to be sure at this distance.

The Gothmobile was between her and the house. But could she get to it and start it without tipping off those psycho motherfuckers? She had to try.

Her pulse quickened the closer she got to the Gothmobile. Just as she reached her car, the wail of a police siren pierced the quiet neighborhood. She ducked behind the front bumper.

Two figures emerged from the house and went to the sports car parked in front. It hummed to life and flew past with a whisper. An electric vehicle, Avery guessed. Meanwhile, the police sirens were drawing closer from the opposite direction.

When the sports car was out of sight, Avery slipped into

the Gothmobile. The engine rumbled to life, and she drove off, keeping an eye out for signs of the other car and cops.

Her heart rate didn't slow until she turned onto Nineteenth Avenue and had crossed Bethany Home Road.

Traffic was light, and she soon pulled into the Seoul Fire parking lot. It was empty. No one hanging around.

Inside, she grabbed a used cardboard box from the back room and carried it to her station. She filled it with her tattoo machine, inks, clean needles, gloves, and other supplies. Her autoclave was too bulky to fit in the box, so she dug out a package of disposable tubes she'd ordered way back when. They'd have to do.

When she had everything ready to go, she wrote a note for Bobby and left it at his station.

*Appa,*

*Sam's dead. She tried to quit working for Bramwell. Guess you were right. Now I think they're after me too. Gotta get out of town for a while. Not sure when I'll be back. Thank you for everything you've done for me. You were the father my bio dad never was. I love you. Sorry to leave like this.*

*Avery*

She wiped the tears from her face and carried her stuff to the Gothmobile.

# CHAPTER 10
# INCRIMINATING EVIDENCE

DETECTIVE PIERCE HARDIN signed in to the crime scene and donned a pair of nitrile gloves and booties. He found his partner, Detective Lorenzo Valentine, just outside the single-occupancy home, talking to one of the patrol officers, a guy who looked barely old enough to drive.

*Or maybe I'm just getting old,* Hardin thought.

"What do we got?" he asked the two men.

"Deceased white female, signs of torture," Valentine replied, studying his pocket-sized notebook. "Neighbors reported hearing screaming around 0100 hours, then gunshots about ninety minutes later. No eyewitnesses so far, but we've got patrol canvassing the neighborhood."

"Well, let's take a look at the scene."

Valentine led the way through the front door. He'd only recently made detective and seemed like a decent guy. Hardin had so far worked two cases with him, and the man seemed eager to prove himself. Maybe too eager. He had a habit of jumping to conclusions without the evidence to back it up.

Hardin studied the disaster area that had been the living room.

"Looks like someone tossed the place searching for something," Valentine said.

"We have any idea what?"

"Money or drugs would be my bet."

They continued into the kitchen. The brutality of the scene penetrated even Hardin's jaded psyche. Half the victim's head was gone, with blood and brain matter splattered on the wall. The rest of the body was covered in knife wounds, burns, and bruises. Fingers were broken and twisted in all directions.

"Damn," Hardin said. "Someone took their time with her."

"Cause of death appears to be the gunshot wound to the head," Valentine explained. "Multiple slugs in the walls in both the kitchen and the living room. Probably what woke the neighbors."

"We got an ID on the vic?"

"Found a wallet in some clothes on the floor near the sink." Again, Valentine pointed. "Victim's name is Samantha Ferguson. Address shows her to be the resident."

Hardin took in the scene. Something felt off. He opened a cabinet. It was empty. He checked a few more, then some drawers. "Where's all her stuff? Dishes, pots, and pans. Looks like she moved out."

"I was wondering the same thing," Valentine replied.

Hardin continued down a hallway to the bedroom. Like the living room, it had been tossed and the mattress torn apart. "What do we know about the vehicle in the driveway?"

"A 2015 Audi A4. Belongs to the victim. Doors and trunk were found open. You ask me, looks like a drug deal gone wrong."

"Maybe. Appears someone was searching for something specific and tortured the victim to find out where it was," Hardin postulated, trying to make sense of the chaos. "Who is that someone, what were they looking for, and did they find it?"

"Detectives." A patrol officer stepped into the room with an evidence bag in her hand. "Found this in the backyard. Glock nine millimeter. Smells like it's recently been fired."

Hardin offered her a grim smile. "Nice job, officer. Maybe we'll luck out, and the shooter left some fingerprints."

# CHAPTER 11
# TAGGING ALONG

AVERY KNOCKED TENTATIVELY on the door to Kimi's apartment. In her left hand, she carried one of the suitcases that Sam had packed for her. Under her right arm, she held Rainbow the Unicorn.

The door creaked open. A bleary-eyed Kimi Asato gasped. "Oh my God! Get in here, sweetie."

Avery let her take the suitcase from her, then she sat down on a couch and bawled her eyes out. A well of sorrow the size of the Pacific Ocean shook her body like a rag doll. A stack of tissues was placed in her hand. She blew her nose, but the anguish kept flooding through her.

She couldn't get the image of Sam's tortured, broken body out of her mind. It bled into a six-year-old memory of walking into the house that she and the other Lost Kids had been squatting in. The horror of their bullet-riddled bodies and the crushing guilt that she had led the shooter to their door had nearly driven her to take her own life.

When Avery had cried herself out, she felt Kimi's head on her shoulder, her arms holding her tightly.

"Thank you," Avery managed to say.

"Aw, sweetie. You don't need to thank me. We're sisters, you and me. This is what sisters do for each other. You've helped me out plenty of times in the past. Like when that stalker wouldn't leave me alone."

"Yeah."

"You able to talk about what happened?"

At Kimi's words, Avery's throat and chest tightened, as if she were being strangled by a python. She forced air into her lungs and held it.

*"Breathe in peace,"* Bobby J.'s words whispered in her mind. *"Hold to serenity. Release fear."*

She let go of the breath and took another. "Sam called me earlier tonight. Or I guess it was now last night. While I was at work. She said... she said she had a surprise for me. Asked me to meet her at the Ocotillo Inn."

"That shithole? What'd she want you to meet her there for?"

Avery shook her head. "When I got there, she told me she quit her job, that we were moving up to Seattle."

"You're moving to Seattle?"

"No—I mean, yes. We were. I don't know. That was her surprise. Some friends of hers up there were going to let us stay with them until we got settled."

"But why leave so suddenly?"

"I... I don't understand completely, but it was because she worked for Theodore Bramwell."

"Bramwell? Ugh. That guy's some sort of mob boss. Sam worked for him?"

Avery nodded.

"So, what happened?"

Another wave of grief hit her like a left hook, this time accompanied by guilt. "It's my fault, Kimi. My fault."

"What? What's your fault?"

"She's dead. They killed her."

"Who? Bramwell? Why?"

"She was afraid they'd come after her. Maybe Bramwell thought she'd ratted him out or something. I don't know.

She never said. But that's why we were spending the night at the motel."

"But if they killed her, why would it be your fault?"

"I made her go back to the house." Sobs racked her body once again. "I told her I couldn't leave without Rainbow. It's my fault, Kimi."

"Aw, baby." Kimi pulled the stuffed unicorn out from under Avery's arm. "I remember what Rainbow means to you. If my mom had died, I would've wanted to hold on to something she gave me too. That doesn't make it your fault."

"But she never would've gone back. She'd still be alive."

"So, they killed her when she went back?"

"Not just killed her. They tortured her. I barely recognized her."

"Was she going to rat on them to the cops?"

"Doubt it. But they killed her anyway. If I hadn't sent her back there…"

"Listen to me, Avery. What they did to her, that's on them. Not you. You had no idea that would happen."

"Still feel it's partly my fault."

"Not even a little. Guessing you didn't call the cops?"

Avery shook her head. "Bobby told me Bramwell's got cops on his payroll. It's why Bramwell's never been busted."

"Shit. That's messed up. So, he can just murder people, cover it up, and get away with it?"

"Power of the patriarchy. Rules don't apply to powerful white men the way they do the rest of us."

"I hear you. The cops wouldn't do shit when that asshole was stalking me. Kept saying, 'We can't do nothing till he actually does something illegal.' Stupid, lazy motherfuckers. Like I'm going to wait around for him to assault me or worse. That's why I'm glad I had you to help me. Avery the Avenger."

"No, not Avery the Avenger. Avery the Avenger's who got the Lost Kids killed. Avery the Avenger died that day."

"That wasn't your fault, hon. You didn't shoot them."

"No, whoever did was looking for me. It was retaliation for me offing that junkie pimp. It was karma."

"You don't know that. They never found out who killed your housemates. As for that junkie pimp, from what you told me, he had it coming. And let's face it, it was only a matter of time before he overdosed anyway. All you did was speed up the process."

They didn't speak for ten minutes.

"I'm afraid, Kimi."

"Well, yeah, who wouldn't be? A gangster just murdered your girlfriend. If someone did that to Chupa, I'd be terrified out of my mind."

"Not just that."

Visions of the dead pimp flashed hard in her mind, along with all the excitement that had led up to that moment. The planning and strategizing. The glee when she tracked him down. The thrill of finding him passed out among his buddies after they'd been partying. Creeping into the apartment. Filling that syringe and sticking it in his arm. The satisfaction of pushing the plunger. The anticipation of feeling his pulse stop. And then the unexpected, horrible realization. She was a murderer.

Maybe he'd deserved it. He'd been brutalizing one of her fellow squatters. But what gave her the right to kill him?

His dull eyes had haunted her dreams ever since, even as her friends thought of her as a hero. She hated that word. Heroes didn't murder people in their sleep.

And when she found the Lost Kids dead a few weeks later, she knew that the universe was punishing her for her crime. Her karma had gotten them killed.

And now Sam was dead. And she wouldn't have been if Avery hadn't been so damn sentimental about a stuffed toy unicorn. More bad karma.

"What, Avery? What else are you afraid of?"

"Of becoming what I was when I killed that pimp."

Kimi nodded. "You were someone who helped a friend. That's it."

"I killed a man. Murdered him. And as a result, the Lost Kids are dead. Melissa's dead. And now Sam. It's my fault. I'm like a death magnet. I should probably go. Don't want to risk you getting killed too."

Avery started to stand, but Kimi pulled her back down.

"You're not going anywhere, sweetie. And you are definitely not a death magnet. Though that sounds like a cool name for a goth band."

Avery gave her a halfhearted smile but said nothing.

"Think of every time that junkie pimp beat up your friend. Not to mention the time he put her in the hospital and refused to pay for the medical expenses. If he had killed her before you killed him, how would you have felt then? You did what you had to do. It wasn't out of spite or for the joy of it."

"But I did enjoy it, Kimi. I enjoyed tracking him down. I got a thrill out of sneaking into his place, plotting my revenge. It was fun. And she ended up dead anyway, along with the others."

"You did it to protect someone. Even in the legal system, defense of another is the same as self-defense. You got nothing to feel guilty about."

"I just don't want to become that person again. Some vigilante who takes delight in hurting people. Even if they deserve it. That's not the person I want to be."

"Then don't be. Be the person you want to be. I've know you as since before you transitioned. You are a good soul."

"I just want to live a normal life, creating tattoos, working with Bobby and everyone from the shop, going to clubs to hear you and the band play. Having a girlfriend who loves me for who I am, even if she doesn't get my love of gothabilly culture. Maybe that's not everyone's normal, but it's what I've dreamed of. It's my normal, and I want it back."

"Well, who's to say you can't get it back?"

"I'm just afraid Bramwell's guys are going to come after me."

"Why would they come after you?"

"I'm a loose end."

"You don't know anything about what Bramwell does in his business. Legal or illegal. Hell, they probably don't even know you exist."

"Sam's partner knows. I met him a few nights ago at Club Elektronik. And he was there tonight at the house. He and some Black guy with him tried to kill me too."

"I still don't think you have anything to worry about. The police will find her body and do their investigation thing. And if Bramwell's got one of his cronies working on the force, they'll probably make the whole thing disappear. Which sucks, but they won't find you. And in the meantime, I get to have my sister come on tour with me." Kimi kissed her on the cheek.

"And when the tour's over?"

Kimi shrugged. "I don't know. But you'll figure it out. Have you talked to Bobby?"

"I left him a note when I collected the stuff from my station at the studio."

"What'd you tell him?"

"That he was right about Sam being involved with bad people and that I needed to take off."

"Call him after you get some sleep. And after you get cleaned up. Is this blood?"

For the first time, Avery realized she had blood on her hands. Sam's blood. The sorrow hit her again, but she was all cried out. "I shouldn't be here. What if Bramwell tracks me down? I could be putting you all in danger."

"Nonsense. We're going on the road. New Mexico,

Colorado, Texas. By the time we get back, I'm sure this will have all blown over. I mean, obviously, Sam will still be gone. But hopefully, you can get back to some semblance of your normal."

"I won't even have a place to live."

"We'll worry about that when the time comes. I'm sure Bobby wouldn't mind putting you up in your old room until you find a place. And if he won't, you can crash on our couch for as long as you need. Okay?"

Avery felt dead inside—ironic considering her love of all things goth. "Okay."

"Come on." Kimi helped her to her feet. "Let's get you cleaned up. I'll grab some sheets and a pillow for you to sleep on."

"Thank you, Kimi. You've always been there for me. Even when my asshole bio dad kicked me out of the house."

"I just wish I'd been able to convince my folks to let you move in with me so you didn't end up on the streets."

"You stayed in touch. That was more than anyone else did. And for the record, I didn't hurt your stalker. I just talked to him."

"What'd you tell him?"

"That Chupa was ex-Special Forces and if he didn't leave you alone, your husband would rain hellfire down on his ass."

"Chupa wasn't Special Forces. He was an army supply clerk."

"But your stalker didn't know that."

# CHAPTER 12
# THE PRICE OF FAILURE

CUERVO PRESSED the front doorbell to his boss's sprawling estate and waited.

The house, dubbed by Mr. Bramwell as the Raven's Nest, stood atop a summit in the Biltmore Highlands neighborhood. The rugged beauty of Piestewa Peak and the Phoenix Mountains Preserve rose around them.

"Helluva view here, ain't it?" Luther said.

"Let's hope it's not the last thing we see," Cuervo replied glumly.

The door opened. A slender man in his sixties with thinning hair and wearing a black suit acknowledged them with a nod. "Mr. Bramwell is in his study."

"Thanks, Jeeves," Luther said.

It wasn't the man's name, but for the life of him, Cuervo couldn't remember what the butler's real name was.

Cuervo trudged the hardwood floors as if he were walking to his execution. Sam had been his partner, so he was already under suspicion by association. If he didn't recover the money soon, it could easily look like he was involved in the theft.

He knocked on the heavy oaken door to Mr. Bramwell's study.

"Come in." The desk Bramwell sat behind was the twin to his office at the club. "Where is my money, gentlemen?" The man spoke the words so evenly and calmly, it only added to the implied threat.

Cuervo glanced at Luther, hoping he'd take the brunt of Bramwell's wrath.

"You were right. The girlfriend showed up," Luther muttered humbly. "We almost got her."

"Almost?" Bramwell's face was expressionless.

"She slipped out the back and jumped the back wall to the neighbor's yard."

"And you gave chase, surely."

"Bitch was too fast. Like a fucking gazelle."

"I don't give two shits about the girl's athletic prowess. Where is my money?"

"We're sure she has it," Cuervo chimed in. "I talked with our guy in Phoenix Homicide. He's working with us to track her down. We'll have the money back soon. I swear."

"And what do you two intend to do in the meantime? Sit on your hands like little girls? This thing happened on your watch." He pointed a finger at Cuervo. "She was your partner."

Cuervo wanted to remind the man that he and Luther had been providing security for Bramwell and his Las Vegas guests when Sam broke into the safe.

But he didn't think pointing that out would go far in tempering the man's anger. They didn't have the money and didn't have any leads on where Avery or the money might be. But he did have Sam's phone.

"Don't worry, sir," Cuervo said. "I'm going to get the money back. Every dollar."

"You better do so and quickly, or we'll all be hanging from a bridge with our guts ripped out."

# CHAPTER 13
# ROAD TRIP

SLEEP CAME to Avery in brief gasps. Her body still ached from the beat down at the club. Lying on Kimi's lumpy sofa didn't help.

When she finally drifted off, her slumber was haunted by a highlights reel of her trauma. Murdered lost kids. Melissa's body riddled with shrapnel from a terrorist bomb.

Grief hung on Avery like a lead-lined coat. And when the anguish ran its course, all that remained was the urge to avenge Sam's death. And that frightened her all the more.

Bobby J. had warned her against vengeance, saying that if she planned to hurt someone, she should dig two graves in the shifting sands of Tatooine—one for her enemy and one for her.

He was always mixing Buddhist wisdom with *Star Wars* references. She never understood his fascination with the sci-fi franchise, but she loved him, so she played along like a dutiful daughter. At least most of the time.

He'd once compared Theodore Bramwell to Jabba the Hut, to which she'd replied that would make Sam a female Han Solo. No wonder she had fallen in love with her. Who didn't love Han?

He had smiled and tapped the Princess Leia inked on his

arm. "I guess that would make you the princess of this story."

She was going to miss his nerdy sense of humor and goofy smile. Even his corny dad jokes.

She tried to tell herself she would be back. Just didn't know when or how. Not while Bramwell and his goons were looking for her. Not that she knew anything. Sam hadn't even told her where she worked, much less who she worked for, until a few days ago. But Bramwell and his thugs didn't know that. And they clearly didn't like loose ends after what they did to Sam.

"Morning, sleepyhead."

Avery's heart jolted at Kimi's voice. She forced open an eyelid to the horror of daylight streaming between the slats of the blinds.

"Morning."

Kimi plopped down beside her and offered her a mug of coffee. "Get any sleep?"

"Some."

"I'm so sorry this happened, Ave. Can't imagine if something happened to Chupa. I'd probably just crawl inside my string bass and never come out again."

Avery sipped her coffee. "At least Chupa wouldn't be involved with a mobster like Theodore Bramwell."

As soon as she said the words, she felt pangs of guilt for blaming Sam. Pressure built behind her eyes as if she would cry again, but she didn't have any tears left. She felt like a dried-out husk of her former self.

"The psychos that hurt Sam, they the ones who did this to your face?" Kimi asked.

Ave touched a finger to her cheekbone, which was still tender from her encounter with the frat boys at Club Elektronik. "This? No. Tried to protect a woman from a couple of drunks at Sam's club. Stupid me."

"I spoke with Chupa about your situation. He's cool with you tagging along."

"I can be your roadie, helping you set up and sell merch. And you won't even have to pay me. I just need to be with my best friend and somewhere those murderous fucks can't get to me until this blows over."

"If you work, we're going to pay you. But that's entirely your choice. You're family."

Avery nodded wordlessly.

"Were you wanting to drive your Caddy, or did you want to ride with us in the Tahoe? Torch and McCobb will be driving the equipment van."

"I'd prefer to ride with you, if it's okay. Not sure what to do with the Gothmobile, though, since I don't have a home anymore. Don't feel safe leaving it at Seoul Fire."

"You can park it at McCobb's place. He normally keeps the van inside his backyard fence. I'm sure he'd be cool letting you stash your car there while we're on tour. No one will bother it."

"Thanks."

"No problem. Well, we better get ready. First stop's Tucson. And there's always a traffic jam somewhere on the 10."

Avery took a quick shower and got dressed. Marco "Chupa" Melendez, who was Kimi's husband and the lead singer and guitarist for the band, helped her carry her bags to their Tahoe. He was a tall brawny guy with a goofy laugh, reminding her a little of Seth Rogen.

Two of the bags belonged to Sam. Obviously, Sam would no longer need whatever was in them, but she didn't have the emotional energy to go through them just yet. And she didn't feel right about leaving them at Kimi's. So they agreed to let her bring them with her.

When everything was packed, Avery climbed into the Tahoe, sitting behind Chupa, who was in the driver's seat.

She slumped against the door as lifeless as a pile of discarded clothes.

Any other time, she would have a blast going on tour with Damaged Souls. Laughing and chatting with Kimi and Chupa. Singing along to the Coffinshakers and the Horror-pops on the stereo.

But after the events of the night before, Avery simply stared out the window, feeling empty and dead inside. She ached for Sam's arms around her, to kiss her lips and tell her it would all be okay. But that would never happen again. All the love in the world had evaporated.

"What do you want from inside? Breakfast burrito? Donuts? Something to drink?"

Kimi had turned in her seat to face Avery. They had stopped at the Love's Truck Stop, the last place to gas up before the hundred-mile stretch of desert between Phoenix and Tucson. Parked next to them sat a white van emblazoned with the Damaged Souls logo.

"No thanks. Not hungry."

"Babe, you have to eat. I know grief is a horrible appetite killer, but starving yourself won't bring Sam back."

Avery said nothing.

"Avery Siobhan Byrne, I love you more than air. But if you don't eat and drink, I'll instruct Torch and McCobb to force-feed you. And believe me, no one wants to see that."

Torch Shaheen and Michael McCobb were the band's lead guitarist and drummer, respectively. They were also notorious for playing pranks, especially on the band's manager, Scott Murray. Kimi had shared countless stories of the pair's antics.

During one tour, Torch and McCobb had twice sent strippers—one female, another male—dressed as cops to Murray's motel room in the middle of the night.

At the next stop on the tour, they called in a noise complaint that had resulted in real cops showing up. Only

Murray wrongly assumed they were more strippers. Murray spent a night in jail for shoving one of the cops, though the charges were later dropped.

Avery was surprised Murray hadn't fired the band. Turned out Murray was more interested in payback. He knew Torch occasionally had nightmares of glowing red eyes in the dark. Something to do with reading *The Amityville Horror* as a child.

Murray arranged for a bouquet of flowers to be delivered to the motel room Torch and McCobb shared. What they didn't know was he had slipped a Bluetooth device into the flowers.

That night when Torch was asleep, Murray activated the device, which made grunting pig sounds and had LED lights that resembled demonic red eyes. Torch's screams woke the entire floor.

McCobb didn't escape unscathed either. At a gig in Las Vegas, Murray released a jar full of moths into the cab of the equipment van after learning that McCobb had an intense phobia of flying insects. No one knew where or how Murray had acquired the jar of moths. But the pranks had been going back and forth ever since.

Before Avery could agree to Kimi's suggestion of food, Torch and McCobb appeared outside her door. Avery lowered the window.

"Hey, Torch! Looks like we got ourselves a stowaway," McCobb teased.

Torch shook his head in mock disapproval. "Murray's gonna flip his toupee! He hates surprises."

"Hey, guys." Avery managed a weak smile. "How's it going?"

"Better now that you're along for the ride." Torch rested his arm on the window. "Saw you on the cover of *Inked Magazine* a few months ago. Very impressive. What's a celebrity tattoo artist like you doing slumming with the likes of us?"

"Maybe she can be our new mascot! Ever since that one groupie broke her foot—what was her name?"

"Beatrix."

"Right! Ever since Beatrix broke her foot after trying to jump the stage, we've been without a mascot."

Avery wasn't sure how seriously to take this discourse. "Just needed to get out of town for a while."

"Oooh, intriguing. On the run, are we?" McCobb joked. "Were you the one who robbed that bank on Camelback and Seventh Avenue? The security footage they showed on the web was grainy, but that woman looked familiar."

"Guys, leave her alone. She had a rough night." Kimi pushed them away from the car.

"Chill, Kimi," McCobb replied. "We're just kidding around. Avery looks like she could use some cheering up. Right, Torch?"

"Exactly. Besides, I've been needing a new tat. I'd love for her to do it. Your work's amazing, Avery. Would you be willing?"

"The last thing she needs is you clowns putting her to work," Kimi said, still trying to shoo them away. "She needs some R & R."

"I'll do it," Avery said.

"See?" said Torch. "Whatever you normally charge, I'll pay it."

"Fine. But not now," Kimi insisted. "Last thing she needs right now are you two knuckleheads pestering her."

"Excuse me," Torch said. "I'll have you know that I'm the goofball. McCobb's the knucklehead. Or is it the other way round? I forget."

"You're both going to be dead meat if you don't get back to the equipment van."

"Bye, Avery! See you in Took-son," McCobb said, deliberately mispronouncing Tucson.

"I bought you a chicken-and-cheese breakfast burrito. I also have a bag of other unhealthy delights. Fried pork skins, candy bars, beef jerky. In short, essential road trip fare." Kimi offered her something wrapped in an orange paper wrapper then held out a plastic bag filled with drinks. "Also got some sodas, bottled water, energy drinks, and juice. You need to hydrate, baby."

Avery took the burrito and selected a bottle of water from the bag. "Thanks, sweetie. I appreciate you looking out for me."

"Don't mention it. Now, if Murray ever shows up, we can finally get on the road. He always throws a snit fit anytime one of us shows up a minute late for sound checks."

Just as she said it, a black Mercedes Benz with peeling paint and a missing hood ornament pulled up next to them. A heavyset man in his fifties with doll-like hair plugs climbed out. His suit was rumpled, as was his expression. Scott Murray, the manager, no doubt.

"I hate the idiot drivers in this city. Two cars driving ten miles an hour under the speed limit next to each other on the highway. Damned rolling roadblock." Murray's eyes locked onto Avery. "Kimi, who the hell is this? Not another one of your vagabond groupies?"

"Scott Murray, meet Avery Byrne. She's my sister from another mister. I invited her along."

"And where does she plan to sleep? In your car? Because I haven't booked any extra rooms."

Avery realized why Torch and McCobb loved pranking him so much. The man had all the charm of an oozing cold sore.

"Relax, Murray," Kimi soothed. "I'm sure we can accommodate her somehow."

"I can pay for my own room," Avery volunteered. "I'll even help run the merch table if you like."

Murray looked back and forth between the two women. "Next time, clear it with me first. We ready to roll?"

Kimi exchanged a bemused glanced with Avery. "Torch and McCobb are in the van. We're all just waiting on you."

"Fine. I'm going to hit the can, and we can get on our way." He marched off to the convenience store.

"Charming guy," Avery said.

"Don't take it personal, Ave," Chupa said. "Just his way of making himself feel he's in charge."

"Why have him around if he's that much of an asshole?"

"Because he gets us good gigs. Not an easy thing for a gothabilly band these days."

"And he got us that record deal with Evil Empire Music," Kimi added. "Doubled the advance from their initial offer, got the royalty rate bumped up by seven percentage points, and made them remove a bunch of rights-grab clauses from the contract. He's a bit of a jerk sometimes, but the dude knows how to manage a band."

A few minutes later, Murray emerged from the store and slipped into his car without a word.

"And away we go," Kimi said, cranking up the stereo.

# CHAPTER 14
# IN THE NEWS

THE BREAKFAST BURRITO was tough and chewy. Probably from being under the heat lamps too long. But it was warm and spicy and left Avery feeling a little less dead inside.

As Avery ate, she checked the internet news feeds and found a local story about a woman shot to death in West Phoenix. Though they didn't mention Sam by name, the story quoted police as saying the victim appeared to have been tortured prior to being shot. Police stated they were following multiple leads but refused to mention any suspects.

A chill ran down Avery's spine. How long before the police considered her a person of interest or even a suspect?

Her instinct was to call them to explain what had happened and clear her name. But if the detectives on the case were on Bramwell's payroll, that would only get her arrested, or worse.

Her phone rang.

"Hello?"

"Avery? Tell me what's going on, kiddo." It was Bobby J. His tone was that of a concerned parent.

"Appa." She felt as if her ability to put words to her feelings had been sucked out of her. "I… I put it in the note."

"So, Sam's dead. I am… I'm so sorry, sweetie."

She caught herself crying again. "I'm so… so…"

"Hey, kiddo. I get it. You're probably feeling a thousand different emotions. Grief, anger, fear. But why would they kill her?"

"I think because they'd be afraid she'd talk to the cops. She wasn't real specific. It's all my fault."

"Your fault? How could it possibly be your fault?"

"I told her about Bramwell's thugs putting you in the hospital. My words must have hit home, because I think that's why she quit working for him. And then I sent her back home to pick up Rainbow."

"The toy unicorn Melissa gave you? Oh, honey, that doesn't make it your fault. Clearly, something else was going on. News said she'd been tortured." There was a long pause.

"She was. I found her at the house, Appa." The horrific image of Sam's body shook her. "She was tied to a chair. She looked… They did all kinds of horrible things to her. But she was still alive. At least until they came back. They saw me and started shooting. I barely got out of there."

"Oh, my sweet girl. How horrible and terrifying! Did you call the police?"

"No. You'd said Bramwell's got cops working for him."

"He does. Or at least he did. I can't imagine things have improved. So where are you?"

"Don't want to say."

"Okay. Fair enough. Are you safe?"

"I think so. At least for now."

"Good. I want you safe. Is there anything you need? Anything at all I can do to help you?"

"No, I'm good for now. I'm with friends."

"Avery, I wish I could be wherever you are. You're my daughter. I love you, and I'm worried about you."

"I know. I love you too. Just don't want to put you in danger too." Avery glanced up to catch Kimi looking at her with a worried expression. She wondered if joining the band for their tour would bring trouble their way.

"Appa, why have so many people in my life died?" she whispered. "The Lost Kids, Melissa, and now Sam."

"I wish I had a good answer for you."

"I'm cursed."

"No, you are not cursed."

"God is punishing me for killing Vinnie D. Or maybe for being transgender."

"Stop it, Ave. You know that's not true. If there is a God, a loving God, he wouldn't make you trans and then punish you for it. Nor do I think it's because of what happened with Vinnie D. The Buddha teaches that all things are impermanent. As a goth, you understand the concept of memento mori. We all will die one day."

"It can't be a coincidence all these people in my life are dead at such a young age. It's bad karma. My bad karma."

"That's not how karma works, kiddo. Nothing you did caused these things to happen. As the Buddha says, 'Shit happens.'"

"I don't think the Buddha ever said that."

"Maybe not in so many words. Although the First Noble Truth is that life is suffering. Kinda the same thing. Regardless, none of what has happened is your fault. Not Sam, certainly not Melissa. Not even the Lost Kids, despite what you might think."

"Sam quit because of me. She kept saying I inspired her to be a better person. She'd still be alive if it weren't for me."

"People who work for gangsters like Bramwell end up dead or in jail eventually. That's the life they choose. That was her karma."

"Don't blame Sam," Avery snapped.

"I'm sorry. I know how much you're hurting. When

Missy died, I was so angry. Not just at the terrorists who set off the bomb but at myself for encouraging her to come with us to that damn rally. I was pissed at the entire universe. It's okay to be angry and sad and whatever else you are feeling. But don't get stuck there. Don't let yourself become consumed with the fear and anger and hate. Remember that fear leads to…"

"Don't be quoting Yoda to me, Appa. Not right now."

"Okay. I won't. Just know I'm here for you."

"I know. For all your Jedi Buddhist fanboy whatever, you showed me what unconditional love was. If it hadn't been for you, I'd probably be dead or in jail right now."

"And you helped me after Missy died. You really did. We're good for each other. So promise me you will come back. And that until you do, you will keep yourself safe."

"I promise, Appa. Salanghaeyo."

"Love you, too, kiddo."

Avery hung up. They never said goodbye to each other. They always parted with "I love you."

She felt a hand on hers and looked up to see Kimi with tears streaming down her face. She didn't say anything. But she didn't have to.

## CHAPTER 15
# THEORIES OF THE CASE

"I'M TELLING YOU, LT, Theodore Bramwell's connected to this somehow," Hardin said as he stood in Lieutenant Ross's office. "The way this poor woman was tortured. Haven't seen anything like this in a while. Just like the Gibson case from six months ago."

"Which you never closed," Ross finished.

"Because Bramwell is one slippery son of a bitch. He knows how to cover his tracks, but it's got his name all over it."

"How so?" Ross had always been a slender man in the years that Hardin had known him. But after his wife, Angela, had left him a few months earlier, he'd started putting on weight and had grown a caterpillar under his nose that didn't fit his face.

"For starts, the victim, Samantha Ferguson worked for the bastard. As did that Whitmore guy who went missing a few days ago. And Bramwell owned the house where she was living."

"You think Bramwell tortured one of his own?"

"I don't know. But it looked like she was moving out. Maybe she crossed Bramwell. The feds have been after him for years. Maybe they flipped her and he found out."

"I need more than maybes, detective."

"We'll know more when we get the forensics. I notified Ferguson's parents but they claim they hadn't spoken with her in several years. Apparently, she'd been in trouble a lot in her youth. Juvie and then served some time in Florence for aggravated assault."

"Thinking they may have been involved?"

"No. Dysfunctional family to be sure but didn't strike me as giving two shits about the girl. Not enough to murder her like this. I'm still trying to get hold of this Avery Byrne, the woman who lived with the vic."

"What do we know about her?"

"Avery Siobhan Byrne, age twenty-two. Formerly Avery Stephen Byrne. Roommates, maybe lovers."

"This Byrne person got a sheet?"

"Two busts when she was a teen, one for solicitation, the other for trespassing. Served a few months in juvie for solicitation. Trespassing charge was dropped. Ended up in a foster home at sixteen until she aged out of the system. Nothing since then."

"What about her family?"

"The birth father, Joe Byrne, claims she ran away at thirteen, but I got the impression he kicked her out for being trans. Foster father is a Kwang-Sun Jeong. No sheet. Runs a tattoo parlor near Camelback and Seventeenth Avenue. I'm going to talk to him soon as Valentine gets back from the crime lab."

"Okay, keep me posted," Ross replied.

Hardin returned to his desk and was digging deeper into Avery Byrne's background when Valentine strode into the bullpen, holding up a folder. "We got a hit on the gun."

Hardin looked up from his computer. "Yeah? Whaddya got?"

"The Glock is registered to Ferguson."

"So, she was shot with her own gun?"

"The fatal shot was a through-and-through. Preliminary ballistics report suggests the slugs pulled from the walls match the gun. And we got latent prints off it belonging to Avery Byrne, the roommate." Valentine said, using air quotes on the last word. "I'm thinking maybe a lesbian lover's quarrel. Or Ferguson found out that Byrne used to be a dude, and we get the whole fucking *Crying Game* scenario."

"I turned up something interesting too. Ferguson worked security for Club Elektronik, which is owned by Theodore Bramwell, head of the Desert Mafia, as is the house where Ferguson and Byrne lived."

"*Rumored* head of the Desert Mafia. Last I checked, he's never been convicted of anything."

"Listen, youngblood, just because the man's too slick to do his own wet work don't mean he's clean. Only reason he isn't behind bars is because the few who dared cut a deal turned up dead before they could testify. With this Whitmore guy missing at the same time Ferguson turns up tortured to death, my instinct says Bramwell's involved."

"But to kill one of his own? Seems a little thin." Valentine made a face. "Could be a rival gang with a beef against the Desert Mafia. Maybe the 4-17s, Los Jaguares, or the Freedom Brotherhood."

Hardin shrugged. "I don't know yet. I'm thinking we should bring the Gang Crime Unit in on this one."

"We got Byrne's prints on the gun. She's clearly our shooter. Let's bring her in. See what she has to say. Any idea where the girl might be?"

"From the looks of the house, I'm guessing she's moved out and in the wind. Last place of employment was Seoul Fire Tattoo, same place her foster father works. I'm thinking we pay the man a visit."

~

"You doing okay?" Bobby J. asked the young woman lying on his table. He was outlining a blossom-laden cherry tree that would eventually stretch across her back and around her hip.

"Yeah," the woman replied quietly.

"Let me know when you need to take a break."

"Okay."

The chimes over the front door rang. Possibly a walk-in or a curious inquirer considering their first tattoo. A folding privacy screen he'd setup for his client blocked his view of the door.

Butcher was working on a client nearby, but he wasn't much of a conversationalist. Frisco was still on vacation. And Avery… he had no idea where she was, but he hoped she was safe. That left him to deal with this visitor.

"I'm afraid I'll have to see who that is. Would you care for something to drink?"

"No, I'm good," the woman said dreamily.

Bobby switched off his machine, removed his gloves, and walked around the screen to greet the visitors.

Two men in suits stood at his front door—a Black man in his late fifties, the other in his thirties and of Mediterranean ancestry. He didn't need to see their badges to know they were cops.

"Can I help you gentlemen?" he asked.

They flashed their detective's shields.

"Detective Hardin, Phoenix PD Homicide," the older man said. "This here's my partner, Detective Valentine. We're looking for Avery Byrne."

"I'm afraid she's not in at the moment." He considered saying she'd had a death in the family but didn't want to let on that he'd spoken with her or knew anything about Sam's murder.

"Do you know where we can find her? It's urgent that we speak with her."

Bobby regarded them with suspicion. The young guy looked familiar, but he couldn't place him. "I'm sorry. I do not know where she is. Perhaps try her at home."

"You got a phone number for her?" Valentine asked.

Bobby considered saying no. The last thing he wanted to do was put Avery in further jeopardy, especially if one or both of these guys were in Bramwell's pocket. Even if they weren't, he had heard horror stories of how cops treated trans women.

But stonewalling them would look suspicious, especially if they knew she'd been his foster daughter.

He rattled off a phone number. It was Avery's number, except that he gave them a 602 area code instead of the correct 623. A plausible mistake. It might not stop them from eventually finding her, but could slow them down enough that they might find whoever was actually responsible for Sam's murder first.

Valentine wrote the number in his notepad. "Were you expecting her in today?"

"She sets her own hours, depending on her clientele."

"Did she contact you and say why she wasn't coming in?"

"She didn't mention anything when she was here yesterday. Is she in some kind of trouble? Has something happened?"

"We just need to ask her some questions about a case we're investigating," Hardin said, his face an unreadable mask.

"You said you're with homicide. Someone was murdered? Who?" Bobby tried to appear genuinely shocked. And in truth, Sam's death troubled him, if only because it added to the many traumas Avery had already faced in her young life.

"Samantha Ferguson," Valentine replied. "You know her?"

Bobby wrestled with how much to share. "Avery and Sam lived together."

"Were they a couple?" Hardin asked.

"Yes. For a few months now."

"They having relationship troubles?"

"Not at all. They seemed very much in love according to Avery."

Valentine locked eyes with him. "How long you known Avery?"

"Several years. I was her foster father. And her employer here. She's a talented artist. That's some of her work there."

Bobby pointed to some photos taped to the wall. One depicted Yama, a Hindu god of death. Another was a stylized version of the Pale Man from the movie *Pan's Labyrinth*. A third looked like exposed muscle, blood vessels, and bone on the inside of someone's forearm. There were also zombies, demons, and and other dark fantastical creatures.

Valentine sneered. "Looks rather twisted, you ask me. Like something only a seriously disturbed individual would create. And that," he said, pointing to a back piece depicting an adult woman's head emerging from a vagina, "is obscene."

"That, detective, was inspired by a Frida Kahlo painting and represents a woman giving birth to herself. It is neither disgusting nor obscene. It is simply art."

"Whatever you say. But you can't tell me a woman who drew this stuff didn't have dark thoughts. If you know where she is, I strongly advise you to tell us. Obstructing a murder investigation is a serious crime. We could charge you with conspiracy murder after the fact."

"I honestly have no idea where she is, detectives."

"Has she been in touch with her birth family?" Hardin asked.

Bobby snorted. "Not since her parents kicked her out of the house when she was a teenager. She's mentioned having a younger brother, but I don't think she's in contact with him."

Hardin was scribbling furiously in his notebook. "Do you know how we can get in touch with them?"

"Nope."

"What about him? He know anything?" Valentine pointed to Butcher, who was inking a man's shoulder. "Sir, could you come over here a minute?"

Butcher looked first at Hardin then at Bobby.

"He doesn't know anything either," Bobby assured him.

"We'll be the ones to decide that." Valentine strode over. "What's your name, buddy?"

After a long minute, he replied, "Butcher."

"Great, another sicko."

"His name is Ethan Butcher." Bobby stepped toward them, but Valentine held out a warning hand.

"Fine, Mr. Butcher. Any idea where we might find your coworker, Avery Byrne?"

Butcher shook his head.

"You friends with her?"

Butcher nodded.

"Not much of a talker, are you?"

Butcher shrugged.

"You hiding something?" Valentine's tone turned acid. "Or you just a retard?"

"That's enough," Bobby said, stepping between the detective and Butcher. "I will not tolerate ableist slurs or harassment in my studio. We don't know where Avery is. I gave you her phone number. Whatever you may think of her art, she's a good kid. Keeps her nose clean. If she's mixed up in Sam's death, then she's another victim, not a perpetrator."

The two men stood glaring at each other until finally Hardin said, "Come on, Lorenzo. I think we're done here. Thanks for your assistance, gentlemen."

The two proceeded to the entrance. Just as he was

walking out, Valentine turned and said, "I find you holding out on me, Mr. Jeong, there's gonna be hell to pay."

Bobby watched them get into a black Ford Explorer and drive out of the lot.

"Child, what have you got yourself mixed up in?" he whispered.

# CHAPTER 16
# A BAG FULL OF TROUBLE

AVERY SLEPT for much of the drive down to Tucson. She woke to the sound of car doors being slammed shut.

"We here?" she asked groggily.

Chupa laughed his goofy Seth Rogen laugh. "Yep. End of the line, girly girl. Everyone off the train."

She dragged her fatigued body out of the truck. The sun was glaring and the air hot, close to a hundred degrees. Not unusual for the first of May.

They were parked in a motel lot. A sign proclaimed it the Sunrise Inn, part of a chain of moderately priced motels in the southwest. She had stayed in one when she'd attended a tattoo arts festival in LA a few years back with Bobby J.

"Hope they have a room for me," she whispered to no one. The parking lot already looked three-quarters filled. Who knew how many more people already had reservations?

"Don't worry." Kimi put an arm around her waist as they walked behind the guys. "If they don't, you can always bunk with Chupa and me."

"Crash the love nest? I don't think so."

"Or take the spare bed in Murray's room, though somehow, I don't think he'd be too eager for a roommate. You could even bunk with Torch and McCobb. They'd love to have you, I'm sure."

Avery laughed for the first time in what felt like forever. "Not sure I'd survive that one. Suddenly, the love nest doesn't sound so bad. But I'd rather have my own room, if they have one."

By the time Avery and Kimi reached the front desk, the guys had all checked in.

"I need a room too," Avery told the man behind the counter. "Preferably near theirs."

The guy behind the counter typed away on his keyboard. "We do have a room that is four doors down from them. Will that be okay?"

"So long as it has a bed, I don't care."

"It does. Two queen-size beds."

"Do it."

"Okay, that will be one hundred and forty-nine dollars for the night. I'll just need a credit card."

"A hundred and fifty bucks? No, it's just me in the room."

"I understand. If there were more in the room, the price would be an additional twenty-nine dollars per person. Would you like the room? We may have one with one double-sized bed for one twenty-nine a night, but it would be on the other side of the motel."

"Avery, if you want, I can ask Chupa to bunk with the boys, and you and I can be roomies. I'm not sure you should be alone anyhow, given what you've been through."

Avery considered it. The last thing she wanted was to inconvenience the band. But if she kept having to pay these rates every night, she'd be running low on funds pretty soon.

"I'll take the room." She handed the man her card.

Fifteen minutes later, Chupa and McCobb carried Sam's two bags while Avery hauled her own suitcase and a computer bag. Torch carried the box containing her tattoo equipment and supplies.

"What do you got in this blue gym bag? Bricks?" Chupa asked. "Must weigh about fifty pounds."

"Maybe it's drugs," McCobb teased. "Party in Avery's room after the show!"

"They're Sam's. Not sure what's in them."

McCobb set his down. "Maybe we should look inside."

Before he could unzip the top, Chupa kicked him. "Hey, nosy! Your job's to carry the lady's bag. Not poke your nose in her business."

"Fine, be a spoilsport." McCobb picked the bag back up again and resumed hauling it to Avery's room.

When they reached the door, Avery opened it with her key card and thanked them after they left the bags and the box inside.

"We'll let you get settled," Chupa said before they left. "We'll be heading out to do a sound check soon."

The room was standard motel-chain-vanilla blah. But after the night before, she could use a little blah.

She hefted the blue gym bag onto the bed, unzipped it, and froze.

Countless stacks of hundred-dollar bills filled the bag. Her first thought was that they had to be fake. Her second thought was to wonder how much was in there if it was real.

She opened the bag more fully and counted roughly six stacks wide, five stacks long, and eight stacks deep. According to the gold-and-white band around the stacks, each one comprised ten grand worth of C-notes.

It took her a moment to do the calculations in her head. When she was done, she gasped. The bag contained nearly two and a half million dollars. *Where the hell did Sam get…?*

"Fuck me."

The room tilted, and she fell onto the bed, spilling bundles of cash onto the floor.

*Sam, what did you do?* she wondered, heart thundering in her chest. She felt sick to her stomach. Why would Sam steal millions of dollars from Bramwell? And how?

No wonder they'd tortured her. They were trying to get their money back. Money that she now had.

"Fuck me," she repeated.

A knock on the door pulled her from her thoughts. "Ave?" It was Kimi.

"Just a minute," Avery replied. She frantically gathered up the stacks of bills that had fallen out of the bag, crammed them back in, and zipped up the bag before hiding it on the other side of the bed. "Coming."

She opened the door. "Hey."

"You seem out of breath. You okay?"

"Was on the toilet." Avery stepped aside to let Kimi in.

"Just wanted to make sure your room was suitable."

"The room? Oh, yeah, it's fine. It's a motel room. How bad can it be?"

Her words triggered the memory of her and Sam at the Ocotillo Inn. Sadness stabbed at her, but this time, the sharp steel of anger accompanied it. Partly at herself for asking Sam to go back for the unicorn. Partly at Sam for being stupid enough to rob Bramwell.

But mostly at Bramwell and his thugs. Somehow, someday, she would make it right. She would see Bramwell and whoever else was involved in Sam's death get their just deserts.

"Okay, good," Kimi replied. "Me and the band are going to the Batfish Theatre to set up for tonight and do a sound check. Should take us about an hour or so. Did you want to come with, or did you want us to pick you up afterward for dinner?"

"I'd just as soon stay, if that's all right."

"Of course. Whatever you want. You doing okay? I mean, considering."

Avery felt the urge to tell Kimi about the money. She'd never kept secrets from her before. And here Kimi was letting her tag along with the band, being there for her.

But she couldn't bring herself to tell Kimi that Sam had stolen over two million dollars from a sadistic mobster. And because she now had the money, they all had a big fat target on their backs.

"Of course, you're not okay. You just had one of the worst nights of your life, and that's saying something." Kimi side-hugged her. "But you're going to get through this. We're going to help you."

"Thanks, girl," Avery replied. "I don't know what I'd have done if I didn't have you."

"Don't thank me yet. You have an entire tour of having to deal with Torch and McCobb's shenanigans and Murray's incessant griping. You may regret tagging along before it's over."

"Better than being tortured and killed by Bramwell and his men."

"Yeah, no arguing there. Okay, I gotta jet. I'll see you in about an hour. You need anything—toiletries, food, a book to read, whatever—call me. I can pick them up on my way back. In the meantime, there's a vending machine in a hallway about three doors down."

"Okay, thanks again."

"Anytime."

After Kimi left, Avery sat staring at the bag of money. What was she going to do with millions of dollars in stolen Desert Mafia money?

Her phone rang. She figured it was probably Kimi calling to tell her one last thing. Her heart leapt into her throat when she saw the caller ID. It was Sam's phone.

For an instant, she dared to think that maybe, just maybe, Sam was still alive. But no. Those fuckers had blown her brains out. Her death was on the news. So who the hell was calling?

After four rings, it stopped. A few minutes later, a chime showed the caller had left a voicemail. The phone shook in her trembling hand.

Finally, she gathered her courage and played the message.

"Hey, Avery. It's Cuervo."

## CHAPTER 17
# AVERY THE AVENGER

"HEY, Avery. It's Cuervo. We met the other night at the club. I want you to know it wasn't me who hurt Sam. I did everything I could to prevent it. But I guess it doesn't matter, does it?

"Thing is, she took something. Something valuable that didn't belong to her. It belongs to Mr. Bramwell. And I need it back. I think you know what I'm talking about. Least, I hope to God you do."

There was a long pause before he continued. "I don't want anything to happen to you. Sam always said you were a nice person, and I believed her. So, if you return what Sam took, I'll do everything in my power to keep you safe. But if you don't, well, there'll be a lot of trouble. For you. For all of us. Mr. Bramwell has a lot of connections. More than that, there are some bad people who are also after you know what. Worse than Bramwell or any of the folks who work for him."

Another pause. Avery realized she was trembling.

"Do all of us a favor, Avery. Call me back on Sammy's phone. We can arrange to meet. You return what she took. It ends there. I promise. You get on with your life. Okay, I hope to hear from you."

The message ended.

Avery struggled to catch her breath, while her body convulsed with a mixture of fear, anger, and confusion. How could she trust Cuervo? He'd been there at the house along with another man when the shooting began.

Even if she did turn over the money, what was to stop them from killing her too? He'd obviously betrayed Sam, who had been his partner. Or was she just assuming that because they showed up when they did? She couldn't remember if she shot first or they did.

She didn't even want the money. Who knew what horrible things Bramwell's organization had done to earn it? How many lives destroyed? How many people traumatized by violence? It was blood money, pure and simple. And it was nothing but trouble.

And yet she couldn't just dump it. Not that much money. Two million bucks? If they ever tracked her down, there was a chance she could use it as a bargaining chip. It would be stupid to get rid of it. And yet, carrying it around also seemed like a risk. Not just for her, but for Kimi and the band as well.

She powered off her phone and popped out the SIM card. The last thing she needed was for Bramwell to have his cronies or the cops in his pocket tracking her down. She probably shouldn't be using her bank cards either. Nothing that left an electronic trail. But that meant she needed to use cash.

Again, she stared down at the bag of money. The money that cost Sam her life. She unzipped the top, took out a bundle, and thumbed through it, all crisp hundred-dollar bills. The yellow ochre band had the number $10,000 printed on it. Ten grand in this small stack. It was mind-boggling.

She tore off the band and stuffed the cash into her purse then tossed the torn paper strip back in the bag and zipped it closed again.

A thrill ran through her. She had money. A shitload of money. And yeah, those assholes were out hunting her to get it back. But this also gave her power. Leverage.

She thought back to the person she had been before she'd met Bobby, when she and her fellow homeless teens, who called themselves the Lost Kids, were squatting in that empty house downtown on Portland Street in Downtown Phoenix.

She'd been reading a dog-eared copy of *Peter Pan* at the time. Not the Disneyfied version, but the original story by J. M. Barrie. Part of her felt like Wendy Darling, looking after the Lost Boys.

And part of her felt like Peter Pan, bold and wild and willing to do whatever it took to protect those in her care. Pan the Avenger, he called himself when he showed up to rescue Wendy and the Lost Boys from the pirates.

One morning, three suits had showed up at the house—a tall woman with blond hair and two forgettable-looking men. The woman screamed at them, saying the house was hers and that they were trespassing. One of the men called the cops.

Avery and a few of the older kids hurriedly rousted everyone from sleep to get out of there, with no choice but to leave behind most of their belongings.

Avery had been furious. They were only there because they had nowhere else to go. The church-run teen shelter had been a viper pit of drug dealers, pimps, and pedophiles. And the foster system wasn't much better. This blond bitch, who obviously owned multiple houses, couldn't let them have a half-decent place to sleep?

Just as Avery had helped the last of the littles to escape, one of the suits had grabbed her and held her until the cops arrived.

She was arrested and spent a night in jail. She had spent a few months in juvie for solicitation a couple of years earlier. A sick joke, considering the shit that happened to her once she was in the boys' detention facility. Sex work was illegal, but prison rape was ignored. No wonder the officers were called "screws."

When Avery was taken for her court appearance on the trespassing charge, she noticed the written complaint listed the blond woman's name and address on it. A plan formed in Avery's mind. She slipped a copy of the complaint into her DOC jumpsuit when no one was looking.

As the overweight bailiff was about to recuff her on her the back to lockup, Avery used her gymnastic skills to escape his grip and sprint out of the courtroom. *Bad cop,* she thought. *No doughnut.*

Once she'd ducked out a fire exit, she disappeared onto the street and shed the jumpsuit in favor of some clothes she found in a donation drop site. And that was when Avery the Avenger was born.

Using the computers at the Burton Barr Library, she learned that Chloe Howard, the owner of the house they'd been squatting in, was an investment banker. A little digging turned up that Howard owned a dozen properties across the Valley, including a low-rent apartment complex in central Phoenix. Something about it caught her attention. Not that she wanted to live there. *Hell no. But maybe, just maybe…*

She took a bus to the complex. Mountain View Terraces. The name sounded nice. The place was a dump. Boarded-up windows. Overgrown shrubs. Gang graffiti. Roof rats scurrying about.

When Avery talked to the tenants, she learned it was even worse than it appeared. Calls for maintenance went unanswered. Apartments had electrical problems, toilets that wouldn't flush, and broken refrigerators and stoves. In one building, the air-conditioning had been out for a month with no sign of a repair person, despite repeated requests. And it was almost June.

In another building, the roof leaked, and black mold had spread across the ceiling and down one wall. Chloe Howard was a freakin' slumlord.

Avery recorded videos of her interviews with the tenants and took dozens of photos of the violations. She compiled them onto a USB flash drive and took a bus to Howard's office in Scottsdale.

She got past the receptionist by convincing him she was Chloe Howard's daughter.

Once Avery was in the office, Howard glared at her. "What are you doing here?"

Avery reclined in the leather guest chair. "Nice digs you got here. You must make a lot of money doing what you do."

"If you don't tell me what this is about, I'm calling the police."

Avery sat up and smiled. "Please do. And then I can give them this." She held up the flash drive.

"What is that?"

"Evidence."

"Evidence of what? You and your fellow vagrants breaking into my house downtown?"

"I took a little trip to Mountain View Terraces." Avery thought she saw the faintest flicker of concern in the woman's eyes.

"If you think I'm going to rent you one of those apartments, you're sadly mistaken."

"No, I got no interest in living there, despite the lovely view of North Mountain. But I did interview many of the residents there. Took loads of photos and videos. Black mold. Leaky roofs. No air conditioning. And no matter how many times they call the management company, no one ever shows up to fix anything. I'm no lawyer, but I think the legal term is *uninhabitable*."

When Howard didn't reply, Avery continued. "I read there are laws against that sort of thing. Massive fines. Possibly jail time. Ever been to jail? Probably not. Not a rich white girl like you.

"And then there's the publicity. I bet Channel 3 would love to run a story like this on their consumer advocate segment. *Phoenix Living* could do a whole feature on Phoenix's sexy blond slumlord. Maybe even get your pretty face on the front page, you holding your hand out to ward off the camera. 'Don't take my picture. No!'"

Howard stared at her for a long time without speaking. Eventually, she said, "What is it you want?"

"Right to business. I like that. Here's what I want. My friends and I get to live in the house on Portland Street. Rent free, utilities included. And you drop all charges against us."

"Not a chance." Howard snorted derisively.

"Hold on. I'm not finished yet. You also have to hire a real management company to fix everything wrong with the Mountain View Terrace. Get rid of the mold. Fix the roof. Replace the broken appliances. Everything."

"And if I do all that, what?"

"I'll keep quiet about what I found. Do the right thing, and this goes away. No county health inspectors breathing down your neck. No reporters knocking on your door. Oh, and your husband never has to find out about your affair with your daughter's science teacher. Mr. Woods. Cute guy, by the way. Is he the father of your one-year-old son?"

The mirth in the woman's expression evaporated into a simmering hatred.

"Extortion is a serious crime, too, young lady. A lot more serious than criminal trespass."

"Look, all I'm asking for is a decent place for me and my friends to live."

"You want a decent place to live, go live with your families."

"My father threw me out a few years ago. He's a major asshole."

"Teen shelters. Foster care."

"Don't even get me started. Look, we'll keep the place up. I swear. Be a lot easier with utilities. And those nice families at Mountain View Terraces deserve a nice place to live too. You're a businesswoman. I'm simply making a business offer."

Again, the long stare. Avery waited her out.

"Fine. You can stay on Portland Street with utilities. And I will drop the charges against you."

"Don't forget the nice people at—"

"Yes, I will contact one of my other property management companies and get them started on the needed repairs. Anything else?"

"No, that'll do." Avery stood and extended her hand. "Pleasure doing business with you, Ms. Howard."

Howard shook her hand. "Now leave my office."

Sitting in the motel room in Tucson, Avery savored the memory of her friends' joy-filled faces when they'd learned they had a home. No more squatting in a house without air-conditioning or running water. Avery had enjoyed being a hero.

But it hadn't ended there. She'd turned the tables on a cop who had planted drugs on one of the Lost Kids. She'd helped bust the assistant director of the teen shelter after he sexually harassed a couple of her friends. When a hipster restaurant near the library refused to seat her, she'd taken some photos and gotten them shut down on several health-code violations.

She'd developed a reputation as the righter of wrongs among the street community. Avery the Avenger. She liked it. Not just the reputation of being a bit of an antihero for the underdogs but the excitement of seeking out some asshole's vulnerability and exploiting it.

But eventually, she took it too far. A pimp named Vinnie D was beating up the girls working for him. Avery learned he was a dope fiend and liked to get high with his buddies at his shithole apartment. Her first move was to call the cops and get him busted.

Problem was, he got out a few days later and took out his anger on the girls. So Avery switched to plan B. She broke in when they were all passed out and shot him up with enough heroin to kill a horse. She was careful to wipe down anything she had touched before she left.

She didn't bother to call the cops this time. Word eventually filtered back to her that he was dead, presumably from an "accidental" overdose.

She should have been happy the fucker was dead. And really, he probably would have been dead soon enough on his own. She'd just hurried the process along before he could hurt anyone else.

But she couldn't shake the guilt. She was a murderer. A killer. She'd gotten drunk for a week until some of her housemates started complaining. One of the younger girls, whose name was Maggie but everyone called Knife, had nursed her through a bitch of a hangover. Knife had served as lookout when Avery went in to take care of Vinnie D.

"I know you're sad," Knife said to her one morning at breakfast. "But imagine how much sadder you would've been if Vinnie had killed Jessie or Lindsey or one of his other girls. I heard he once killed a girl for not giving him the money she'd made. He and his buddies stuffed her body in a dumpster like she wasn't nothing but trash. You did the world a favor."

"Maybe." *Wisdom from the mouths of babes,* Avery had thought.

"And it ain't like you going to jail for it. Cops wrote it off as an overdose. You're in the clear."

But it hadn't ended there. A few weeks later, she'd come home to find the Lost Kids dead. Every one of them, including Jessie and Lindsey. Maybe one of Vinnie D's buddies had seen her kill him. They were dead because she'd wanted to play the hero.

She had enjoyed killing Vinnie D. She'd cherished the sense of power it had given her. And there was a part of her deep down that wanted to do it again to someone else who was hurting innocent people. There was a monster inside her. Maybe her bio father had been right after all. She was possessed by a demon, and now she was being punished for it.

That monster or demon or whatever it was now wanted to kill Bramwell and Cuervo and anyone else who was hurt Sam. And Avery wouldn't let them go quietly, slipping away into oblivion like Vinnie D. No, she wanted them to suffer.

This, more than anything else, was what terrified her now, sitting alone in the motel room. If she avenged Sam, who else would be hurt or killed as a result? Bobby J.? Kimi?

A knock on her door made her jump. "Who is it?" She glanced around the room, looking for something to use as a weapon.

"Avery? It's me. Kimi. You okay in there?"

## CHAPTER 18
# FRESH INK

AVERY OPENED THE DOOR, trying her best to appear calm and her usual self. Kimi, on the other hand, looked worried.

"You okay?" asked Kimi a second time. "I tried to call you to let you know we're meeting for dinner at Manuela's Cucina a couple of doors down. Did your phone run out of juice?"

Avery felt heat rush to her face. "No, I turned it off. I was afraid the people who killed Sam might track me."

"Shit. I didn't even think of that. Can they do that?"

"I dunno. Bobby says Bramwell's got cops on his payroll. Didn't want to risk it."

"You always were the smart one." Kimi chucked her on the shoulder.

"Yeah, right."

"Come on! Grab your purse. I'm starving. We're going for pie afterwards."

"Pie?" Avery raised an eyebrow as she followed Kimi to the SUV.

"It's a sort of tradition. The band always gets pie right before a gig. Sydney's Sweet Shoppe has the best pies in Tucson."

"Sounds good."

"Oh, I thought of some new ironic characters."

It was a thing they'd done since they were in English class together. Avery wasn't really in the mood, but she said, "Go ahead."

"A landscape architect named Roxanne Flowers."

Avery couldn't help but chuckle. "Good one. I have one. A somnologist named Mella Tonin."

"Somnologist?"

"Sleep doctor."

"Ah, got it. Clever," Kimi said as they walked outside. "I swear one of these days, I'm going to write them all down and put them into a book. Maybe a cozy mystery or something."

"I'd definitely read it."

"Hey, speaking of cozies, did you see Mia Manansala has a new book out? *Halo-Halo and Homicide*. I don't know what's more delicious. The story, the characters, or the recipes."

At dinner, Avery tried to relax in the band's company. It felt good to listen to their banter and laughter, even if she wasn't really taking part. And the blueberry rhubarb pie at Sydney's revived her flagging appetite.

"Yo, Avery," said Torch, pulling her out of her daze. "We have a few hours before the show starts. Think we have enough time for you to ink me?"

"Depends. What'd you have in mind?"

He pulled something out of his shirt pocket and handed it to Avery. It was an ultrasound of a fetus.

"It's my kid. Farrah and me went to the baby doc a couple days ago." He started to tear up. "Can't believe I'm really gonna be a daddy."

"Let me see." Kimi leaned over. "Oh, how adorable! Let's hope the baby looks more like Farrah and less like you."

"Funny."

Avery thought it looked like a gecko with a giant Frankenstein head. "Cute."

"Can you do it before the show?"

"You want this as a tattoo?"

"Absolutely." Torch patted his chest. "Right here above my heart. The first photo of my kid."

"We'd need to make a photocopy onto regular paper. I wouldn't want to put the photo through my stencil machine."

"There's a photocopy shop down the street," McCobb added.

"Yeah, I can probably do it. Or at least get a good start on it."

"Awesome! Thanks, Avery! How much would you charge?"

"Nothing. You guys letting me tag along is payment enough."

"No!" Kimi replied. "You're already paying your own way. If you're doing actual work, something that requires your experience and skill, you deserve to be paid."

With all the cash sitting in her motel room, and even the stack of bills in her purse, she wasn't exactly hurting for money. "Normally, I'd charge a few hundred bucks. But I'll give you the friends and family discount. Say a hundred even."

Torch looked like he would burst with joy. "Deal!" He extended his arm and shook Avery's hand.

After dinner, they stopped at the copy place before returning to the motel. Avery set up a makeshift tattoo station on the desk in her room.

She ran the photocopy of the ultrasound through her printer to generate a copy that would transfer the image onto Torch's chest. When the ink and her machine were ready, she gloved up and set the transfer on his left pect.

"That placement look about right?" she said when she peeled away the transfer paper.

"It's fucking wicked. Perfect."

"Great. I'll get started."

She started out using an outlining needle. The chest could be a sensitive area, but Torch seemed unbothered as Avery worked.

"That your unicorn?" he asked.

Avery glanced at the stuffed animal sitting atop the nightstand. Somehow, having it there made her feel less alone.

"Her name's Rainbow. My foster mom gave her to me after they took me in. I keep it to remember her."

"She died?"

"Yeah." She didn't feel like elaborating.

"That sucks."

The conversation lulled for a bit until he asked, "How come you're tagging along with the band? Not that I mind, obviously. But Kimi was rather light on details."

Avery didn't like these kinds of distractions when she worked. Light banter was one thing. But emotion-laden discussions pulled her out of the zone. She was tempted to not say anything, but the question alone was enough to bring up the horrific memories.

"I'd really rather not talk about it." The fewer people who knew, the better.

"Okay, sure. Sorry, didn't mean to pry."

She shrugged and tried to focus on the work. Her hands trembled, and not just from the vibrations of the machine. She took a calming breath. Positive, calming energy in. Fear and anger out.

"Mind if I ask you something?" she asked.

"Shoot."

"You're Muslim, right?"

"More or less. Not as devout as my folks. Why?" There was a wariness in his voice.

"I thought Muslims weren't allowed to get tattoos."

"Depends. Not technically forbidden in the Quran. And until a few hundred years ago, tattooing was quite common in some Muslim cultures. These days, it's kind of frowned upon. But my family's more liberal than most."

Avery nodded. The conversation lagged, but it allowed her to get deeper in the zone.

After forty minutes, she switched needles and began filling and shading. As expected, Torch fidgeted a little.

"You okay?" she asked.

"Of course." But even his voice gave away his discomfort. "Probably nothing compared to what Farrah will go through when the baby comes."

"No doubt."

When Avery was done, she wiped away the blood and excess ink from the freshly minted tattoo. "What do you think?"

He stood and spent several minutes staring at his reflection in a mirror. Avery peeled off her gloves and held the original ultrasound photo next to it.

"I just can't get over it. My kid. That's my kid there."

"Well, an image. I'm sure they'll look a lot cuter when they're born."

"Still." Tears trickled down his cheeks. "Never been so proud. Thanks, Avery. You are amazing."

"Okay, let me put some antibiotic ointment on it and wrap it. You'll have to keep it covered during the concert."

"What? No! I wanted to show it off to the fans."

Avery shook her head. "Better if you let it heal for a day or so."

She donned a fresh pair of gloves, applied the ointment, then covered the design with a large sterile pad, which she secured with medical tape.

"You're the boss," he said, somewhat glumly.

She tossed the gloves into the bag she was using for biowaste and withdrew two small bottles from her box of supplies. "This bottle is fragrance-free soap. This other is moisturizer. Use them along with the antibiotic ointment once in the morning and once at night. It will keep the tat from getting infected and help it heal faster."

He nodded, pulled out his wallet, and handed her three hundred-dollar bills.

"I said it was only a hundred."

"Yeah, but this is my kid. And you did a helluva job."

"Thanks." Avery palmed the cash. "Let me get everything cleaned up."

"You want to help McCobb and me with a prank?"

"On Murray?"

He grinned. "Who else?"

"I don't know. I think he already hates me tagging along on the tour with you guys."

"Which is all the more reason for us to prank him. The man desperately needs a sense of humor transplant. I like to think of it as an intervention or therapy."

She put the used needles in an empty water bottle, sealed it, and bagged it along with her soiled gloves, wipes, and other waste. She didn't have any red biowaste bags.

"I don't know, Torch. What did you have in mind?"

"McCobb is out buying as much cling wrap as he can get a hold of. Then tonight, after the show, we're going to wrap his car with the stuff. Completely harmless. But funny as hell. You look like you could use a laugh. And we could use an extra hand."

"Yeah, okay."

# CHAPTER 19
# ACCUSATIONS AND UMBRAGE

HARDIN PORED over the call detail records he'd received on Avery Byrne's cell phone.

The phone number Mr. Jeong had given him turned out to be assigned to an auto repair shop that insisted they'd never heard of either Avery Byrne or Samantha Ferguson.

Hardin checked Ferguson's call log and found a nearly identical number except for the area code.

Had Avery's foster father made an honest mistake? Both 623 and 602 were local area codes. Or had he intentionally given them the wrong area code to protect Byrne? And if so, was he involved with the murder?

Valentine was on a call in the cubicle next to him, making notes. "Nothing? When was the phone last used? Really? What number was dialed? Can you ping that number? Yeah, yeah. Warrant. But this is a murder investigation. If that murderer skips town just because... okay, fine. I'll get a damn warrant."

"What'd you find out?" Hardin asked him when he hung up.

"Couldn't get a current location for the vic's cell. Whoever took it must've turned it off and pulled the SIM card. However, a call was made earlier this afternoon." Valentine showed Hardin the number.

"Avery Byrne's cell."

"Call lasted less than two minutes. I'm thinking Byrne murdered her girlfriend with an accomplice. Her accomplice takes the victim's phone. Maybe they were having an affair."

Hardin considered the theory. "Possible. You get a location for Ferguson's phone?"

Valentine plugged the latitude and longitude into Google Maps. "A bar on Jefferson Street, downtown. Justeen's Tavern. Probably a dead end, but still worth checking out."

"That's just a few doors down from Theodore Bramwell's Club Elektronik."

"So?"

"So maybe there's a connection," Hardin explained. "Think about it. Ferguson worked for Bramwell. She's dead and tortured. This other guy, Whitmore, is reported missing by his girlfriend about the same time. He also worked for Bramwell. And now whoever called Ferguson's girlfriend makes the call on Ferguson's phone next door to Bramwell's base of operations. Looking more and more like some sort of gang war."

"Still, it's obvious Byrne is involved, despite what her boss said," pressed Valentine. "Her fingerprints were on the gun. What if Byrne is involved with a rival gang to take down Bramwell?"

Hardin considered and shook his head. "Naw, doesn't feel right. Not saying she didn't kill our vic, but she didn't strike me as a gangster. Let's talk to Bramwell, see what he has to say."

Valentine sighed. "Worth a shot, I guess. If we can actually get in to see the man."

~

It was six thirty in the evening when Hardin pounded on the front door of the nightclub. When there was no response, he wondered if they would be open on a Sunday but pounded again anyway.

A minute later, the door opened. A mountain troll of a man stood there with a bar towel thrown over his shoulder. "Don't open till seven."

Hardin and Valentine flashed their shields.

"We need to talk to your boss, Theodore Bramwell," Hardin said.

"You got a warrant?"

Hardin narrowed his gaze. "We need a warrant just to talk to the man? We're not here to search the place."

"Sir," Valentine injected, "we believe someone is targeting his organization. We're hoping by speaking with him, we can prevent any further harm."

The bartender studied them for a moment then said, "Wait here. Lemme see if he's in."

The door shut. Hardin checked it. Locked. Figured.

After a few long minutes, the bartender reappeared. "He'll see you in his office. Follow me."

Hardin and Valentine trailed the large man through the drab, dimly lit interior. The residual odor of sweat and booze hung heavy in the air. Probably seeped into the walls after a while, Hardin figured.

The bartender led them up a metal staircase. Hardin felt every step in his knees. His doctor had hinted that eventually he'd need a knee replacement, but he'd been putting it off. He didn't like the idea of someone cutting him open. But moments like this made him reconsider.

At the top of the stairs was a chain with a sign saying VIP Guests Only. The bartender stepped over it nimbly, as did Valentine. Hardin unlatched the chain and resecured it when he'd gone through.

The three of them continued down a hallway. The bartender opened a door. "In there."

Hardin and Valentine stepped inside. The room looked less like a business office and more like a study in some Victorian mansion. Wood-paneled walls. Gorgeous antique desk. A bookshelf filled with hardback books and a few intricately carved beer steins.

Behind the desk sat a stocky man a few years younger than Hardin. He stood when they entered and extended his hand with a warm smile.

"Evening, detectives. To what do I owe this honor? Chad mentioned something about my business being in danger."

Everything about the man looked like money, from his suit to his haircut to the painting on the wall behind him that looked like something that belonged in a museum. The fly in the ointment was the framed portrait of the former president, though it was no surprise that a guy like Bramwell was a fan.

Hardin laid three photographs on the desk—Ferguson, Byrne, and the recently missing Whitmore. "Do you recognize these people?"

Bramwell reached for a pair of reading glasses then appeared to study each of the photos. "Two of them are my employees. Miss Ferguson and Mr. Whitmore. But this one in the middle, I don't recognize. Who is she?"

"You've never seen her?" Hardin wasn't sure whether to believe him or not.

"Sorry, she doesn't look familiar to me."

"When was the last time you saw either Ms. Ferguson or Mr. Whitmore?"

"Oh, let me think. Please, gentlemen, sit." Bramwell gestured toward the two guest chairs in front of his desk. He sat as well.

"I haven't seen Mr. Whitmore in a week or more. But Miss Ferguson, must have been the day before yesterday?

She missed one of her shifts. She's not in any sort of trouble, I hope." The concern in his voice sounded almost genuine.

"We think a rival organization may be targeting your people," Valentine said.

Hardin didn't approve of Valentine's spurting out this theory of the case but let him run with it for the time being.

"A rival organization? What kind of rival organization? I am simply a humble businessman."

Hardin couldn't help but smirk. "Who has been repeatedly charged with racketeering, extortion, drug trafficking, and several other related offenses. It's no secret you're the head of the Desert Mafia."

"That is a damn lie," Bramwell replied, his tone sharper. "For reasons unknown, the county prosecutor has a grudge against me. A bleeding-heart commie liberal, no doubt. But in every case he's brought against me, I have been exonerated. I own several properties throughout the Valley and operate some honest businesses. That is all."

"Mr. Whitmore's girlfriend says she hasn't seen him in a few days. And Ms. Ferguson was found dead the other night," Valentine said. "It appears she was tortured prior to her death."

Bramwell's umbrage turned to concern. "Tortured and killed? That's horrible. Simply horrible."

"Tell me, Mr. Bramwell. What did Ms. Ferguson do for you?" Hardin pressed.

"Miss Ferguson worked as one of my security managers here at the club. A truly woman. She knew how to handle herself in difficult situations. She has saved my life on multiple occasions."

"I had no idea being a real estate tycoon such as yourself was such a dangerous business."

"We live in a world of haves and have-nots, Detective Hardin. The have-nots are jealous little creatures who are not above using violence to get what they want from those of us who have earned it."

*Earned through criminal means,* Hardin thought.

Valentine asked, "Any reason why someone would want to harm Ms. Ferguson?"

"None that I can think of. Thought I don't know much about her personal life."

"Her murder may be connected to your organization. We'd like to speak with the people she worked closely with," Hardin said. "Starting with your other security managers."

Bramwell made a face. "I do not see why that would be necessary."

"You don't see why that's necessary? One of your security managers is tortured and killed, but now you don't want us speaking with her coworkers? If someone is indeed targeting your so-called honest business, I'd think you'd be a little more forthcoming. Unless, you have something to hide."

"What Detective Hardin means to say is, perhaps this other security manager can point us to some leads that will help us find whoever did this to poor Ms. Ferguson. Perhaps we can prevent any further harm to your business."

"What about Benjamin Whitmore? What was his position?" Hardin asked, hoping the change in direction would throw Bramwell off his game.

"Mr. Whitmore worked in my accounts receivables department."

"But he hasn't been in touch for more than a week?"

Bramwell threw up his hands. "I have many people in my employ, detective. Not unusual for him not to contact me daily."

"So, it would surprise you to learn that his girlfriend reported him missing a couple days ago?"

"You think this is connected with Miss Ferguson's untimely death?"

"One employee tortured and murdered, another missing?" Valentine replied. "I'd say it's concerning, wouldn't you?"

"I'd call it downright suspicious," Hardin added. "And you not wanting us to speak with Ms. Ferguson's coworkers? Makes me wonder what you're hiding."

Bramwell glared at him before turning to Valentine and answering. "Cuervo. Julio Cuervo. He worked closely with Miss Ferguson." The man scribbled the name and a phone number on a slip of paper and handed it to Valentine.

Valentine offered him a smile. "Thank you for your cooperation."

"Now, if you don't mind, I must get back to my work. Good evening, detectives."

"You got an elevator?" Hardin asked as he stood up. "I'm not much for stairs."

"Down the hall, to the left." Bramwell sat back down and returned to the paperwork on his desk.

Hardin followed Valentine to the elevator and pressed the call button. "That man is clearly hiding something."

Valentine shrugged. "Or he's tired of being accused of things he didn't do."

"Oh yeah, a real Mother Teresa, that one. No, he's hiding something. Let's see if we can't track down this Julio Cuervo."

## CHAPTER 20
# A NIGHT AT THE BATFISH

PRIOR TO THE SHOW, Avery worked the Damaged Souls merch table. She wore a black off-the-shoulder bustier dress decorated with red roses, paired with a matching red rose hairclip. Sterling skull earrings and a black lace choker completed the ensemble.

The sheer number of people who lined up to buy CDs, postcards offering digital downloads, T-shirts, posters, mugs, and stickers surprised her. *Who knew there were this many gothabilly fans in Tucson?*

The fans frequently asked if she was a member of the band herself and when the actual band members would be out to sign autographs. She assured them she was not and that the band would be happy to sign autographs after the concert.

Despite the endless and sometimes inane questions, she found herself feeling in her element for the first time in a long while. The chaos of selling the merch helped to keep her trauma at bay. And the energy of the crowd got her excited to see her friends perform.

When music thundered from the auditorium, the few people still in line ran to find their seats. Avery closed everything up and secured the cashbox and merch in plastic crates with padlocks as she'd been instructed.

She flashed her VIP badge to a staff member at the door, who led her to a seat front and center. The band was midway through the title track of their album *Vampire Vacation*. The huge room thrummed with energy and sound.

Kimi was made-up like a Día de Muertos Catrina, an homage to her mother's Mexican heritage. Chupa's hair had been slicked back, exposing his widow's peak. He also sported vampire teeth that looked frighteningly real.

Torch looked like a goofy Frankenstein with a T-shirt that read Feed the Monster. McCobb had donned a lab coat spattered with fake blood and round spectacles that reminded Avery of Thomas Dolby's mad scientist in the "She Blinded Me with Science" video from back in the 1980s.

The music was so loud, her clothes vibrated to the beat. She slipped the earplugs Kimi had provided into her ears to keep from going deaf. She never understood why so many bands felt the need to play at such an ear-splitting volume, especially in a small auditorium no bigger than a high school gymnasium. Loud was one thing, but literally deafening seemed pointless. Then again, she was a tattoo artist, not a musician. Kimi and the boys must have had their reasons.

A few songs in, Chupa welcomed the audience to the show and introduced the band members—Kimi on string bass, McCobb on drums, and Torch on lead guitar.

Torch stepped up to his mic after he was introduced. "Pardon me, Chup. I just want to share a bit of personal news. My girlfriend, Farrah, and I are expecting a baby monster."

The crowd erupted into applause.

"To celebrate this special occasion, I asked my amazingly talented friend Avery Byrne to create a new tat of our baby's ultrasound. This is the first photo of my child, and she was able to ink the image right above my heart."

Torch set down his guitar, tore off his T-shirt, and peeled off the bandage. When he beckoned the camera operator, a close-up image of the tattoo appeared on the video wall behind the band.

For a moment, Avery felt a blush of pride, followed quickly by a wave of terror as she realized the danger Torch had put her in. What if this announcement led Bramwell's men to her?

"There's our girl," she heard Torch say. "Ladies, gentlemen, and people of all genders, please give a big round of applause for master inkster, Avery Byrne!"

A spotlight blinded her in a flash of light and heat. Her ears began ringing. Not from the unfathomably loud sound system but from panic. She'd been trying to hide out, and now her face was on the giant screen.

"Thanks, Torch!" Chupa said in a hurried tone. "Now who wants to hear another song from our latest album, *Vampire Vacation*?"

The crowd roared in response, and the band started playing again.

Avery fled the auditorium, shaking with rage and fear. She wanted to punch Torch's lights out. How could he do such a stupid thing? He knew she was hiding, didn't he? She couldn't remember how much she had told him. It was all a blur. Even if he didn't know, putting her in the literal spotlight could lead Bramwell and his cronies to her and place the entire band in danger.

She needed to take control of the situation. If all she did was hide, Bramwell would eventually find her. It was only a matter of time. And she couldn't live a life always looking over her shoulder. But what could she do to stop Bramwell and the Desert Mafia?

Her mind drifted back to when she was looking out for the Lost Kids and the fierce protective energy she'd felt any time one of them was being harassed or threatened. As homeless kids, they were always being threatened by someone. Cops, pimps, gangbangers, drug dealers, and anyone else who saw them as easy prey or a nuisance to civilized society.

She had pushed back then, exploiting the vulnerabilities of those who threatened the people she cared most about. She had even killed to protect them.

Was she willing to be that ruthless again? To risk becoming a killer again? To once again be Avery the Avenger? And to what end? To avenge Sam, who had gotten her into this situation in the first place? Just to protect her own ass? No, not just her ass. Now, because of Torch, they were all in danger. She had to protect Kimi and the band. But how?

She thought about Cuervo's call. Did he genuinely want to help her? Or had he murdered Sam and was now trying to bait her so he could get the money back and tie up loose ends? Something about when he'd showed up during the scuffle at the club told her she could trust him.

A Batfish Theatre employee walked past.

"Hey!" Avery called out. "Is there a place that sells cell phones nearby? A Target or Best Buy or something?"

He turned. "There's a Walmart about half a mile from here. Take Sixth Avenue south to Broadway then a few blocks west. Not sure what time they close, though."

Avery looked at her watch. It was nine forty. *Shit.* "Okay. I can get back in with this, right? I'm with the band." She held up her VIP badge.

"Oh yeah, no problem."

"Thanks."

She rushed out of the building and ran down Sixth Avenue, hoping she was running the right way. In Phoenix, she always had a good sense of direction, even at night. But she was less familiar with downtown Tucson.

Fifteen minutes later, she located the Walmart. She raced

through the aisles to the electronics section, found a pre-paid phone that fit the bill, and hurried to the checkout.

The dull-eyed guy at the register barely noticed her in her full goth pinup attire—a relief since she was in no mood to be gawked at. And considering it was ten o'clock on a Saturday night, they probably got a lot of odd characters here at the downtown Walmart.

With her phone paid for, she stepped out into the parking lot, activated it, then logged into her email account. If Cuervo had Sam's phone, maybe he could access her email as well.

*Subject: Answers*

*Tell me the truth, Cuervo. Who killed Sam?*

She waited for about ten minutes, but there was no response. *Shit.* She tucked the phone into her purse and ran back to the club.

She flashed her badge at the door and sat at the merch table. The band would finish up soon. And after Torch's little stunt, she didn't feel much like going back into the auditorium.

She was in the middle of laying out the merch again when her burner phone chimed. She opened the mail app.

*Luther Jackson killed Sam. He hurt her to find what she took. I wasn't a part of it. I told him to stop. She was one of us, even after what she did. Where are you? We need to talk.*

Avery sat staring at the phone, trying to decide if she could really trust Cuervo. Sustained applause came from the auditorium, muffled by the closed doors. The concert was wrapping up. The band would probably play an encore or two. That was Avery's cue to finish setting up the table.

Avery missed Sam so much, her chest hurt. Sam could be idiotic and impulsive at times, but despite Bobby's misgivings, she'd had a good heart. She'd treated Avery like a princess. And Avery being trans or into gothabilly was never an issue with Sam. But now she was gone.

"Hey!" Kimi's voice brought Avery back into the present. "What'd you think of the show?"

Avery looked up to see the band standing next to her and crowds of fans pressing in. She narrowed her gaze at Torch. His makeup was runny with sweat, and he was still shirtless. She rushed him and punched him in the gut.

"What the hell were you thinking?" she screamed.

Torch managed to stay on his feet and looked at her, dumbfounded. "About what?"

"Calling me out like that!"

"I was praising your work, silly girl. Thought maybe you'd get some more business out of it."

"You're such an idiot!" Avery stormed off to the ladies' room and sat in one of the stalls while a squall of emotions screamed through her.

Once she had calmed a little, she opened her phone and stared at Cuervo's reply asking where she was. She sure as hell wasn't going to tell him.

*If I have what Sam took and if I return it, what's to stop this Luther asshole from killing me?*

The restroom door opened. Whoever came in knocked on her locked stall door.

"Occupied!" Avery snapped.

"Ave, it's Kimi."

Avery put away her phone and opened the stall door. "I'm sorry for blowing up like that. It's just..."

"Hey, I get it. After Sam being killed, you're terrified they're going to come after you. I'd feel the same way if someone had hurt Chupa. Thing is, I didn't tell Torch what all happened. Need to know, right? So, he figured you were just taking some time off, not that you were hiding from murderous gangsters."

"Shit. I'm sorry."

"Not me you should apologize to."

"Yeah." She followed Kimi out of the bathroom.

The other band members were at the merch table, talking with fans and signing CDs, T-shirts, and other merchandise. Avery slipped in and began taking payments for purchases while feeling like a total heel.

When the last of the fans were gone, Avery turned to the band. They stared at her stone-faced, much the way normal people stared at people like her.

"Torch, I'm sorry for blowing up at you. And for hitting you."

"Yeah," McCobb said. "What's that shit about?"

"My girlfriend, Sam, was murdered last night. I'm afraid the people who did it might try to do the same to me."

"Shit. And here I literally put you in the spotlight." Torch put a hand on her shoulder. "If I'd known, I never would have…"

"I know. You were just trying to be nice."

"Do the police know who killed her?" Chupa asked.

"Sam…" Avery debated how much to say. "Turns out, she worked for some bad people. And she wanted out. But they don't like loose ends."

"That's the understatement of the year," McCobb said. "Murdering someone for wanting out? That's insane."

Avery shrugged. "Yeah."

Kimi sat down next to her and leaned her head on Avery's shoulder. "Are we in danger now, you think?"

"I don't know. I probably just overreacted. Chances of one of Bramwell's guys being here are pretty remote."

"Bramwell?" Chupa asked. "As in Theodore Bramwell, the head of the Desert Mafia? That's who's after you? Fuck me."

"Now that we know, we'll do everything to keep you safe, girl," Torch said. "I promise."

"Thanks. And thanks for not hating me."

"You're a victim in this," Kimi said. "We get it. But more important, you're our friend. And friends stick together."

Avery felt an impulse to tell them about the money. But she wasn't ready to share that just yet. It might put them in more danger.

Murray came striding out of the business office next to a lanky guy with wild hair. No doubt the Batfish's manager. "Okay, kiddies! Business is concluded. Time to pack up and get the heck out of here."

## CHAPTER 21
# THE NOOSE TIGHTENS

"SO WHERE ARE we with the Ferguson case?" Lieutenant Ross asked the next morning.

Hardin frowned. "Not as far as I'd hoped. Valentine's convinced it was just a lover's spat with the girlfriend, Avery Byrne."

"But you're not?"

Hardin shrugged. "Her prints were on the gun. But someone called Byrne yesterday from the victim's phone."

"Another lover perhaps?"

"Maybe. But Ferguson was tortured before she was killed. Didn't strike me as a crime of passion. More like someone trying to extract information from her. This looked like the work of a pro."

"You get a location on either phone?"

"By the time we got the warrants, both were off the grid. On the plus side, we determined that the call from the victim's phone originated at a bar down the street from a club that Bramwell owns."

"You still think this ties back to Bramwell?"

"Plus, there's this other missing person case..."

"You have anything solid pointing to Bramwell?"

"Not yet. Just a hunch. He got squirrelly when we questioned him."

"Seems thin. You talk to the victim's neighbors?"

"We did. None of them admitted to being close to Ferguson, and even less so to Byrne. A few stated that since she moved in a few months earlier, there'd been an increase in car break-ins, vandalism, and vehicles with loud engines."

"Was there?"

"I talked to Daniels in Property Crimes. There was a string of break-ins back in March. But footage from one homeowner's security camera showed the culprits were two teen boys who were later arrested. Byrne had nothing to do with it."

"Still doesn't rule out Byrne for the murder of her girlfriend."

"No. One neighbor, a guy named Leeburg, took a strong dislike to her. Said, and I quote, 'You could tell she was trouble just by looking at her.' Apparently, she dresses like a goth version of a 1950s pinup model. I pressed him if he'd witnessed the two women having any sort of altercation?"

"And?"

"Claims to have witnessed them arguing a few times. Nothing physical. The man's convinced 'the creepy chick'—his words—must have murdered Ferguson. "

"Sounds like trouble in paradise. Byrne does have a jacket, right?"

"Just the one solicitation conviction and the dropped trespass charge. Nothing recent. No history of drugs or violence."

Ross sat back with his arms folded. "You ask me, I'd have to side with Valentine. This girl disappears right after her girlfriend's murder and then gets a call from someone with the victim's phone? Has all the markers of a love triangle gone wrong."

"I know, nine times out of ten, it's the spouse or lover.

But the torture just doesn't feel like a domestic violence situation to me."

"Sounds to me like an emotionally driven homicide. Where do you have the most intense emotions but in a relationship gone bad? If Byrne's one of those kinky goths, she could well be into the whole BDSM scene, right? Maybe they were getting freaky at home and things got out of hand. Or maybe Ferguson was cheating, and Byrne found out."

Hardin considered it, but it still didn't fit in his mind. "Maybe."

"You said Byrne was trans, right? Maybe Ferguson found out after months of living together and tempers flared. A thousand and one possible scenarios, all pointing back to the girlfriend."

"Possible."

"Find the girl and talk to her," Ross said. "I want a suspect in custody soon. The media's already whipping this into a frenzy, especially the torture and goth angle..."

"Yeah, it's a real shitstorm. I've been fielding calls from all kinds of crazies. Nothing solid."

Valentine appeared in the doorway, holding his phone. "We caught a break."

He tapped the screen, and a video started playing. A strange-looking band dressed as movie monsters was on a stage. A guitarist was talking to the audience, then he tore off his shirt and exposed a tattoo on his chest.

"There's our girl," the guitarist said. "Ladies, gentlemen, and people of all genders, give a big round of applause for master inkster Avery Byrne!"

The video tilted to a large screen above the band. A woman with black hair squinted in the glare of a spotlight.

"That's her!" Valentine stopped the video. "That's our perp!"

"Where was this taken?" Hardin stared at the blurry image of Byrne on the screen.

"A club in downtown Tucson. Can you believe this shit? A woman gets KO'd, and the next night, the girlfriend's partying the night away at a punk rock concert."

"How'd you find this?"

Valentine hooked a thumb back toward the bullpen. "Richardson's son is a student at U of A and into the weird college music scene. Overheard his kid playing the video this morning at breakfast when he heard Byrne's name mentioned."

"Lucky break," Ross said. "Issue a BOLO and coordinate with Tucson PD to bring her in."

Hardin still wasn't convinced it was Byrne. It just felt wrong. But at the moment, she was their best lead. He followed Valentine out of the office.

"We know which club?" Hardin asked.

"Some place called the Batfish Theatre on Congress Street. The band's called Damaged Souls. Based here in Phoenix. Must've booked an out-of-town gig."

Cuervo turned to Luther, who was driving, as they pulled up to the tattoo studio. "Just take it easy on these people, Luther."

"Easy? You think them Mexicans gonna take it easy on us when they show up and we ain't got their money? Fuck that shit!"

"I'm just saying these people don't have anything to do with Sam taking the money. We just need them to tell us where Avery is. You'll get more flies with honey than vinegar. It's why torturing Sam didn't work."

Luther glowered at him. "Bitch, don't ever tell me how to do my job! Your cunt of a partner got us in this mess. She deserved what she got. Maybe you should stick to babysitting the boss's whore. Seems the only thing you're good at."

Luther turned off the ignition and hopped out of the car. Cuervo followed him into the building.

A petite white woman with sea-foam-green hair was working on the back of a man lying on a padded table. On the other side of the room, an Asian man was inking a sleeve on the arm of a woman whose leather vest identified her as a member of the Athena Sisterhood Motorcycle Club.

Luther drew his piece and pointed it at the green-haired woman. "You Avery Byrne?"

"Dude, put it down. That ain't her." Cuervo put a cautioning hand on Luther's gun. "Sorry, he's a little agitated."

Luther shrugged Cuervo away. "I don't get answers, I start shooting. Ya feel me?"

The Asian man stood up and approached. "Ms. Byrne isn't here," he said sternly. "Take whatever this is out of my studio."

Luther cocked his head. "You look familiar. I know you from somewhere?"

"I don't think so. As I said, Ms. Byrne is not here. Please leave before someone gets hurt."

"Where she at?" Luther turned the gun on him.

"I do not know. I haven't seen her for a couple of days. What do you want with her?"

"She took something that don't belong to her, and we want it back. How we get a hold of her? You got her phone number, right?"

"It wouldn't do you any good. I've called her several times myself. She's not answering her phone."

Luther pistol-whipped him and pressed the muzzle of his gun to the man's temple. "Bitch, I decide what's good and what ain't."

"Put it down," growled the woman in the biker vest. She aimed a large-caliber revolver at Luther.

"Everyone, please put away your guns." The Asian man wiped blood from his nose. "Please, Fuego. Put it away."

"Come on, man," Cuervo said to Luther. "No call for this craziness. They don't know where she is."

A cell phone rang loudly, sending a ripple of alarm through the room. Cuervo half expected Luther and the biker chick to start shooting at each other.

Luther reached into his pocket and answered his phone. "Yeah? Tucson? Really? Fuck, yeah." He hung up. "The bitch is down in Tucson."

Cuervo shot the Asian man an apologetic glance then followed Luther out of the shop.

"Who was that?" Cuervo asked in the car.

"Our contact in Phoenix Homicide. They came across a video showing the bitch at a rock concert down there. She better hope she still has the money. Else I swear…"

"If she has the money and gives it up, that's the end of it. Right?"

"It means you and me don't end up swinging from a bridge, if that's what you're asking." Luther pulled onto the street heading for the freeway.

"And we let the girl live, right?"

"Let her live? Are you stupid?"

"She doesn't know anything except that Sam took the money," Cuervo explained.

"We don't know what she knows. She's a loose end. Boss don't like loose ends."

"Look, it's bad enough we tortured and killed one of our own."

"Man, you got the hots for this freaky chick? You know she's into pussy not dick, right?"

"It's not like that, ese. Yeah, Sam was stupid for stealing from Mr. Bramwell, but she paid the price. We get the money back, no need to hurt Avery too. Another body just puts us at further risk of getting busted. There's always a chance that CSI forensics shit could come back to bite us."

"Man, you been watching too much TV. That CSI stuff is bullshit." Luther slowed when a Phoenix Police cruiser pulled onto Camelback in front of them. "It's Bramwell's call. Whatever he says do, I do. And so do you, got it?"

"Fine."

Cuervo opened the mail app on his phone.

*Avery,*

*Get out of Tucson. You're blown. Doing what I can to protect you. If you give me what Sam took, no harm will come to you. Please contact me. Let's schedule a meet.*

*Cuervo*

He put his own cell phone number after his name.

"What are you doing?" Luther asked.

"Emailing one of my brothers. We were supposed to have dinner tonight. Letting him know I won't make it."

# CHAPTER 22
# GOING ON OFFENSE

AVERY STARED out at the endless scrub desert on the long drive to Las Cruces.

After the previous night's drama, she'd told Torch she was too exhausted to help him and McCobb with their prank.

She did chuckle when she saw Murray the next morning cursing as he used a car key to cut away the many layers of cling wrap on his car. But then she remembered all the times she had been on the butt end of other people's pranks. She grabbed a pocketknife from her purse and went outside to help unwrap the Murray's car.

He didn't say anything, but his expression toward her softened. He almost looked thankful.

On the road, she tried her best to be sociable with Chupa and Kimi. When Kimi came up with a string of ironic character names like an insurance rep named Justin Case, a woman running a dating service named Anita Mann, and a mystery author named Paige Turner, Avery failed to come up with any of her own. Her mind simply wasn't in a creative or funny space.

Her body ached for Sam's gentle and passionate touch. She craved the solace of Sam's embrace while telling her about the awful things that had happened to her over the past couple of days. Only, Sam was dead and would never hold her again.

At least Kimi and the band were willing to hide her for the time being. But what would happen after the tour was over? Guilt stabbed at her conscience for keeping the money a secret. It was putting a big target on their backs, and she was too selfish or paranoid to tell them.

She had to find a way out of this, to track down this Luther asshole and put him and Theodore Bramwell in the ground.

Of course, killing a powerful man like Bramwell would likely lead to an extensive police investigation to find his killer with unlimited media coverage. The cops would eventually track her down, and she'd end up spending the rest of her life in prison.

Worse, as a trans woman, they'd likely throw her in a men's facility. Didn't matter whether she'd had gender confirmation surgery or not. They had already stuck a woman she'd known in a men's prison where the screws turned a blind eye, and she was brutalized. And that was on murder charges that were later dropped when the real killer was arrested. Was avenging Sam worth all that?

The memory of Sam's swollen, blood-flecked face blazed vividly in Avery's mind, followed by the thunderous gunshot that had torn away half of Sam's skull in an explosion of gore taking all of Avery's dreams of a happy life with it.

The answer was a resounding yes. Knowing these monsters couldn't do that to anyone else would be worth the consequences. Even Bobby's warnings couldn't dissuade her. She would get her revenge. And the world would be a better place for it.

But she had to be smart about it. Perhaps pin their deaths on someone else, someone equally deserving. But who? A rival gang, perhaps? One of Bramwell's cops on the take? Maybe a disgruntled employee?

And how exactly would she accomplish that? She didn't have a gun. She didn't even have her car. And she was actively being hunted.

"Pit stop!" Chupa pulled off the highway. "Welcome to the bustling metropolis of Benson, Arizona. Population: four thousand."

Avery started at the world outside the car. Nothing but a Chevron station and a few abandoned buildings in sight. She recalled visiting Kartchner Caverns a few miles south of here with Sam. The once-happy memory of the spectacular underground rock formations was now poisoned with immense sadness.

Her phone chirped. An email from Cuervo. They knew she'd been in Tucson. She nearly stumbled while stepping out of the car.

"Shit. Shit, shit, shit!" Panic crushed Avery's chest.

"What's wrong?" Kimi appeared beside her.

"They know I was in Tucson."

"Who's they?"

"Bramwell's men."

"How do you know?"

Avery showed her the email.

"Who's Cuervo?"

"He worked with Sam. He has her phone and has been emailing me."

"Can you trust him?"

"I… I dunno. Maybe. I mean, he sent this. But…"

"What does he mean by this thing Sam took?"

*Fuck,* Avery thought. She had forgotten Cuervo mentioned it in his email. "I… I don't know."

"You sure?"

Kimi met Avery's gaze. They'd been friends for so long, Avery wondered if Kimi could tell when she was lying. She wanted to tell her. But if she did, Kimi and Chupa might dump her here in Benson. Even friendship had its limits. So she kept quiet.

"Sam told me she was afraid Bramwell would try to kill her for leaving." It was technically the truth. "When I found her at the house, she only uttered one word before she died. 'Run.'"

"Maybe whatever they're looking for is in one of her bags. Have you looked inside them?"

"Just books. She was a big reader."

"Okay."

Shame piled onto Avery's already troubled mind. She was a shit friend.

*Maybe I should find some way back to Phoenix. I could rent a car or catch a bus once we get to Las Cruces. Not like money's an issue.*

But the thought of being on her own felt so desolate. So vulnerable. So terrifying. She'd have to think about it.

While Chupa gassed up the SUV, Avery went to the restroom to pee. Sitting in the stall, she stared at Cuervo's message, debating whether she could trust this man she'd only met once. Finally, she dialed the number.

"Hello?" Cuervo answered.

"It's me, Avery."

"¡Hola, Luis! ¿Cómo estás?"

*Luis? What the hell?* It took Avery a second to realize he was saying he couldn't talk freely now. Maybe he was with that Luther asshole who'd tortured Sam.

"I'm still not sure I can trust you, Cuervo. You said you tried to stop Luther from hurting Sam. So either you're incompetent or a liar."

"How could you say that? I'd never do you wrong, bro. You know that. I'm down in Tucson right now. It's a work thing. But I promise, soon as I'm back in town, I'll come over and give you a hand. Call you later, hermano. Okay? ¡Bien!"

"Whatever." Avery hung up and called Bobby.

"Seoul Fire Tattoo, Bobby J. speaking."

"Appa, it's me."

"Oh my goodness, kiddo. Are you okay? I've been so worried."

"I'm all right for the moment."

"Are you safe?"

"I think so."

"The cops showed up at the shop looking for you, followed by a couple of Bramwell's goons."

"Shit. I'm so sorry, Appa. I never meant for any of this to happen. Are you okay?"

"Everyone here is fine. But the goons apparently know you're down in Tucson."

"Don't worry. I'm no longer in Tucson. I'm with Kimi's band. We're headed to Las Cruces."

"Avery, I think they're looking for something Sam took from Bramwell. Do you know anything about that?"

She couldn't lie to him. Bad enough she was keeping secrets from Kimi and the band. "She took a bag of money," Avery whispered, in case someone was in the stall next to her. "A lot of money."

"Figured it was something like that. You have it with you?"

"Yeah. I don't know what to do, Appa. I'd happily give them back the money if they'd leave me alone afterwards, but I don't think it would be that easy. Not after what they did to Sam."

"You're probably right. Bramwell doesn't strike me as the 'live and let live' type. What are you planning to do with it? Nothing crazy, I hope."

"Everything's already crazy right now." Avery scoffed. "I want to hurt these people for what they did to Sam. I want to tie them to the bumper of the Gothmobile and drag their bodies through the street."

"I understand how you feel. I felt the same way after Melissa was killed. But, kiddo, killing Bramwell and his crew won't bring Sam back. And it could well end with you either in prison or dead yourself. As Yoda said—"

"Please, Appa, no Jedi wisdom right now."

"Okay, but remember what Confucius said about the two graves?"

"Trust me, I don't want to be that person again. Avery the Avenger is dead. But right now, they're not giving me a lot of choice. Even if I return the money, they're going to kill me."

A heavy silence hung on the line for a minute. "I don't know what to tell you, kiddo. I hate that I can't fix this for you or at least do more to keep you safe."

"You've done plenty to keep me safe. You're the best dad I ever had."

"Considering your last father threw you out, it's not exactly a high bar."

Avery managed a chuckle. "Suppose not."

"Is this a number where I can reach you in the future?"

"Yeah, it's a prepaid. No one but you has the number. I pulled the SIM card from my regular phone."

"Smart girl. Woman, I should say. What's your next move?"

"I've been in contact with Sam's old partner, a guy named Julio Cuervo. He says he'll help protect me if I return the money."

"You believe him?"

"Not sure yet. Could be a setup. I'll let you know as soon as I'm ready to make a move. I just have to figure this out."

"If anyone can figure a way out of this, it's you. You're a survivor and one of the smartest people I know. As Obi-Wan said—"

"Appa, please! Leave poor Obi-Wan out of this for once. I'll talk to you soon, okay?"

"Stay safe. Watch your back. I love you, Avery."

"Love you too, Appa."

She picked up some snacks from the convenience store and met Kimi and Chupa in the car. "Sorry for taking so long."

Kimi gave her a sympathetic smile. "No problem. You okay?"

Avery nodded as their caravan of vehicles drove back onto the highway. "Talked to Bobby J."

"He must be awfully worried."

"Yeah."

## CHAPTER 23
# GOT THE T-SHIRT

IT WAS NEARLY five o'clock when Hardin and Valentine pulled into in Tucson. They would have arrived sooner, but Valentine had insisted on taking the South Mountain Freeway to avoid the congestion of downtown Phoenix. And it would have been a faster route had a truck not jackknifed near the Vee Quiva Casino exit.

As it was, they spent an hour stuck in sweltering traffic before they ever got out of the Valley. When they finally reached Tucson, they checked in with Tucson PD then proceeded through rush hour traffic to the Batfish Theatre.

The half-filled lobby contained a bar and a smattering of small tables that looked like they'd been acquired from garage sales or thrift stores.

"We need to speak with the manager," Hardin said, flashing his badge to the bartender.

The bartender nodded, gave a "follow me" gesture, and led them down a narrow corridor past the closed doors of the auditorium.

A woman with an explosion of bloodred hair sat at a keyboard in a cramped office. The bartender knocked on the already open door then vanished back down the hall toward the barroom.

"Can I help you?" the woman asked in an exasperated tone.

Hardin badged her and introduced himself and his partner. "You the manager?"

"Willa Cohen. What do you want? I'm busy."

Valentine held out a photo. "We're looking for this woman, Avery Byrne."

Cohen gave the photo a cursory glance. "Geez, don't you people talk to each other?"

"You people?" Hardin cocked his head.

"Two other guys were here earlier looking for her. Though come to think of it, they never actually said they were cops."

"So, you did see her?" Valentine pressed. "She was here last night."

"Yeah, her and twelve hundred other people."

"Don't get smart with me, lady. This is a murder investigation. We could arrest you for hindering prosecution."

Hardin put a hand on his partner's arm and stepped in. "The woman we're looking for was with the band that performed last night. One of the band members thanked her onstage for doing a tattoo. We could use your help finding her."

Cohen sat back in her chair and met their gaze. "Okay, yeah, she was running Damaged Souls' merch table last night."

"Do you know where the band is staying?"

"You mean, like, which motel? Beats the hell outta me. By now, they've probably checked out and headed to the next gig of their tour."

"They're on tour?" Hardin raised an eyebrow. "Where's their next gig?"

Cohen pulled a T-shirt out of a cardboard box and tossed it to Hardin. "Somewhere in New Mexico, I think."

Hardin examined the shirt. A list of cities had been

printed on the back, starting with Phoenix, followed by Tucson, Las Cruces, Albuquerque, and more. There were dates listed on the right. "Thanks."

"Who'd this girl kill anyhow?"

"Her girlfriend," Valentine replied. "But only after sadistically torturing her for God knows how long."

"We think," Hardin added.

"Wow," Cohen replied. "Didn't strike me as the type, you know."

Hardin exchanged a glance with Valentine. "You said two other men were looking for her. Could you describe them?"

"A big Hispanic guy, nearly six foot. And a little Black guy, about like Prince. But creepy, you know? Like seriously creepy. Major bad energy."

"Were they with Tucson police?"

"Never said. Though I could tell they were armed. If they were cops, they were probably dirty."

"They give you their names?" asked Valentine.

"They did not."

"You have contact information for this band Damaged Spirits?"

"Damaged Souls. Manager is Scott Murray." Cohen pulled up her phone and gave them Murray's phone number and email address.

"What about the band members?" asked Hardin.

"All I know is their stage names. Kimi, Chupa, Torch, and McCobb. What their real names are, I don't know, and I don't care. They fill the house when they're in town. That's enough for me."

"Okay, thanks." Hardin turned to leave.

"Whoa, whoa, whoa. That's thirty bucks for the shirt."

Hardin regarded the shirt in his hand. Might come in handy in case they didn't catch Byrne in Las Cruces. He turned to Valentine. "Pay the lady, youngblood."

Once they were outside, Hardin called Ross. "Hey, LT. Looks like we missed our girl here in Tucson."

"Dammit. Any idea where she is?"

"She's tagging along with that band onto their next gig in Las Cruces."

"New Mexico?"

"That's where they keep it. The band's scheduled to play at a venue called Gothique. I'm thinking we can catch her there."

"No, we can't afford to be sending you two on a multi-state manhunt after this girl. Call Las Cruces PD. See if they can detain her. Y'all just head home. Plenty other murders here to solve."

"He wants us back to Phoenix," Hardin said to his partner.

"Gimme the damn phone." Valentine snatched it out of Hardin's hand. "LT, we can't just let this girl go. Not after what she did to the vic. Someone like that is violent and unstable. Who's to say she won't return to the Valley and start brutalizing more people?"

Hardin watched his partner grow increasingly agitated as he listened to Ross's response.

"I don't believe this was just a domestic situation that got outta hand, LT. This woman's clearly disturbed. All due respect to Las Cruces PD, Hardin and me need to be the ones to bring her in. If we don't get her now, who knows how many people she could kill. Just give us forty-eight hours to close this. We'll get her." Valentine paused a moment. "Thank you, sir. We'll get her. I promise."

Valentine ended the call and handed the phone back to Hardin, a supreme look of satisfaction on his face.

"I take it you convinced him to let us go to New Mexico," Hardin said.

"Yes. We're gonna get this bitch."

After dinner, Avery joined the band for pie at the Pie Hole, voted Best Desserts of the Mesilla Valley by the Las Cruces Bulletin for three years running. At least according to the plaques on the wall.

It had been difficult to choose just one kind of pie, but Avery had to admit her strawberry rhubarb was a wonderful explosion of sweet and tart flavors.

"You need a disguise," Kimi said between bites of Dutch apple pie. She held up her phone. Avery's driver license photo was at the top of a news article about Phoenix PD's pursuit of a murder suspect.

"Shit," Avery murmured. She choked on a piece of rhubarb stuck in her throat.

"She's wanted for murder?" Murray asked, his face turning as purple as his sugar-free blueberry pie.

"She didn't do it, Mur," Kimi replied sharply. "But whoever did tried to make it look like she's the killer."

"She should go back to Phoenix. While I am appreciative of her help, we don't need her problems becoming ours. I busted my ass to book this tour. Last thing we need is trouble from the cops."

"Chill, Murray," Chupa replied with a bit of meringue on his cheek. "She's one of us. And we protect our own."

"Maybe Murray's right," Avery said. "I don't want to get any of you in trouble. Or put you in danger. This is..."

A sudden surge of emotion choked off her words. She couldn't get the image of Sam's swollen, blood-streaked face out of her mind. Or the instant when the bullet ripped her out of Avery's life forever in an explosion of gore and heartbreak.

Kimi's gentle hand squeezed her shoulder. "You're safe with us. No one knows where we are. Besides, you and me, we're family. I couldn't be there for you when your bio dad kicked you out. But I can be here for you now. And goth forbid, if those assholes who hurt Sam find us, Chupa and Torch will kick their asses."

"Hey!" McCobb piped in, gesturing with a bite of chocolate cream on his fork. "I can kick asses too. Don't listen to Murray, Ave. We got your back. And you were a real hit at the merch table. Much better than Murray ever was."

"Gee, thanks a lot!" Murray sneered at him.

Avery took a deep breath, drawing in energy as Bobby J. had taught her. *You will get through this,* she told herself. *You are resilient, resourceful, and radiant.*

She always chafed at Bobby's suggestion that she was radiant. Made her sound perky and cheerful, which she wasn't. Bobby had assured her that in her case, she radiated her confidence and power. And so, she included it in her affirmation.

"I appreciate you looking out for me, but now that the cops have put my photo out there, I don't know."

"Thus, the need for a disguise," Kimi repeated with a mischievous grin.

"I'm thinking Groucho Marx glasses and a mustache," McCobb jibed.

"Funny." Avery rolled her eyes. "I don't think so."

Kimi rested her chin in her hand in a contemplative gaze. "If you change your makeup from goth to more of a traditional glamour style, maybe add a blond wig and a pair of glasses."

"How about a Bride of Frankenstein disguise?" Chupa suggested. "Make her look like a member of the band."

"Ooh, I know!" Torch said. "Frank-N-Furter from *Rocky Horror*."

Avery recalled the first time she'd watched *The Rocky Horror Picture Show* at the midnight showing in Tempe six months before her she was kicked out.

Watching Tim Curry and the cast play with gender and

sexuality with such abandon had both thrilled and terrified her and ultimately woke her up to a dreadful reality. This was her. She was a gender outlaw. And when her true self emerged, her life would be turned inside out.

"I don't know." Avery stared at her plate. "I mean, Frankie was a guy."

"I like it," Kimi replied. "I know it might trigger your dysphoria, babe, but it could also keep you safe if the cops or those murderous psychopaths find us. Besides, Laverne Cox played Frankie in the remake, and she's trans."

Avery considered the suggestion. "Fine. I'll play the sweet transvestite."

"From transsexual…" McCobb sang.

"Transylvaniaaaahhhh." Avery joined the rest of the group in singing.

The other patrons began glaring at them. *Of course, they were already staring, so whatever,* Avery thought. Being with this nutty bunch of musicians filled her with joy.

# CHAPTER 24
# GUTSHOT

THEY ARRIVED BACK at the motel around six, a couple of hours before showtime.

Kimi and the guys helped Avery get made up. She should have been surprised to learn that Torch had packed a corset, garter, lace gloves, and a pearl choker. But the Frank-N-Furter costume had been his suggestion. Kimi provided a pair of fishnets and did Avery's hair and makeup.

When they were finished, Chupa looked her over. "Wow! You make a better Frankie than Tim Curry or Laverne Cox ever did. I don't think even Bobby J. would recognize you, girl."

Avery stared at herself in the full-length mirror on the back door of the bathroom. "I don't recognize myself."

"See?" Torch gave her shoulder a squeeze. "Great idea, huh?"

"If anyone shows up looking for me, tell them I caught a ride back to Phoenix. Hopefully, they'll leave you alone."

"We got your back, girl," McCobb assured her.

"I know. But this can only go on for so long. I've got to figure out a way to end this. Maybe I should go to the cops."

Kimi looked alarmed. "I thought you said you couldn't trust them."

"I don't. Not sure what else to do. But if I don't do something soon, someone else I care about will get hurt because of me. I can't live with that."

"Well, you don't have to decide anything tonight," Kimi assured her. "Tonight, we're gonna rock and celebrate life."

When the band members returned to their rooms and dressed for the show, Avery checked her phone. Cuervo had sent another message.

*A,*

*Please contact me. I'll keep you safe. Only interested in getting the money back. It belongs to the Mexican cartel. Without it, we're all dead. Let's meet somewhere. You can return the money and get on with your life.*

C

Avery considered it for a moment then replied.

*Why should I care if gangsters kill you all? You people tortured and murdered Sam. I hope you die screaming. Fuck you all.*

The Gothique was a smaller venue than the Batfish—more dance club than concert hall. But the fans who showed up were no less enthusiastic than the people in Tucson.

Avery got a lot of compliments on her costume while she ran the merch table prior to the show. A few asked whether she was really a guy or a girl, to which she would just smile and reply in a gender-neutral pitch, "Wouldn't you like to know?"

To her surprise, playing the part of a cross-dressing man didn't trigger her dysphoria as much as she'd feared it would. For a while, she was actually having fun. Until it all went to shit.

The first sign of trouble was someone shouting her name near the club's entrance. A palpable wave of fear rippled through the crowd, reaching Avery a heartbeat before two men pushed their way to the merch table.

Avery instantly recognized Cuervo, along with the skinny Black guy she'd seen with him at the house. Luther Jackson. Something about the man triggered a sensation of spiders crawling across her body.

"Where's Avery Byrne?" Luther held a large gun in his small hand.

Avery dropped the pitch of her voice and spoke in a shaky masculine monotone. "She… she went back to Phoenix."

"Bullshit!" Luther growled in anger and aimed the gun at her face. "Where the fuck is she, you goddamn faggot?"

"G-Gone." She caught Cuervo studying her intently, as if sussing out her identity. "S-Sorry."

The sound of someone tuning an electric guitar caught her attention. At the other end of the club, Kimi and the band had stepped onto the stage.

A roar of applause rose but was quickly squelched when Luther fired a shot in the air and marched toward the band. The fans stampeded toward the exits.

Avery watched in horror as Luther pointed his weapon at Chupa. "Where the fuck is Avery Byrne?"

Chupa towered over the armed thug. "She caught a ride back to the valley, asshole. Now get the fuck out before we call the cops."

"I ain't playing, freak. Tell me where she's at, or so help me, I'll blow your fucking head off."

In a blur of movement, McCobb grabbed Torch's spare guitar and brought it down on Luther's arm like a sledge-hammer. The gun fired and dropped to the floor. Chupa fell, screaming.

McCobb raised the guitar again, but Luther dashed out the back entrance, cradling his arm.

Avery sat frozen in terror. Suddenly, she was back in the

house, kneeling in front of Sam's brutalized body. Begging her to still be alive. Hearing the front door open. Raising Sam's pistol toward the men coming in. Her world shattering once again.

"Avery?"

She looked up to see Cuervo still standing there, staring at her.

"No!" She shoved the table over onto him and ran, hurtling like a meteor out the front door and down the sidewalk.

A car nearly clipped her as she dashed across a side street. She ran until her lungs burned and her legs were numb, collapsing onto the concrete.

"No, not again. No, please, Mother Goddess, please, not again."

The steady beat of footsteps approached. Cuervo loomed over her.

"Get away from me!" she roared, her voice ragged and labored.

"Avery." He held up his hands in a calming gesture. "All we want is the money. Just the money, and we're gone."

She pulled herself to her feet and swatted away Cuervo's outstretched hand.

"Just the money?" she croaked. "You fucking killed my girlfriend and now one of my friends. Don't tell me it's just about the money."

She punched his face as hard as she could. Jolts of pain shot through her fist.

Cuervo backed up a step, his face bleeding, but remained standing.

"I'm sorry, Avery. Luther's a loose cannon. I begged him not to torture Sam. But I didn't hurt her or your friend."

"Bullshit! I saw you coming into my house. You were there."

"Look, just give us the money, and it stops. I promise."

She got in his face. "I. Don't. Believe. You." She kneed him in the crotch. When he doubled over in pain, she kneed him in the head.

He fell to the ground, blood pouring from his nose. She kicked him several more times with all her strength. "I don't believe you. I don't believe you. I don't fucking believe you."

Exhausted, she hobbled back toward the club. The four-inch heel on one of her shoes was broken. She kicked them both off and walked in her stocking feet the rest of the way.

She didn't know if Cuervo was dead or alive. Nor did she care.

# CHAPTER 25
# THE LIMITS OF FRIENDSHIP

WHEN SHE REACHED GOTHIQUE, the crowd of fans had become a mob of lookie-loos crowding around the entrance. She pushed past them to the front door, where a brawny man barred her way.

"Sorry, dude. The place is closed. There's been an incident."

Being called "dude" felt like a stiletto to the heart, but she ignored it. "I'm with the band. I was running the merch table."

The bouncer looked uncertain then said, "Yeah, okay. Come on. Cops'll be here any minute. Probably have to talk to them."

It was the last thing Avery wanted to do, but if it got her inside, she'd agree to just about anything. "No problem."

She found Kimi and the others circled around Chupa, who lay onstage, groaning. Blood was everywhere. Torch knelt over him, apparently applying pressure to the wound on his abdomen.

Guilt sucker punched Avery in the soul. "Oh fuck. No, not again."

"Avery!" Kimi gasped and hugged her hard. "Thank goth you're okay."

"I… I… I'm so sorry."

Kimi hurried her toward the same back exit the gunman had vanished through. Avery caught a glimpse of medical personnel and uniformed cops stepping through the front entrance.

"Ave! Listen to me," Kimi said in a harsh whisper while opening the door. "You need to go."

"Go? Where? How?"

Kimi pressed a set of keys in her hand. "Back to the motel. Stay in your room. Don't answer the door for anyone but me."

"But Chupa…"

"Chupa… Chupa's…" Kimi swallowed a breath and met Avery with a steely gaze. "Look, Avery, I don't want you here. You gotta leave."

Kimi's loyalty had reached its limits now that Chupa was dying. Not that Avery blamed her. She should never have asked to tag along on the tour. This was all her fault.

She slipped out the door into the dark alley, broken and ashamed. For an instant, she wondered if Luther might be waiting for her in the shadows. Not that she cared. She deserved whatever she got.

"I'm such a horrible person," she told herself when she climbed behind the wheel of Kimi and Chupa's SUV. It took her a moment to find the headlights and adjust the mirrors and seat so she could drive.

"I should have been the one he shot. Not Chupa. Mother Goddess, please let him be okay."

At a stoplight, she caught her reflection in the rearview mirror. She now looked like Frank-N-Furter after the movie's pool scene, her makeup smeared and runny. "So pathetic."

A moment later, she realized she was in her dark motel room, sitting on the floor with her back against the bed. She had no memory of pulling into the parking lot or walking up the stairs to the room.

Chupa's body on the stage loomed large in her mind, accompanied by those last moments with Sam, the horror of finding the Lost Kids murdered, and that terrifying moment when the bomb at Bolin Plaza had exploded and killed Melissa.

Bobby J. kept talking about the two graves. And yet despite all of her acts as Avery the Avenger, she was still here. It was the people around her, the people who loved her, who were filling the other grave. Even after she'd given up pushing back against the bullies in her little world. Karma was a relentless bitch.

Her heart nearly stopped when her phone rang. She fumbled it out of her purse, half expecting it to be Kimi calling from the hospital. But it was Bobby J.

"Hel… hello?"

"Hey, kiddo. Are you okay? The news is reporting a shootout at a Las Cruces nightclub. They said the shooter was shouting your name."

A glance at the clock on the nightstand told her it had been two hours since the shooting. It felt more like two minutes.

"Bramwell's guys found us. I don't know how. They shot Chupa."

"But you're okay, right?"

"No, Appa! I'm not okay! He could die because of me. I'm cursed, like a bad luck charm. I'm a danger to everyone around me."

"Listen to me, sweetheart. None of this is your fault. None of it." His tone was full-on father mode. "This is on Bramwell's men and—I hate to say it—on Sam for taking their money. But none of this is your fault. You are not cursed. You hear me?"

"I should have given back the money soon as I found it. If I had, maybe Chupa wouldn't have been shot."

"I don't have an answer for that. But if you had, you could have been shot."

"And if I had, who cares?"

"I care, Avery. As your father, I care very much. You know that."

"I do, Appa. I do. But..." She sobbed. "I don't know what to do. I can't keep putting people's lives in danger. It's selfish of me."

"Maybe you should just fly back here. I can pay for a plane ticket. We'll figure it out together."

"Then I'd be putting you in danger. I should just disappear for good. Live off the grid for the rest of my pathetic life. I've done it before."

"Avery, that's no way to live, and you know it."

"What choice do I have? Unless you want me to try and kill Bramwell and those motherfuckers who work for him."

"I don't want you killing anyone. I want you living a life of joy and creativity."

She remembered Cuervo lying on the sidewalk, where she'd left him bloody, possibly dead. "I don't see how that will happen at this point."

Her phone chimed. She glanced at the screen and saw Kimi was calling. "Appa, I gotta go. Love you. I'll call you soon."

"Aver—"

She switched to the incoming call. "Kimi, how is he?"

"Stable and out of surgery. Bullet went through his left side and penetrated his large intestines. Missed the major organs and arteries, thank goth. They're pumping him full of antibiotics but expecting him to recover."

"I'm so sorry, Kimi. I never should have come with you on this tour."

"Stop it, Avery. This isn't your fault. I don't blame you. I only sent you away to save you from talking to the cops."

Kimi's kind words only piled onto the guilt Avery felt.

She needed to come clean about the money but couldn't do it over the phone. "Should I come to the hospital?"

"Not a good idea. Cops were here earlier, asking about you and Sam's murder. They have one of those BOLOs out on you. I told them you went back to Phoenix. Not sure if they believed me or not. There's a guard posted outside Chupa's hospital room. Don't know if it's for his protection or to see if you show up."

"Shit." She took a deep breath. "Kimi, there's something I need to tell you."

"What?"

"Not over the phone. Can I pick you up at the hospital and grab a cup of coffee somewhere?"

There was a pause before Kimi answered. "Yeah, okay. I'll meet you in front of the main entrance of MountainView Regional Medical Center. It's on Lohman Avenue. Looks like the east side of the city, according to the map."

"I'll find it. I'll see you soon."

# CHAPTER 26
# A SLAP IN THE FACE

AFTER LUGGING the bag of money into the back of the SUV, Avery punched the location of the hospital into her phone's navigation app and drove the speed limit to the hospital.

She was no longer angry or afraid. Just numb. Dead. A meat sack in motion. She deserved to be rotting in an unmarked grave.

Kimi stood outside the hospital's main entrance, arms wrapped around her as if she were cold, despite the lingering warmth of the day. She climbed into the passenger seat without a word. She had washed off Her stage makeup had been washed off, leaving her looking as tired and wan as Avery felt.

Avery drove a half mile to a twenty-four-hour restaurant called Mom's Diner.

"What'd you want to tell me?" Kimi's tone was quiet and unreadable.

"Better if I show you." Avery climbed out and opened the back of the SUV. Kimi came around the other side.

"One of Sam's bags."

"The one with the books in it?"

"Not books, it turns out." Avery unzipped the bag.

Kimi stared at the stacks of cash as if turned to marble. No words. Not even a change in expression.

"I..." Avery fumbled for words. Her throat tightened. "My best guess is that Sam... I think she robbed her boss. Theodore Bramwell."

When Kimi still didn't react, she added, "I didn't know what was inside until after we got to Tucson."

"You knew before that psycho shot Chupa. But you knew but kept it a secret."

Avery stared at the ground. "Yes."

"You knew they wanted their money back."

"Yes."

Kimi slapped her hard, but the guilt hurt far more than the blow ever could.

"I'm so sorry, Kimi. It should have been me who got shot."

Kimi stepped into Avery's space. She was four inches smaller than Avery, but her ferocity blazed as if she were as tall as her husband. "I'm so pissed at you."

"I know."

"Do you know why I'm pissed at you?"

"Because I put you all in danger and lied about what was in the bag."

"No! That is not why."

Avery said nothing.

"I knew it was a risk to protect you. We all did. And we accepted it. I am pissed because you didn't trust me enough to tell me about this."

"It's yours if you want it."

"You think I want Theodore Bramwell's blood money? Hell no! I want my friend to be honest with me. To trust that I will stand by her no matter what. Not to keep secrets and hide things from me."

Avery let that process for a moment. "I'm sorry."

Kimi reached up and cupped Avery's face in her delicate

but strong fingers. "I love you, Avery Siobhan Byrne. You've been through unimaginable shit. But you also have friends who are here for you. And you owe us the courtesy of your honesty."

"You're right. I do."

"Is there anything else we should know?"

Avery told her about her communication with Cuervo and her encounter with him on the street.

Kimi picked up a stack of bills, thumbed through it, then cocked her head. "What's that?"

"What's what?"

Kimi put down the cash and pulled up a rectangular black plastic object roughly the same size as the stack. "This."

Avery took it from her and examined it. There was a USB port on one side. "Must be a power bank. Sam used to carry one with her because her phone was always running out of juice."

"Why would Sam put it in with the cash?"

"Beats me. Sam did a lot of things I didn't understand. Like why she fell in love with me in the first place."

"Oh, please," Kimi said. "I need a drink. Looks like there's a bar down the street."

Avery handed the keys to Kimi, and they drove to the bar called Ain't Nobody's Bizness. A neon rainbow flickered above the entrance.

"Any idea how Bramwell's men found us?" Kimi asked as they sat at a secluded table. A Melissa Etheridge tune played on an old jukebox.

"I've racked my brain and came up empty. Maybe they figured out I was riding along on your tour. I should email Cuervo and tell him I've decided to give back the money." *Assuming I didn't kick him to death.*

"And then what? What's to stop them from killing you?"

"I don't know. But I'm tired of putting my friends in danger. Even putting on a disguise didn't help."

"I don't want you to risk your life over this. It's got to blow over eventually."

"Not with me carrying around two million bucks of Theodore Bramwell's blood money."

Kimi nearly spilled her drink. "Two million bucks? In cash? Damn. What I could do with that kinda money."

"You want it? It's yours. I owe you for whatever Chupa's medical bills are going to be. Not to mention pain and suffering."

"Hell no. I want nothing to do with that money. Give it to a children's charity or something."

"Cuervo said it belongs to a cartel south of the border. And if they don't get it soon, the Mexicans will kill Bramwell and all his guys."

"So there's a bright side after all."

"Maybe."

They didn't talk for a while. Avery played through several possible scenarios of returning the money, but nothing she came up could prevent Bramwell from making her disappear once he had the cash back.

"I've got one for you." Kimi's voice shocked Avery back into the present.

"What's that?"

A faint smile played at the corners of Kimi's mouth. "An ironic character name."

"Lay it on me."

"A woman who runs a car rental agency named Lisa Carr."

Avery winced. "Okay, I got one. A civil rights attorney named Frieda Peeples."

# CHAPTER 27
# LEVERAGE

AVERY'S EYELIDS were growing heavy by the time Kimi drove her back to the motel.

"I don't know what to tell you." Kimi put the SUV in park. "I know you loved Sam. And I am truly sorry she's dead. But what she did was stupid and selfish. Stealing money from a mobster like Bramwell? She put everyone in danger."

"I know." Avery's voice choked with tears. "Which is why I need to stay away from you and everyone I care about. At least until I can figure a way out of this."

"I hate to admit it, but you're probably right. I'm sorry I wasn't there for you when your father kicked you out. And I hate to goth that I'm abandoning you again."

"You were there for me, Kimi. We kept in touch. Your calls and texts got me through a lot of shit. Wasn't your fault your folks didn't want to take me in. And you let me tag along with the band after Sam was killed. Only, things got too crazy. And now Chupa's been shot because of me. I will figure a way out of this. Go be with Chupa."

Kimi hugged her. "Love you, girl."

"Love you too." Avery climbed out of the SUV, grabbed the bag of money, and went up to her motel room.

She pulled the power bank out of the bag of money and examined it. *Should probably make sure it's fully charged in case I need to charge my phone,* she thought.

Dreary-eyed, she dug into her laptop bag and found an adapter cord that was standard USB on one end and mini-USB on the other. She searched the power bank for the charging port. Most of the ones she'd seen had a mini-USB port for charging the power bank itself and a standard USB port for charging devices. But this one only had one port, and it was standard USB.

She stared at it for a moment, trying to brush away the cobwebs in her brain. An idea formed that drove away the blanket of sleep.

She grabbed a different cord, one that was only a foot long but standard USB on both ends. She connected the device to her laptop and confirmed her suspicion. It wasn't a power bank, but an external hard drive. And it was full of files.

Suddenly, all fatigue burned away like a morning fog as she browsed through the vast array of folders and files. Accounting spreadsheets. Email backups. Text conversations. Contact lists. It soon became apparent why Sam had put it in with the bag of money.

# CHAPTER 28
# QUESTIONABLE ANSWERS

DETECTIVES Hardin and Valentine strode down the hospital corridor, escorted by Francesca Ruiz, the Las Cruces PD detective investigating the Gothique shooting incident.

Ruiz was maybe in her early thirties. Hardin's initial impression was that she was sharp but relatively inexperienced at investigating serious crimes.

"We identify the kind of gun the shooter used?" Hardin asked.

"Found a .45 ACP casing at the scene. Bullet mushroomed when it hit the victim but seems consistent with a .45 slug. I'll send you the ballistics report when I get it."

"Thanks."

"Gotta tell you, Detectives, these rock band members are pretty tight-lipped. Couldn't get much out of them. But I suspect they know more than they're telling."

"Don't worry," Valentine replied. "We'll open them up like a cheap can of ravioli."

"Slow your roll, youngblood," Hardin cautioned. "These people are the victims, not the perpetrators."

"Maybe of this crime, but you and I both know they've been protecting Avery Byrne."

Hardin stepped in front of his partner and locked eyes

with him. "I realize you're anxious to prove yourself to the lieutenant and make the collar on this horrible murder. But let me remind you we follow the clues. We may form a theory of the case, but sometimes that theory is wrong."

"Byrne's prints were on the murder weapon."

"But that doesn't prove she was Ferguson's shooter. They could have been on there before."

"Don't lecture me on procedure, old man. I scored the top of the list on the detective's exam."

"Oh, so I guess you know everything, huh?" Hardin wondered why the man was so hellbent on arresting Byrne. Was he dirty? "Tell me, smart guy, if Byrne shot Ferguson, how come some guy shows up tonight, guns blazing, with a hard-on for this woman almost as big as yours?"

"Maybe Bramwell's looking for payback for doing one of their own."

"Or maybe Bramwell's crew is covering something up." *And maybe you're in on it,* Hardin pondered.

"Gentlemen…" Detective Ruiz stood a ways down the corridor, an impatient look on her face.

"I've been doing this job since before you were eating paste in kindergarten. Follow my lead. And maybe, if you pay attention, you'll learn something about solving a murder."

Hardin caught up with Ruiz. "Apologies, Detective. Lead the way."

They found the victim, Marco Melendez, asleep in his room next to a woman dozing in a chair and wearing a Damaged Souls tour T-shirt.

Her eyes opened when they entered. "What do you want?"

Hardin introduced himself and his fellow detectives.

"We already gave our statements to the patrol offers and again to her," the woman said, nodding toward Detective

Ruiz. "We got no idea who the shooter was. He just stormed in, shot Chupa, and ran out. End of story."

"Chupa?" Hardin raised an eyebrow, even though he knew she was referring to the man in the bed beside her. He just wanted to see how she'd react, throwing her off-balance.

"My husband, Marco Melendez. Don't you people talk to each other?" The woman grasped the sleeping man's hand. His eyes fluttered open.

"I understand." Hardin glanced at his notes. "You're Kimiko Asato, correct?"

"What of it? And what're a couple of Phoenix cops doing out here? Not exactly your jurisdiction."

"I'm really sorry about what happened to your husband, Kimiko. We're believe tonight's shooting is connected to an incident that took place a few days ago in Phoenix." He pulled up a chair next to her and showed her a photo of Avery Byrne. "I'm guessing you know this woman."

An expression of panic flashed across her face, followed by more suspicion. "Why?"

"We're hoping to talk with her about her girlfriend's recent death."

"So you can frame her for murdering Sam?"

"Hey, if the shoe fits," Valentine said. "We found her prints on the murder weapon."

Hardin shot him a withering glance. "No, we're not interested in framing anyone. We simply want to find out what happened. Personally, I don't think Avery did it. Especially after this evening's shooting. But I could use your help and hers to bring Sam's killer to justice."

Asato didn't answer right away. Valentine started to say something, but Hardin held up a hand to silence him. The tension in the room grew, but Hardin knew that worked in his favor.

After five minutes, Asato said, "Sam worked for Theodore Bramwell."

"The real estate tycoon."

"The head of the damn Desert Mafia. He's the one who killed her. Or had her killed."

"Why would he do that?"

Again, the waiting game ensued. Hardin used the time to study everything he could about the woman. The blood on her shirt. The callouses on her fingertips. The way she avoided his gaze. The alcohol on her breath.

"Hey, Kimi! They didn't have Diet Dr Pepper, so I got you…"

A couple of young men stood in the doorway. Hardin recognized the one holding up a Diet Coke can as Omar "Torch" Shaheen, the same man who'd credited Byrne for a new tattoo at the concert in Tucson.

The round-faced man next to him reminded Hardin of the musician Ed Sheeran. Michael McCobb, no doubt. Hardin wondered if that was his real name or something he'd adopted as part of this goth band aesthetic.

"More cops?" Shaheen asked with a sneer, lowering the can of soda. "Great."

Hardin smiled at him. He preferred to interview witnesses separately, but in this case, her bandmates might set Asato at ease and make her more talkative.

"Come on in and join us, gentlemen. Everything's okay."

"Yeah, absolutely peachy. Just ask Chupa," McCobb added derisively.

"You don't wanna talk here? We'd be happy to drag your asses down to the station if you'd be more comfortable," Valentine said.

"Forgive my partner's rudeness," Hardin replied. "We really are here to help. We're worried about your friend, Avery Byrne. Kimiko here was telling us she suspects Sam's boss was behind both shootings."

McCobb and Asato exchanged a glance. The two men entered the room and stood against the far wall. Shaheen handed Asato the soda, which she placed on a bedside table.

"You were explaining why Mr. Bramwell had Sam murdered."

Again, Hardin watched the wheels turning in Asato's head as she debated what to say.

"All I know is what Avery told me," Asato replied. "Sam quit working for Bramwell and was afraid he'd come after her. Maybe he thought she might talk to the cops or the feds. I don't know. They were moving to Seattle to get away from him and make a fresh start."

"Seattle?" This was the first he'd heard of that, but it explained why the house was empty except for some basic furniture. "Is that where Avery is now?"

"Beats me. She left after our Tucson concert. Headed back to Phoenix."

"So Bramwell was afraid Ms. Ferguson was informing on him to the police. That's why he had her killed?"

"Or maybe he didn't like loose ends," McCobb added.

"Or he's a fucking psycho," Shaheen replied. "Take your pick."

"The evidence suggests that the people who killed Sam were looking for something. Perhaps drugs or something else of value worth torturing and killing for. What do you know about that?"

Shaheen and McCobb looked at each other with expressions of befuddlement. Asato simply stared down at her husband's hand. She knew something.

"Kimiko? Any idea what Bramwell might be looking for?"

She met his gaze. "No."

Hardin considered his options. "But Avery would probably know, right?"

Asato shrugged.

"I want the people who hurt Chupa and murdered Sam

brought to justice so they won't hurt anyone else," Hardin said in an assuring tone. "But to do that, I need to talk with Avery. How can I get in touch with her?"

"How do we know you're not working for Bramwell?" Shaheen asked. "Word is he has dirty cops in his pocket."

"I have no way of proving to you I'm not, I suppose," Hardin admitted. "Honestly, dirty cops make me sick. They make it harder for the rest of us to do our job. And I'll be the first to admit that Phoenix PD has had its share of bad apples."

Shaheen and McCobb both snorted with derision.

"Like when you people accused Black Lives Matters protestors of being part of a gang?" Shaheen glared at him. "Yeah, we know. Sounds like a whole barrel full of bad apples."

"Can I confide in you? I see Avery as an innocent victim in all of this, which is why I want to protect her. I suspect Bramwell had Sam killed, and I fear he's now after Avery. Tonight's shooting only confirms this. I would love nothing more than to slap the cuffs on Bramwell and whoever else was involved in these two incidents. You want to see these bad people punished as much as I do. So we're on the same team, right? So help me protect Avery and tell me how I can get in touch with her."

Again, he was met with a wall of silence.

"Fucking pathetic!" Valentine said. "You people call her your friend but won't help us find her."

"It's okay. You're not sure you can trust us with Avery's safety," Hardin said, resisting the urge to slap the hell out of his partner. "Why don't we focus instead on what happened tonight at the bar?"

"Asshole shot me," Melendez said, his eyes now open. The numbers on his vitals monitor climbed steadily.

"Hi, Chupa. Nice of you to join us. How are you feeling?"

Melendez groaned. His eyelids drooped.

"I'm sorry that man shot you. Can you tell me what you remember?"

"Getting ready for our first set. Black man rushed the stage." Melendez winced and continued, his breathing labored. "Little guy. Had a gun. A 1911A. Chrome."

"Did he say anything?" Hardin pressed.

"Looking for Avery. Told him to fuck off."

"I disarmed him with one of Torch's guitars," McCobb said quietly. "Unfortunately, the gun still went off and hit Chupa. Sorry, man."

"Better in the belly than in the head." Melendez managed a weak smile.

"Then what happened?" Hardin asked.

"We tried to stop the bleeding." Asato's voice was full of emotion. "I thought he was going to die."

"And the gunman?"

"Ran out the back," Shaheen said. "Like the chickenshit punk he is."

"He was cradling his arm and screaming," McCobb added. "Hope I broke the bastard's arm."

"I commend you for protecting your friend. Such loyalty is sadly rare. Help me do my part. If I can find Avery, I can protect her. But I can't protect her if she's out there on her own."

"Went back to Phoenix," Melendez said.

"Why would she do that?" Hardin pressed. "Why not stay with you?"

"Because of me," Shaheen said sadly. "I blabbed about her during our concert in Tucson. Didn't realize she was hiding from Bramwell's goons until after."

Hardin studied all of their faces. He could see the lie in their eyes. "You sure she's gone? I can't help her if you're not honest with me."

"You see her here?" McCobb gestured in a sweeping motion.

"Maybe she's back at your motel," Valentine chimed in. "What room is she staying in?"

Again, the silent treatment.

"So, she is at the motel?" Hardin asked.

"No," Asato said assertively. "She left when we were in Tucson, like we said. We don't know where she is. Now leave us alone."

"What's her phone number?" Valentine asked.

Asato rattled off a number. It matched the one he already had for her cell phone, the one that didn't show up when they tried to get a location on it.

"She got a burner?" Hardin pressed.

Asato shrugged. "If she does, I don't know the number."

"What motel are you all staying at?"

"I'm staying right here with my husband," Asato insisted.

"And the rest of you?"

Ruiz pulled a notebook out of her pocket. "Days Inn on Avenida de Mesilla. Rooms 319, 321, and 323."

The musicians' expressions hardened.

"Check all you want," Asato replied. "You won't find her in our rooms because she went back."

"And where's your manager? Scott Murray?"

"He went on a food run. Should be back in thirty."

Hardin sat for a moment to see if she or the others would offer anything else. Eventually, he nodded to his partner and Detective Ruiz. "Mr. Melendez, I hope you feel better soon and can resume your tour. In the meantime, I will do what I can to bring Sam Ferguson's killers to justice. With or without your help."

He handed each of them a business card. "If you hear from Avery, have her get in touch. I only want to protect her and bring these shooters to justice."

As soon as they were back in the corridor heading to the parking lot, Valentine said, "They're full of shit. She's in town here. You can read it on their faces."

"I suspect you're right." For all the young detective's impulsive nature, he'd gotten the same read on the band that Hardin had. "Let's wait for the manager to get back and talk to them. If we still get nothing, we can go knocking on doors at the motel."

"This whole thing about Theodore Bramwell is a smoke screen. I'm telling you, Avery Byrne killed her rug-munching lover, pure and simple. And this satanic cult band is protecting her."

Despite the fingerprint evidence, this still didn't feel to Hardin like a domestic dispute gone bad. "Even if Byrne is Ferguson's killer, it doesn't explain tonight's shooting. But you're right, the band is definitely covering for her."

"My guess is Byrne killed her girl. Then Bramwell found out someone did one of his people, and now he's out for revenge."

"Maybe. Detective Ruiz, let us know once you've gotten the security footage from the bar. Perhaps we can help you ID the shooter."

"Roger that. My sergeant says he's still waiting on the warrant. But as soon as we got it, I'll give you a call."

"In the meantime," Valentine added, "keep checking with all the hospitals in town to see if they've admitted anyone matching the shooter's description with an injured arm."

Ruiz gave him a glare. "This is not our first rodeo, Detective Valentine. We know how to run a murder investigation."

"Come on, youngblood," Hardin pointed toward a dumpy white man walking down the corridor with two large paper sacks marked Golden Dragon Chinese Restaurant. "Looks like we found our band manager."

# CHAPTER 29
# LIABILITY

CUERVO WASN'T sure which ached more, his balls or his head.

He had hunkered down next to Luther's car, which was parked in a lot off of Main Street about a mile from Gothique.

He had to hand it to Avery. The woman knew how to defend herself. Or maybe he had just underestimated her while dressed up like Tim Curry in that weird movie. He hadn't even been sure it was her until she pushed over the table and ran.

He didn't blame her for being mad at him. He should have stopped Luther from torturing Sam. She'd always felt like a kid sister to him. Sure, what she'd done was stupid, robbing the boss then trying to run. *But still...*

There was only one way to make it right. Or at the very least, less wrong. He had to protect Avery. None of this was her fault. He owed it to Sam to keep her safe. At the same time, he had to get the money back, or they'd all be dead.

Only now Luther had fucked things up by shooting someone in the band, attracting unnecessary attention to the situation. Now, the entire Main Street area was crawling with patrol cars, their lights turning the street into a disco of blue and red.

A sound nearby caught his attention. He drew the small pistol from his waistband and groaned as he got to his feet. A shadow approached. Cuervo raised his weapon. He lowered it again when Luther's wiry frame emerged into the glow of a streetlamp, cradling his arm.

"Fuck, man." Cuervo tucked the pistol back in its holster. "Where the hell you been?"

"Got fucking turned around in this goddamn Podunk town."

"What happened to your arm?"

"Faggot musician hit it with an electric guitar. Think it's broke."

"You won't be able to drive like that. Best give me the keys."

Luther eyed him suspiciously. "Let you drive Veronica? I don't think so."

"You named your car after a character from Archie's comics?"

"No. I named her after my aunt. She was a badass."

"Whatever. You really think you can drive with your arm like that?"

Luther stared at him for another minute then spat. "Fuck." He dug out a set of keys and offered them.

"Let's get the hell out of here." Cuervo opened the door.

"That bitch still has our money. And she still in town. I can feel it. Those vampire freaks were lying their asses off, saying she went back to Phoenix."

"She is here," Cuervo replied. "I spoke with her."

"You what? Where?"

"Out in front of the club. She was dressed like Tim Curry from that weird midnight movie."

"That faggot at the merch table? That was her? She sounded like a guy."

"She lowered her voice to make her sound like a guy." Sam had told him Avery was trans, but he didn't feel the need to share that tidbit.

"Fucking faggots, man. Can't trust any of them. So d'you get the money?"

"Not yet. We're supposed to meet her."

"Fucking A, man! Then we cap her ass."

Cuervo drove them south and turned right onto Lohman Avenue. After a mile or so, he pulled around behind a shuttered bowling alley. The only light came from the smattering of stars and a sliver of a moon.

"We're meeting her here?" Luther asked.

"That's what she said."

"Fine. But once we got the cash, we gotta score some oxy or some shit. Fucking arm's killing me."

"Come on." Cuervo popped the trunk and got out of the car. "I want to show you something in the trunk."

"In the trunk? When'd you put something in my trunk?"

"You'll see."

Luther got out with a string of expletives and met Cuervo at the back of the car. "What?" he asked impatiently.

"There." Cuervo pointed deep into the trunk.

Luther leaned over.

Cuervo wrapped his arms around Luther's skinny neck in a sleeper hold. "Had enough of your homophobic remarks."

Luther flailed and grunted, but after a few minutes went limp. Cuervo snapped the guy's neck and dropped him on the pavement.

He pulled out the dead man's wallet and relieved him of his watch, a gold chain around his neck, and a diamond ring from his pinkie. Cuervo had no interest in Luther's shit but figured it best to look like a robbery gone bad.

Finally, he took a photo of Luther's body and attached it to an email. Creating a digital trail to a murder was a risky move, but if it convinced Avery to return the money, it was a risk worth taking.

He climbed into Veronica and drove to an all-night diner on the outskirts of town to wait for a reply.

# CHAPTER 30
# NO MORE RUNNING

AFTER SPENDING a half hour exploring the contents of the external hard drive, she received a message from an unfamiliar email address. She nearly deleted it as spam, but saw attached image and gasped.

Luther Jackson lay on the ground, his eyes open but neck twisted at an unnatural angle. He was clearly dead.

The message read:

*The man who tortured Sam is no longer a problem. Sorry I didn't do this before he shot your friend. I'm in your corner. Call me. Let's work this out.*

*C*

Was this a trap? Even if Cuervo had killed Luther, what was to stop him from killing her as well once he got the money? Or from Bramwell from sending someone else to finish the job?

Her phone chimed again, but this time it was a text message from Kimi.

> Cops were here. Phx cops. Looking 4 U. We told them U went back to Phx. Not sure they believed us.

"Shit. Shit. Shit." Phoenix cops had tracked her here too?

How? Were they working with Luther and Cuervo? Had to be.

As her mind raced, a plan to put this entire madness to rest began to come together.

With a trembling hand, Avery replied.

FWIW, Sorry for all the trouble. I'm going back 2 Phx 4 realz. Gotta end this.

A reply came a moment later.

What R U going 2 do? Don't want 2 lose U, Aves.

Avery considered her answer, not wanting to worry Kimi but at the same time let her know that the time for running and hiding was over.

Don't worry. Got a plan. Avery the Avenger is back. I'll be in touch.

She wasn't entirely convinced her plan would work, but running and hiding was no longer an option. To put things in motion, she needed supplies.

A quick web search turned up an OfficeMart a few doors from the motel. Perfect! But they were closing in ten minutes. She had to hurry.

The only person in the store when she raced in was a middle-aged woman working the cash register. Avery rushed through the aisles and picked up two more external hard drives, a package of padded envelopes, and a two-foot-by-three-foot cardboard box.

As she approached the checkout, she saw a display of books on marketing by an author she'd never heard of. She grabbed a dozen of them then put eight hundred dollars cash on a prepaid debit card at the register.

When the clerk gave her a weird look, Avery said in a fake Southern drawl, "I've run away from my abusive husband. I'm afraid he'll track me if I use my regular bank card."

The woman behind the register gave her a knowing nod. "Been there myself, sugar. You call the cops?"

"He is a cop," Avery replied.

"Fucking assholes. You keep yourself safe. Anybody asks, I ain't seen ya." The cashier started ringing up the paperbacks. "So, what's with buying twelve copies of the same book?"

"The friend I'm staying with runs a book club for entrepreneurs."

"Makes sense, I guess. Well, good luck. And watch your back."

"Thanks."

As she reached the top of the motel stairs with her purchases in hand, she spotted two men knocking on doors. Something about their look and the way they knocked triggered Avery's internal warning system. Cops.

"Ms. Byrne, if you're in there, you need to open the door," one of the cops demanded. "It's the police. We need to talk."

Avery stood there frozen like a rabbit hiding from coyotes in a prickly pear patch. If they looked her way, they would see her. But should couldn't will herself to move.

A loud argument broke out in the parking lot on the far end of the building. When the cops looked their direction, Avery hauled ass into the pass-through that led to the her room in back of the motel. She dunked into her room, keeping the lights off and flipping the swing-bar lock on the door in place.

She stopped and listened, but heard nothing.

"Breathe, Avery. Just breathe." *Inhale calm, hold, release fear.*

Her instinct was to run, but there was no way she could get away without leaving everything behind—her suitcase, her laptop, her tattoo equipment, and the money. And where would she go? She had no car. Instead, she curled into a tight ball in the dark room, hoping they wouldn't find her.

Just as she was daring to believe she'd escaped, a loud pounding shook the room.

"Avery Byrne, this is the police. If you're in there, we need to speak with you about a very serious matter."

She held her breath. Her pounding pulse sounded so loud in her ears that she feared they could hear it outside.

"Avery, this is Detectives Hardin and Valentine with Phoenix PD. We just want to talk. It's important. We're trying to keep you safe after what happened earlier this evening. But we can't do that if you don't talk with us."

Avery tried to remember if she'd seen Hardin's and Valentine's names listed in the files on the hard drive, but she was too panicked to remember clearly. The name Valentine seemed familiar, but she wasn't one hundred percent sure. Even if Hardin was legit, she couldn't risk talking to him if his buddy was on the take.

More pounding on the door. "Avery, please. You've been through a lot in the past few days. We only want to help you."

Avery had had enough encounters with cops to know they always talked like worried grandmothers with promises to help—up until the moment they snapped the cuffs on. Still, a part of her wanted it to be true.

Her phone chimed. A text message. *Fuck!* She flicked her phone to silent mode, hoping like hell the cops outside hadn't heard it.

"Avery, I know Sam was involved with some shady

people, but I'm sure she wouldn't want you to come to the same end as her. Just open the door. We can protect you."

Bullshit, she thought.

"She ain't in there," muttered a second voice, the one she assumed was Valentine. "Ten to one, one of those freaks in the band tipped her off."

"Maybe," Hardin said. "Avery, if you can hear me, I'm going to leave my card in the door. Get in touch with me. We need your help bringing Sam's killer to justice. Call me. We will work this out for you and keep you safe."

She waited for what felt like an hour before she allowed herself to relax. Odds were good they were still watching the room. She could only hope they'd give up by morning. She had a plan to set in motion, and then she had to get the hell out of town.

She checked her phone. Kimi had sent another text.

How U getting 2 Phx? Where will U stay? Worried about U.

Avery hadn't given much thought to where she'd stay. Maybe a shithole like the Ocotillo Inn.

Prolly take bus to Deming. Amtrak to Phx. Dunno where I'll stay.

The response came quickly.

Forget the bus. I'll take U 2 train station. Wish I could take U all the way. Stay at our house. Will bring U the keys. Chupa & the guys send their love.

Avery caught herself crying at Kimi's text. She didn't deserve such compassion. She'd been ready to follow Sam in a last-minute move to Seattle without telling anyone goodbye. She was a shit daughter to Bobby J. and a shit friend to Kimi and the band.

In the dark room, she assembled the cardboard box she'd bought at the store, filled it with the cash, made duplicates of the stolen hard drive and stuffed them in the padded envelopes.

Finally, she sent an email reply to Cuervo.

*Meet me Wednesday 2pm. Grumpy's Bar and Grill, Phx. Come alone. I'll give you the money then.*

*P.S. I have dirt on everyone in Bramwell's empire, including you. If anything happens to me, copies will automatically go to the feds and media.*

# CHAPTER 31
# NOT A HAPPY CAMPER

CUERVO HAD BEEN SITTING in a bar, anxious to have the money in hand before leaving town, when he got Avery's email.

"Two days? ¡Hijo de puta!" Mr. Bramwell was going to go ballistic.

And what was this bullshit about having dirt on all of them? Had Sam told her something? And even if she had, what could Avery prove?

He sent a reply demanding they meet now. When she didn't respond after a thirty minutes, he stumbled out to Luther's car.

He was too drunk to start the long drive back to Arizona, so he grabbed a cheap motel room to sleep it off. Maybe Avery would come to her senses and agree to meet.

He woke the next morning to his phone ringing.

Bramwell. Fuck! What was he going to tell the man about the money? Or about about killing Luther? He couldn't ignore the call. That would only make matters worse.

"Yeah?" he muttered after hitting the answer button.

"Mr. Cuervo, where is my money? And why isn't Luther answering my calls?"

"I'm meeting with Avery Byrne tomorrow in Phoenix. I'll have the money then."

"Tomorrow? That is not an acceptable answer. I want my money now. You said that bitch was in Las Cruces. Did you find her?"

"She is. Or rather, she was. I think she's on her way back."

"You think? I do not pay you to think, Mr. Cuervo. I pay you to do exactly as I instruct. And I instructed you to retrieve my money and kill that tranny bitch."

"I will. Just need a little more time, is all."

"Where is Luther? I want to speak with him."

"Luther's dead." No way to sugarcoat it.

"What? How?"

"He shot someone at a bar while looking for the girl. He became a liability. Drawing too much attention."

There wasn't an immediate response on Bramwell's end. Cuervo waited him out.

"I better get my money tomorrow, or I'll consider you a liability."

"There's one more thing. She's got something on us."

"She's got what on whom?" The tone of Bramwell's voice was pure violence.

"Don't know exactly. Just that she had dirt on the Desert Mafia. And that if anything happens to her, it will go to the feds and the media."

"She's bluffing. What could she have?"

"I don't know. Maybe Sam gave her something."

"Then you best get it back before this shit show gets any worse. Do you hear me, Mr. Cuervo?"

"Yes, sir. I'm heading to Phoenix now. I'll be in touch."

## CHAPTER 32
# DIVERSION

AVERY WOKE to the sound of her burner ringing. "Hello?"

"You ready?" Kimi asked. Her voice sounded so tired.

Avery looked at the cardboard box she'd filled. Her box of tattoo equipment and two addressed padded envelopes sat on top. Her suitcase and her computer bag lay packed beside it.

After getting everything else ready, she'd gone through Sam's suitcase. Sam's scent had ripped open all the ragged wounds in Avery's soul.

All she'd found in the bag was clothing, accessories, and toiletries. Nothing worth taking back to Phoenix. Right now, she needed to travel light. Leaving the suitcase behind felt like an abandonment, but it was necessary.

"I'm ready." Avery peeked out the window and spotted a large Ford on the far side of the back parking lot. Two people sat in the front seat. She couldn't be sure, but her gut told her it was Hardin and Valentine waiting to arrest her.

"Kimi, I think those Phoenix cops are in the parking lot, watching my door."

"Not a problem. Murray's got you covered."

"Murray? How?"

A moment later, the band's equipment truck cruised through the back lot and stopped right in front of the detectives' car.

A figure passed in front of Avery's window, followed by a knock on the door. "Open up! It's me."

Avery slung the strap of her computer bag over her shoulder and grabbed the extended handle of her suitcase with her box of tattooing gear strapped on top. She opened the door and handed the suitcase to Kimi. "Gotta grab one more thing."

"Hurry!"

She rushed back and hefted the big box of money. It weighed a ton. She raced out the door, following Kimi back down the pass-through to the street side of the building. She could hear raised voices, one of which was Murray's, apologizing for the truck breaking down right in front of their car.

"What's in the box?" Kimi asked as she lifted the suitcase when they hustled down the steps to the ground floor.

"Guess."

Chupa's SUV was parked at the bottom of the stairs. They tossed Avery's stuff into the back, jumped into the truck, and drove off.

Avery's heart felt like it would leap up her throat. "What about Murray?"

Kimi handed Avery her phone. "Call him. Let him know we're away."

"We need to stop at the OfficeMart before heading to Deming." Avery found Murray's number in Kimi's contacts and hit Call.

"Murray? We're outta there. And thanks!"

"Oh, hi, Kimi! Yeah, the equipment truck broke down. Waiting for a tow. I'll get to the hospital when I can. Toodles." The call ended.

"He okay?" Kimi asked.

"Not sure. He was saying the truck broke down and was

waiting for a tow. He thought I was you." Then she realized. "Didn't want the cops to know it was me calling, I guess."

"That was the plan."

"Kimi, I'm sorr—"

"Don't you dare apologize again."

"Fine. Then thank you."

"You're welcome."

"How's Chupa doing?"

"Complaining about being stuck in the hospital instead of on tour, which tells me he's not in too much pain. Doc wants to keep him there for a few days, possibly a week, to make sure there's no infection."

"Shit. Guess this totally wrecked your tour."

"We'll reschedule Albuquerque and miss the Taos Goth Fest. But we should be back on track soon. Shit happens. On our last tour, we got stuck in Barstow for a week waiting on a back-ordered part for the equipment truck. We'll manage through this."

Avery saw they were sitting in the OfficeMart parking lot.

"What is it you needed here at OfficeMart?"

"I'm shipping the money and my tattooing gear back to Phoenix."

"Is that safe? What if they X-ray the box and take the money?"

"I piled a bunch of paperback books on top of the money. Anyone opens the box, that's what they'll see. Not sure what it will look like on an X-ray, but I'm hoping. I don't feel safe carrying the money back with me on the train."

"Where are you sending it?"

"To my friend Jinx Ballou. Former cop turned bounty hunter." Avery told Kimi about discovering the files on the external hard drive. "I made duplicates and am sending one to Jinx and one to a lawyer friend of mine."

"Why?"

"Leverage."

"Avery the Avenger really is back."

"I just hope no one else gets hurt or killed." Avery remembered the photo of Luther that Cuervo had sent.

"Before you go in," Kimi said, "I brought you something. It's in the back seat."

Avery turned and saw a small cardboard box. Inside, she found a shoulder-length blond wig. She stared at it without a word.

"Figured it'd be a better disguise out in the real world than Dr. Frank-N-Furter. There's a wig cap and some bobby pins in there to help secure your own hair so it doesn't show through."

Avery hugged her. "Don't know what I'd do without you."

"You're a good person, Avery. You've had a lot of shitty stuff happen over the years. I'm happy to help make up for it."

Kimi helped Avery secure the wig in place then smiled. "Who are you, lady? And what have you done with my friend Avery?"

"Does it really look all right?"

"I paid a lot of money for that wig. Trust me. If you want to go unnoticed among normal people, this will definitely do the trick. Let's get these packages shipped and hit the road. I want to get back to Chupa."

A jacket covered most of her tattoos, except the ones on her neck. She might need to invest in some concealer to cover them up when she got back to the Valley.

The man behind the shipping counter was all business, barely giving her a second glance. She felt oddly invisible, having gotten used to the inevitable stares.

# CHAPTER 33
# FACING THE MUSIC

AN HOUR LATER, Kimi exited the highway onto a frontage road in Deming and pulled into a small Chevron station parking lot.

"I don't get it. The GPS says the train station should be right here," Kimi said. "Where the hell is it?"

"I think that's it over there." Avery pointed across a side street that crossed the adjacent train tracks. A beige shelter that looked more like a bus stop stood at the edge of a gravel lot fifty feet from the tracks. There was a green sign attached to the wall.

"That's it? We're in the middle of freakin' nowhere. When's the train supposed to get here?"

"Around three twenty."

"I can't just leave you here all alone for four hours."

Avery met her gaze. "Yes, you can. You've gone above and beyond. Y'all risked your lives enough on my account. Chupa took a fucking bullet for me. McCobb fought off a gunman with an electric guitar. I can't ask any more of you. The weather's nice. I'm going to grab some snacks at the convenience store and just chill. After all the insanity of the past few days, I could use some time to relax."

"I don't know, girl. All this sunlight, a goth like you's likely to burst into flames."

"Let's hope not." The two of them laughed.

"Hey, I've got one for you," Avery said. "A triple, in fact."

"Hit me."

"A bakery run by three people—Ben Yaze, Dee Kaffe, and Cookie Baker."

"That's good," Kimi said with a groan. "I got one for you. A bookstore manager named Bess Sellers."

They sat silently for a bit. Avery didn't want to leave but knew she had to. And Kimi needed to get back to Chupa.

"You need cash?" Kimi finally asked, reaching for her purse. "With the cops on the prowl, you probably shouldn't use your bank card."

Avery waved away the purse. "I bought a prepaid debit card with some of the money Sam stole. Still have a stack of Benjamins in my purse. Should be enough to last me until I get this mess resolved. Hopefully, Bramwell won't miss it when I turn the rest in."

"You've really thought this through."

Avery shook her head. "Don't make me out to be some mastermind. I'm totally winging it. But after living on the streets for a few years, I learned how to survive."

Kimi hugged her. "I'm so worried about you. Keep yourself safe, girlfriend."

"You too. Go take care of Chupa. And thank Murray for the distraction."

Avery got out of the truck and carried her suitcase and computer bag across the street.

Kimi waved with a worried expression on her face as she drove out of the parking lot.

While Avery waited for the train, she opened her laptop and dove deeper into the files on the external hard drive. She pulled out the business card from Detective Hardin she'd snatched it off the ground while rushing out of the motel room.

A search on the stolen hard drive turned up one person with the surname Harding and another with the surname of Pierce. But Detective Pierce Hardin's name wasn't in any of the files.

There was an Antonio Valentine in one of the contact files. She didn't know Hardin's partner's first name. Maybe he worked for Bramwell. Maybe he didn't.

Even if the cops were on the up-and-up, what would she tell them? That the Desert Mafia had murdered her girlfriend for stealing a couple million bucks? What would keep them from arresting her for possession of stolen goods?

For now, she was sticking with the plan. Once she got to Phoenix, she would surrender the money to Cuervo. And then hope the threat of sending copies of the hard drive to the feds and the media would get Bramwell to accept a live-and-let-live attitude.

It wasn't an ideal solution. Her alternative was to wait and hope the Mexican cartel would wipe out Bramwell and the Desert Mafia. After all, why should they escape this mess unscathed after all the lives they'd ruined?

But there was no guarantee when or if that would happen. Bramwell was slippery. And if the cartel didn't kill them all, well, she didn't want to think what might happen.

The train arrived at three thirty and whined to a stop. A uniformed man checked the ticket she had printed at the shelter's kiosk, then helped her carry her bags aboard.

The train was a lot nicer than she had expected. Nothing liked the cramped seating in an airplane. And to her surprise, the train offered free Wi-Fi access. Once settled into her seat, she started doing extensive web searches on Hardin, Valentine, and Cuervo. The more she knew, the more leverage she might have.

Hardin had been a cop with Phoenix PD for decades.

He'd received numerous commendations and seemed like an honest cop, at least on paper.

Valentine's first name was Lorenzo, so not the guy she'd found listed on the hard drive. He'd been a cop for a decade and a detective for less than a year. Not much else turned up for him.

Julio Cuervo was a complete ghost online. Of the many people in the valley with that name, none were him as far as she could tell.

She sent emails to both Jinx Ballou and Kirsten Pasternak, the women to whom she'd sent the backup hard drives. She'd met them years ago through the Phoenix Gender Alliance. They would serve as her leverage.

In her messages, Avery explained about Sam's murder, the money, and the backup drive. She asked that if anything happened to her, they should forward the drives to trustworthy contacts in law enforcement and the media.

Kirsten replied immediately with concern and offered to represent her on the matter and advised her not to talk to the cops without her present.

An hour into the trip back to Arizona, Jinx Ballou replied as well.

*Avery,*

*So sorry to hear about Sam. Also saw PPD have a BOLO out on you. What else can I do to help? Do you need a safe place to crash? Do you need protection? Will keep an eye out for the package. Be careful. Word is Bramwell has a lot of powerful people on his payroll.*

*Jinx*

Avery considered Jinx's offer. The woman was a badass bounty hunter who had tangled with people like Bramwell before. At the same time, Avery feared getting anyone else involved too much, even if they could hold their own in a fight.

A thought occurred to her, and she sent a reply.

*You used to be a cop, right? Ever know a Detective Pierce Hardin or Lorenzo Valentine?*

Ten minutes later, Jinx responded. *Hardin was my Field Training Officer. Called him Officer Hardass. Very by the book. You can trust him. Don't know Valentine. I can run background on him, see if anything pops about him being dirty.*

Avery considered the offer and replied, saying she'd appreciate learning whatever she could find out.

After an hour or so, Jinx sent a follow-up. *Valentine's new in homicide. A few claims of excessive force were filed when he was a boot, but PSB cleared him. Scored high on detective's exam. No guarantee, but my gut says he's clean.*

Avery thanked her, then she pulled out Hardin's business card again and called the number.

"Detective Hardin, how can I help you?"

"It's Avery Byrne. Heard you've been looking for me."

"Miss Avery, I'm very glad you called. Where are you?"

Again, she considered Jinx's email. *You can trust him.*

"Jinx Ballou said I can trust you." She didn't bother to ask if it was true. What would he say?

"How do you know Jinx?"

"She's a friend."

"She's good people. Was a good cop before she left the force. But don't tell her I said that. Probably wouldn't believe you if you did."

Avery didn't respond to his lighthearted banter.

"I know you're in trouble, Avery. Sam's death, coupled with the shooting the other night, tells me it's a lot. But I'm on your side in this. I want you to understand that. I want to help you out of this mess."

"I did not kill Sam. I…" Emotion choked off her words. The trauma of that night punched her in the solar plexus.

"Listen, Avery. I think it's best we do this in person. We're not looking to arrest you. I just want to sort this out and bring Sam's killer to justice. Tell me where you are."

"On a train. Heading back to the Valley."

"Amtrak?"

"Yes."

"Good. That's good. I'm on my way back to Phoenix myself. What time are you expected to arrive?"

"Around nine o'clock tonight."

"Sounds like you're ahead of me by a few hours. My priority is to keep you safe, okay? I can have a colleague meet you at the station. It's in Maricopa, right?"

Once again, fear and paranoia crept up over her shoulders. "How do I know they won't be on the take?"

"Let me talk with my lieutenant, okay? His name's Lieutenant Ross. He'll make sure whoever meets you is on the up-and-up. All right?"

She already regretted calling him. But still, she said, "Okay."

"Excellent. I should get in around eleven. But we will keep you safe."

"Yeah." She hung up.

This was it. The route she would take. Turn everything over to the cops. And when she met with Cuervo, she'd give him a copy of the backup drive instead of the money, with a warning that any retaliation would cause copies of the drive being sent to the feds, the local cops, and the media.

There were still so many ways this could go sideways. She could only hope her plan would keep her and those she loved alive long enough for either the law or the cartel to give Bramwell and his crew the punishment they deserved.

A half hour later, Hardin called back. "I talked with my lieutenant. He will personally meet you at the station. So you don't have to worry about a thing. Okay?"

She stared out at the passing desert landscape. "Yeah, okay."

## CHAPTER 34
# HOME AGAIN

AVERY WOKE to an announcement that the train was approaching the Maricopa station. It was pitch black outside, though she could see the lights slowing as they passed. It was after nine o'clock.

Avery's pulse quickened as she remembered who was waiting for her at the station. She had never liked cops. And even though Jinx swore Hardin was a Boy Scout who would die before taking a bribe, that didn't mean Avery was ready to trust him or his lieutenant.

But she was running out of options. At some point, she would have to trust someone. She wasn't ready to trust Cuervo either, even if he had supposedly killed Luther.

Steel wheels whined, followed by a slight jolt when the train came to a complete stop. Avery climbed out of her seat with her computer bag, suitcase, and purse and followed her fellow passengers off the train.

Unlike the station bus-stop-sized station in Deming, the one in Maricopa had an elevated platform with an aluminum-sided building lit up by exterior lights. The windows were dark. And something about the solid metal doors told her it wasn't open to the public, even during the day. A quarter-mile away, traffic whooshed by on a highway overpass.

She couldn't put it into words, but the desert in Arizona smelled different from New Mexico. Maybe it was the air pollution from Phoenix or smoke from the ongoing wildfires. But it was home, at least.

A man in a suit stood from a bench as she walked across the platform. Square jaw. Serious eyes. He moved like a cop. When they eyes met, he waved and strode confidently toward her.

She tensed as he approached.

"Avery Byrne?" His tone was friendly.

"Yeah?" Her scalp itched under Kimi's wig.

"I'm Lieutenant Ross, Phoenix Homicide. Can I help you with your bags?" He extended a hand.

She slung her purse over one shoulder, her computer bag over another, and let him take the suitcase.

"I'm parked just over here."

She followed him around the building and past an old train car parked on an isolated piece of track and emblazoned with the name California Zephyr. He led her to a dark Ford Explorer and unlocked it with the key fob.

Ross put her suitcase in the back while she cautiously sat in the passenger seat. She shut the door then quickly opened it again. Memories of being trapped in juvie flashed through her mind.

"Something wrong?" he asked when he slid behind the wheel.

She shut the door again. "Just checking."

"Don't worry, Ms. Byrne. I'm not here to arrest you. Also, the safety locks are on the back doors. But you're my guest, so you can ride up front with me." He flashed her a smile, which she didn't return.

"Whatever."

"Put your seat belt on. I'd hate to have to give you a ticket."

He started the SUV and drove to the John Wayne Parkway northbound to Phoenix.

She tried to force herself to relax. *Breathe in. Hold for four seconds. Release slowly.*

"You look different from your picture. Wasn't sure it was you for a second."

Avery didn't respond.

"Not real talkative, huh? Look, I understand. No one likes to talk to cops. Especially homicide cops. And from what I've learned, you've been through the wringer recently. I know Detective Hardin has told you this, but I want to reiterate. We're here to keep you safe from the awful people who hurt your little friend."

"Sam."

"What's that?"

"Her name was Sam. Sam Ferguson. And she wasn't my *little* friend. She was my girlfriend."

"Duly noted. We can talk in more detail once we get to the precinct, where you'll be safe. Okay?"

"Yeah."

She stared out the window at the pitch-black desert and thought about Sam. She longed to lie in their old bed and cuddle, wrapped in the comfort of Sam's muscular arms.

Memories bubbled up of the time at the coffeeshop when she told Sam that she was trans. They'd gone out a few times, and things had been getting serious.

"Something I gotta tell you," Avery had said, staring at her cup.

"Geez, girl, you look like you're gonna confess to murder," Sam had replied lightheartedly.

When Avery didn't answer right away, Sam gripped her hand. "Hey, Ave. Whatever it is, it's cool. I like you. I like that you're different. Granted, I don't really get the whole retro goth pinup thing. But who cares? You be you. If we were exactly alike, one of us would be redundant, right?"

"Maybe."

"Avery, come on. Just rip off the bandage already. Tell me. Whatever it is, I can handle it."

*That's what they all say,* Avery thought. She'd dated a few women, but eventually, the trans thing weirded them out. Or one of their friends shamed them into breaking off the relationship.

To make matters worse, Avery had never been so attracted to another woman before. She had let down her guard and fallen hard. Now she feared the inevitable rejection would crush her worse than when her folks kicked her out. Worse than when she'd found the Lost Kids dead.

"I… I'm transgender."

"You're trans? You mean like you want to be a guy?"

Avery finally met her eyes. "What? No, I'm a girl. But I was assigned male at birth. Transitioned about six years ago."

"Wow." Sam looked stunned.

Avery braced for the punch or slap or the simple walking away as if she were a piece of garbage in the gutter.

"Gotta admit, I didn't expect that."

"Sorry. I won't blame you if you never want to see me again."

"What? Avery, are you serious? Why wouldn't I want to see you again? I like you, girl. You're sexy. You're funny and kind. You're dark but in a cool retro sorta way. And you're a fucking brilliant tattoo artist."

Sam pulled up her sleeve. "I mean, look at this? You didn't even use a transfer or nothing. Just doodled on my arm with a marker to sketch out the basic shape of a dragon and then—wow! I feel like I should be on display at the Scottsdale Museum of Art."

Avery shrugged. "I've done better."

"Please! False modesty doesn't suit you. You're a fucking amazing woman. And I mean that. Trans or cis, you're a woman in my book. Okay?" Sam wiped the tears that had formed in Avery's eyes.

"Thanks."

"You're even sexy when you cry. Not that I want to see you cry. But hell. I'm a lesbian through and through. I've known since I was eight. And pardon my French, but I want to fuck your brains out."

Avery's cheeks grew hot. *Probably the coffee,* she told herself.

"I knew I was a girl when I was four. Didn't really understand what that meant until I was ten."

"Hey, we know when we know. Thing is, if I get to spend the rest of my life with you, I'd say it was a life well lived."

Avery took a deep breath as the lights of Phoenix grew in the distance. She wiped a tear from her cheek, hoping Lieutenant Ross didn't notice.

*Just thought it would be a longer life,* she thought.

Ross turned onto the I-10 south of town. When they were approaching downtown, he asked, "You eat on the train?"

"No."

"You must be starving. I can drive through someplace. My treat."

She wasn't starving, though she couldn't remember the last time she'd eaten, aside from the bag of chips she'd bought at the Chevron convenience store.

"Don't care."

He pulled off the highway at Seventh Street and ordered burritos and sodas at the Taco Bell on McDowell, then he continued on until finally, they pulled into a parking garage on Washington Street.

"End of the line. Everyone out," Ross said.

# CHAPTER 35
# CROSSING THE LINE

SHE FOLLOWED Ross a few blocks to the Phoenix police headquarters building. A security checkpoint with a metal detector and an X-ray machine stood just inside the front door.

"Nothing gets through without being checked, I'm afraid." Ross gave a nod to the officers running the checkpoint and laid her suitcase on the conveyer belt leading into the X-ray machine.

Avery followed suit with her purse and computer bag. She pulled out her laptop and laid it on the bag, then she walked up to the metal detector.

The machine's alarm squawked as soon as she stepped through. An officer approached. "You carrying any change or keys or anything else metal?"

"No." She looked down at her Doc Marten's. Maybe there was something in the boots. She stepped back through, unlaced the boots, and put them on the conveyer belt.

Once again, she stepped through, and the machine squawked.

The officer approached with a wand, scanning her body. It beeped when it got to her head. She flushed.

"Must be the bobby pins holding my wig in place." She pulled it off, along with the wig cap and pins.

The officer rescanned her head. Silence. "You're clear."

She went to claim her possessions but had to wait while another officer finished searching her suitcase and computer bag. When he was finished, he nodded to Ross.

Avery put the wig in the suitcase. It felt good to have it off, and it wasn't doing her any good as a disguise now.

"Okay," Ross said. "Up to the third floor."

Her first impression of the interview room was how much smaller it looked than the ones on cop shows. She hoped she wouldn't have to be there long. Not that she was claustrophobic, but the room definitely gave her the feeling that the walls were closing in.

"I'll put your stuff here by the door for now, okay? Have a seat on the other side of the table and enjoy your dinner. I'll be right back." Ross disappeared out the door.

She pulled a burrito out of the bag and unwrapped it, but despite not having eaten much, she put it down after just a few bites. Nothing wrong with the food itself. She just had no appetite.

As she sipped her soda, she noticed the red light on the camera mounted up near the ceiling blinked on.

Ross returned a moment later and took a seat opposite her.

"Do I need my lawyer?" Avery asked.

"I don't know why you'd need an attorney. You're here merely as a witness. This shouldn't take long."

She considered the situation. Kirsten Pasternak was a friend, but she also didn't work for free. And Avery hated the thought of interrupting her evening. "Whatever. Let's get this over with."

"This is Lieutenant Frederick Ross interviewing Avery Siobhan Byrne at twenty-two forty-one hours on October 19,

2022. Is it okay if I call you Avery? Or would you prefer Ms. Byrne?"

"Avery's fine."

"Excellent, Avery, let's start with you telling me what happened to Samantha Ferguson on the night of her death."

Avery's heart constricted as if a giant hand had reached into her chest and was crushing the life out of it. The air in the small room grew thin, making it difficult to catch her breath.

"I found her in our house. Strapped to a chair. Some-one… someone had beaten and cut her. I almost didn't recognize her."

"Was she alive?"

"Barely. She only said a few words."

"What did she say?"

"That she loved me. Then she told me to run." Avery forced herself not to cry, though it felt like her head would explode.

"Run? Why would she say that?"

"I don't… Two men came in the door. I think they were the ones who tortured Sam."

"Do you know these men?"

Avery considered her answer before she spoke. But she was here. Might as well come clean. "Julio Cuervo and Luther Jackson. They worked with Sam."

"And what happened?"

"They shot at me, so I ran out the back door."

"A gun was found by the back wall of the property. Do you know anything about it?"

A chill ran down her back. She'd forgotten about Sam's gun, the one she'd dropped. They would have no doubt found her fingerprints on it. Lying about it would only make her look guilty.

"It was Sam's gun. She kept it under the seat of her car. I

grabbed it before I went in the house." As soon as she said it, she wanted to slap herself.

"Why did you grab her gun?"

"I… I was afraid something had happened to her."

"Why would you think that?"

Her heart was hammering in her chest as panic set in. This felt wrong, though she couldn't pinpoint why.

"Avery, I'm here to help you. I truly am. But I can't help you if you don't tell me the truth. Did you go in there to hurt Sam?"

"What? No! We were moving. To Seattle. But I'd left something in the house. Sam went back to retrieve it for me."

"What'd you leave?"

"A stuffed unicorn my foster mom gave to me when I was a kid." The pressure in her head was excruciating. But she would not cry in front of this man.

"So how did you end up back at the house as well?"

"She'd been gone for a long time and wasn't answering her phone. I was worried."

Ross nodded knowingly. "You took the gun into the house. Did you fire it?"

Avery tried to remember. Everything had happened so fast. "I may have. I don't remember."

"I understand. It must have been very traumatizing seeing Sam like that."

"I just remember them shooting at me. And Sam's… Sam's head…" She struggled to catch her breath.

"What about her head?"

"Someone shot her in the head. One of the men."

"And what did you do?"

"Ran out the back, like I said."

"Where'd you go?"

"My friend Kimi's. She and I have known each other since we were kids."

"She's in the punk band you were with? Damaged Souls."

"Gothabilly, not punk."

"Gotha-what?"

"Gothabilly. It's like a mixture of... It's not important. Thing is, her band was going on tour. Kimi let me tag along."

"Why did you feel the need to get out of town?"

"Because those guys. I was afraid they'd come for me."

"Why would they do that?"

"They worked for Bramwell."

"Bramwell? Theodore Bramwell, the real estate tycoon?"

"Yeah, but he's more than that. He's also the head of the Desert Mafia." Avery locked eyes with Ross. "Don't tell me you don't know that. You're a homicide cop."

Ross nodded. "We have come across a few cases that had potential ties to him. Nothing stuck so far. But what does any of that have to do with Sam?"

"She worked for him. But she decided to quit."

"What did she do for him? What was her job?"

"Security."

"Security? Like a bouncer?"

"More of a bodyguard, I think. That's what she always said."

"Anything illegal?"

"I... I don't know. Not that she ever told me. She was a good person. That's why she wanted to leave. She was tired of working for a mobster."

"When we arrived it appeared that someone had tossed the house as if looking for something important. Any idea what they might be looking for?"

It always came back down to the money. "I don't know."

Ross stared at her blankly, clearly not believing her. She could see the judgment in his eyes.

"I'll be honest with you, Avery. I don't believe you're

being completely honest with me. Whatever these people were looking for, it clearly had a lot of value. Drugs. Money. Whatever. And it may be tempting to keep whatever it was for yourself. Make the best of a bad situation, right? But they won't stop until they have it. And I can't protect you from them until you tell me the truth."

Ross's eyes felt as if they were burrowing into her skull. Her head was pounding as she wrestled with what to say.

"You got any Advil?"

He sat expressionless and motionless for a few minutes before answering. "Why don't we take a break? I'll see if I can't scare up some Advil for you. Okay?"

"Thank you."

After Ross left, the red light on the camera winked out. Like a tsunami, emotion poured out of her. Sobs racked her body. It couldn't have hurt any worse if he'd ripped open her chest with a serrated knife and then bludgeoned her with a sledgehammer.

When the last of her energy ebbed, she wiped her face as best she could. She took a few bites of the cold burrito and drank her watery soda, the ice having long since melted.

She should have called Kirsten. But now it was too late. He was pressing her like she was hiding evidence. And she was. He had her cornered. She wanted to leave and go home. Only she had no home. She would have to crash at Kimi's. *If I ever get out of here.*

She waited and waited. The room grew chilly, as if Ross had cranked up the AC. She opened her suitcase and pulled on a cardigan decorated with skulls, then she returned to her chair and laid her head on her folded arms.

She jolted awake when the door opened again. "Couldn't find any Advil per se. Will generic do?"

She wiped her face on her sleeve and downed the proffered pills with the last of the watery soda.

Ross sat down again. "Now, you were telling me about what these men were looking for."

"I told you, I don't know. Maybe she made a secret deal with the cops and that's why they tortured her. "

"A deal no one here in the Phoenix police know about. A deal she never told you about. Her girlfriend. The woman she trusted more than any other person in the world. Avery, you are not telling me the complete story. And as I stated before, I can't help you if you're not honest with me. I can't protect you if you're holding back key information."

His words sounded sincere. But there was something in his eyes she didn't trust.

Rather than respond to his question, she held his gaze. Cops liked to play the waiting game. But one thing she had learned from Bobby J. was patience. Be in the moment. She breathed in, held it for four seconds, then released it. *Breath in, hold, breathe out.*

She had no idea how long the two of them sat there staring at each other. She thought of Amanda Palmer's TED Talk about her performing as the Eight-Foot Bride, a living statue.

Avery became a statue. With each breath, she drew in energy. She felt her strength and resolve return. Fear and despair dissipated.

"Avery," Ross finally said. "Tell me about the money."

And there it was. Ross knew about the money. The question was how. Kimi wouldn't have told anyone, not even Chupa. That could only mean one thing.

"I never said anything about money."

"The man who rushed the stage in Las Cruces asking for you and shot your friend. He was yelling about stolen money. So, tell me, Avery. Where is Bramwell's money?"

Had Luther mentioned the money when he barged into Gothique? No, she was sure he hadn't. "I don't know what you're talking about."

"Avery, I can't protect you if you lie to me." His tone was no longer reassuring. It was a threat.

"You picked me up at the train station. You saw everything I had with me. You X-rayed all my bags. I don't have any money."

"You have a stack of bills in your handbag. Shall we check and see if they might all be hundreds?"

She stared at him impassively—bride statue mode. Meanwhile, a plan formed. She would find a way out of here.

"Turn over the money, and this all goes away, Avery. Sam wouldn't want you to be hurt over this. You don't want to be hurt over this. I don't want you to be hurt over this. The ball is in your court."

"You're working for Bramwell."

Ross sat there with his arms folded.

Avery glanced up at the camera. She wasn't at all surprised that the red light wasn't on. The camera was off. "I want my lawyer now."

"We're way past lawyers now, Avery. It's time to do the right thing. The money doesn't belong to you. It belongs to Mr. Bramwell. We both know this. Sam was foolish to think she could rob him. And she paid the price. You shouldn't have to pay the price. We can end this now. You can get on with your life."

"You're full of shit. Soon as I give you the money, you're going to kill me."

"I give you my word that I will not. But I assure you that if you don't give me the money, I will charge you with Sam's murder. And because you are biologically a man, I will put you in men's jail."

A fury erupted that she barely contained. "I. Am. Not. A. Man."

"I'll admit, you don't look like one. But you were born with a penis at Phoenix Baptist Hospital, right? Originally named Andrew Stephen Byrne. And no matter what surgeries you may or may not have had, state law says you belong in a men's correction facility. I don't think a nice girl like you would do well in men's prison, especially not in gen pop. Do you?"

"Fine. I'll tell you."

A Grinch-like smile spread across the man's face. "Proceed."

"I didn't know about the money until we got to Tucson. When I found it, I was scared, so shipped it back to Phoenix. A friend put it in my storage unit."

"Good. That's progress. Don't you feel better getting these things off your chest? A clear conscience will make everything better for all involved. And now you're going to take me to this storage unit, and everything will work out the way it should."

"You're a genuine piece of shit, hiding behind that badge. No better than the scumbags you throw in prison."

"We all do what we have to do to survive in this world." Ross stood. "Now come on. Let's wrap this up. You take me to the money, I will drop you off wherever you like. And this stays between us. If it doesn't, well, this investigation into Sam's death can go a lot of ways. Even if a jury doesn't convict you, who's to say you will survive in jail long enough to see a verdict?"

He stood and grabbed her belongings. "Come on."

# CHAPTER 36
# LOCKED UP

IT WAS NEARLY midnight when they arrived at the Sun Valley U-Store. After hours, the gate only opened with a code. Avery gave it to Ross when he pulled up to the keypad. He punched it in, and the gate slowly clanged open.

"Now where?" he asked.

"Second building on the left."

Ross parked under a security light, and they got out. She stared at the rear hatch of the Explorer. Her purse, computer bag, and suitcase were all locked in the back.

"What about my stuff?" she asked.

"You'll get it back after I get what belongs to me." He drew a gun and aimed it at her. "Are we clear?"

"You're a real piece of shit. You know that?"

She opened the building's metal exterior door and led him down the corridor. When they came to unit C-24, she asked, "So, you gonna kill me after I give you what you want?"

"You show me the money, and then we'll see."

She entered the combination into the heavy padlock. After it opened with a clack, she raised the door and flipped on the light.

Stacks of boxes rose among dusty furniture. Avery had

put it all here when she moved in with Sam earlier in the year. "My friend put the money in the back. It's in a blue gym bag. Two and a half million dollars."

She could almost see dollars signs in the cop's eyes, like in those dorky cartoons. She was surprised when he didn't insist she retrieve the bag. Maybe he was simply too eager to get his hands on the cash. Exactly what she was counting on. He holstered his gun and rushed into the unit.

As he passed her, she clocked him in the temple with the heavy padlock. He stumbled into a stack of boxes. She hit him again. He didn't move.

"Damn dirty cop."

She didn't know if he was alive or dead, nor did she care. With his gun and keys in hand, shel walked out of the unit, flicked off the light, and secured the door with the combo lock.

Above her, a security camera recorded her. Was anyone monitoring the feed, she wondered. And was it recording audio as well as video?

Sitting in Ross's Explorer, she sent off an email to Hardin.

*Jinx said I could trust you motherfuckers! Clearly, she was wrong. You're working for Bramwell. Well, fuck you! I'm going to make you regret it. I'll bring you all down. Just watch.*

# CHAPTER 37
# MISSING

DETECTIVE HARDIN'S phone chimed when he walked into police headquarters. He was exhausted from the six-hour drive from Las Cruces, but he needed to know what Ross had found out from Avery Byrne. Valentine had gone home to get some sleep.

As Hardin stepped out of the elevator, he checked his phone. An email from Avery. He read it but didn't understand it.

He rushed through the glass doors of the Violent Crimes Bureau and stopped at the watch commander's office. Sergeant Gwen Wicker was on duty.

"Where's LT?"

"You missed him about an hour ago."

"He have anyone with him?"

"Yeah, a young woman. White with black hair, looked like she was in her early twenties. Had some bags with her."

"Bags?"

"Suitcase. A computer bag."

"Did Ross say where they were going?"

"Didn't say. Why? Something wrong?"

"Not sure." His stomach felt like the floor had dropped out from under him. He called Ross's cell phone. It rang five times then went to voicemail. "LT, call me when you get this."

When he hung up, he turned back to Wicker. "We need to get a location for his Ford Explorer and his phone."

"What's this about? You think that woman did something to him?"

"He isn't answering his cell. We need to find him."

Wicker opened the program on her desktop to track department vehicles. "Looks like he's in Glendale behind a shopping center. Southwest corner of Glendale Avenue and Forty-Third."

"Get on the horn to Glendale PD. Have them send patrol to make sure he's okay. And just for shits and giggles, try to get a location on his phone too. Just in case."

Without waiting for a response, he strode into the bullpen. A weary-faced Detective Olivos was at his desk, no doubt working on a case of his own.

"¡Hola, Hardin! How was the Land of Enchantment?"

"Less than enchanting. Ross was here about an hour ago?"

"Yeah, had a girl with him. A witness from one of your cases, I thought. Did you ask him to interview her?"

"Interview her? He was just supposed topick her up at the train station and babysit her until I arrived. He questioned her?"

"For quite a while. Why?"

"Pull up the recording."

Olivos did so. "That's strange."

"What's that?"

"He had her in there for a few hours, but there's only about forty-eight minutes of footage. Now that I think about it, I was monitoring the feed when he was in there originally, then he walked out and told me to turn off the camera. I didn't think much about it and went back to working the

Keenan case. But I didn't see them leave until a couple of hours later."

"Dammit."

"What's going on?"

"I don't know. He's not answering his phone, and his SUV's parked behind a shopping center up in Glendale."

"He lives in east Phoenix. You think he took the girl home?"

"I don't think so. Wicker's reaching out to Glendale PD."

Hardin dialed the number Avery Byrne had used the day before. It went straight to voicemail. His next call was to Valentine.

"Sorry to wake you so soon, partner, but we've got a situation."

"What's wrong?"

"LT's missing. And he has Byrne with him."

"Shit. You think she jumped him?"

"Right now, we don't know anything. But Ross interviewed her for three hours, but only forty-five minutes was recorded."

"He interviewed her? He's not a detective. He's a lieutenant, for crying out loud. What the hell's going on?"

"I don't know. Just get your ass down here."

"Be there in thirty, partner."

While he waited for Valentine and to hear back from Glendale, he watched the recorded interview of Ross and Byrne.

## CHAPTER 38
# BACK ON THE RUN

AFTER PARKING Ross's Ford Explorer behind the shopping center, she wiped her fingerprints from his gun and tossed it in the back seat. She didn't know why she'd bothered. She was screwed. If the cops found her, they'd lock her up and throw away the keys for assaulting a cop, grand theft auto, and anything else they could think of.

She grabbed her bags from the back of the SUV, tossed in the keys, and slammed the door closed again. Before walking away, she pitched the SIM card from her burner phone into a nearby dumpster.

It was nearly one o'clock in the morning, and she felt as lost as she had when she was a homeless teen. She needed to get somewhere safe where she could figure out her next move. And she needed not to be recognized.

After considering her options, she pulled back on the blond wig Kimi had loaned her and trudged a half mile to an open 7-Eleven. Inside, she purchased a new SIM card.

Once her phone was working again, she called Jinx Ballou, feeling bad about calling at such an early hour. After four rings, the call went to voice mail. *Probably asleep.*

"Hey, Jinx. It's Avery. I'm back in town. I trusted Detective Hardin, but things didn't work out so well. His boss picked me up at the train station, but…" She paused. "Turns out he's just another cop on the take. Demanded the money Sam stole from Bramwell. He was going to kill me, Jinx. Even if I gave him the money. I don't know who to trust anymore. Please call me when you can. I'm… I'm scared and don't know where to turn."

She downloaded the Uber app, created a new account with her prepaid debit card, and hired a ride to the Denny's on the corner of Camelback and Seventh Street, known affectionately as the "Gay Denny's."

Halfway through eating her Grand Slam breakfast, she got an email from Hardin.

*Avery,*

*I don't know what happened. Clearly, something has gone wrong. I'm worried about you. Where is Lieutenant Ross? Please call me. We can work this out.*

*Detective Hardin*

She stared at the screen of her phone. Ross worked for Bramwell. He hadn't even bothered to deny it. Could she trust Hardin? Jinx had sworn he'd never be dirty. But Hardin had arranged for Ross to meet her at the train station.

*Your boss worked for Bramwell. He kidnapped me. Took me to Sun Valley U-Store at gunpoint. Was going to kill me. All for the money Sam took from Bramwell. Look at the security footage.*

Avery spent the next few of hours digging deeper into the copy of Bramwell's hard drive. She came across some revealing email conversations. One between Bramwell and someone named Dante Nicholson, a border patrol officer near Nogales. Another between Bramwell and Jesus Santiago, one of the Sinaloa drug cartel's enforcers. Santiago was on his way to pick up the money.

After a few hours, Avery's server began asking her every twenty minutes if she needed anything else. Avery ordered a banana split to stop the incessant interruptions.

At four thirty, Avery was struggling to stay awake and

the servers were giving her the side-eye for staying so long. She packed everything up and trundled out to the street. Another Uber took her to Seoul Fire.

The back of the shop was largely used for storage, but Bobby J. kept a folding cot in the broom closet. She set it up, used her sweater for a pillow, and fell into a dreamless sleep.

She woke what seemed like an instant later to Bobby J.'s voice. "Avery? Is that you? Wake up, sweetie."

"Appa?" She opened her eyes.

His normally clean-shaven face was scruffy. He had bags under his eyes, but they were also filled with joyful tears. She sat up and hugged him. He felt like the most solid thing she had held in forever.

"I've been so worried about you. And then to find you here? It's like Christmas come early. Almost didn't recognize you with the wig. It looks nice."

She released him, and he sat on a nearby box, still holding her hand.

"I got in last night but ran into trouble. Didn't know where else to go."

She filled him in on everything.

"Is this police lieutenant alive or dead?" he asked.

"I don't know. Appa, he was going to kill me once he got the money. I had to defend myself."

"Sometimes there are no good options, and we must choose between one bad thing or another. When North Korea invaded during the war, my grandfather, who lived just south of the parallel was conscripted into the KPA. He was forced serve with the North Koreans or die."

Bobby J.'s eyes dropped to the floor. "Fortunately, he helped my grandmother, my father, and my aunt escape to Seoul before the real fighting began."

"Did he find them again after the war?" Avery asked.

"No. My father never knew what happened, but believe he was killed in action."

"Appa, if this was meant to be an inspiring story..."

"All I'm saying, kiddo, is that we make the best choices we can for ourselves and the ones we love. That is what you have done. Now that you are home again, perhaps we can find a way out of this situation together."

Her phone rang. She recognized the caller ID and answered it. "Jinx?"

"Avery, what the hell happened?"

Avery gave her the rundown.

"Shit," Jinx said. "I don't know this Lieutenant Ross, but I swear Hardin is solid. He'd die before he sullied his badge. Still, I would've done the same in your shoes."

"I don't know what to do at this point. I just want to get on with my life."

"How 'bout I pick you up? I can keep you safe until we figure this all out."

Avery looked up at Bobby J. "What about my dad? What if they come after him?"

"Bring him. The more, the merrier, I say."

"Thanks, Jinx. I'll see you soon."

# CHAPTER 39
# DIRTY

HARDIN and the others in the squad spent hours trying to contact someone to open up the storage facility. By the time the manager showed, it was nearly eight o'clock. Hardin and Valentine had obtained a warrant for the security footage and had sent out an APB on both Ross and Byrne.

The storage manager fast-forwarded through the security footage of the front gate until Hardin spotted Ross's Explorer. "Hold it. Play at normal speed."

The manager did so. They watched as Ross entered a code and drove through the gate. The manager then pulled up a different camera feed, allowing them to watch the truck park in front of Building C.

Hardin searched his mind for a rational explanation for Ross bringing a witness here, much less on his own. He couldn't think of one.

On the screen, Ross drew his weapon after he and Byrne stepped out of the truck.

"What the hell?" Hardin said aloud.

"Maybe she confessed to murdering Ferguson," Valentine replied.

"No, this feels all wrong. He was supposed to pick her up at the train station and keep her safe until we arrived. He had no business interviewing her, much less turning off the camera. And taking a suspect out alone like this? No, something is definitely rotten in Denmark."

"What's Denmark got to do with this?"

Hardin shot him a look. "Do they teach you nothing in schools these days?"

He refocused on the screen. The manager had pulled up the feed from the interior of the building. "This thing got audio?"

"Ummm… oh, here it is." The manager clicked on a speaker icon.

Ross and Byrne stopped at a unit.

"So, you gonna kill me after I give you what you want?" asked Byrne, her recorded voice tinny and distorted but still discernible. She was working on the unit's padlock.

"You show me the money, and then we'll see."

Valentine asked, "What money's he talking about?"

Hardin didn't answer right away, focusing instead on the video. Byrne raised the door, and the two disappeared inside.

"You got footage inside the unit?" Hardin asked.

"Sorry, no. You're lucky we got this. Can't afford cameras in the units. Customers wouldn't appreciate that anyway. They like their privacy." The manager paused the footage.

"No, keep playing. At least we'll have audio. What unit is that?"

The manager studied the screen. "C-22. No, wait. C-24."

Byrne's voice brought Hardin back to the recording, though the sound was muffled.

"Play that back and crank up the audio," Hardin instructed.

"My friend put the money in the back," Byrne said, the words barely recognizable. "It's in a blue gym bag. Two and a half million dollars."

"She say two and a half million dollars?" Valentine asked. "Holy shit! For that kind of money—"

"Shhh!"

There was a grunt, followed by a rustling sound. Maybe something being knocked over. A moment later, Byrne emerged from the unit alone and locked it, and for an instant, she looked at the camera. She was carrying a gun—Ross's, from the looks of it. Glendale PD had found it in the trunk of Ross's car.

"What happened?" Valentine asked. "She kill the lieutenant?"

"We need into that unit pronto," Hardin told the manager before turning to Valentine. "Call for medical. Let's hope he's still alive."

They ran out of the office to Building C. The manager used a pair of massive lever-action bolt cutters to make quick work of the padlock. They threw open the door.

"About damn time!" Ross said from the darkness. "You people stop for doughnuts and coffee before coming to look for me?"

Hardin found a switch just inside the doorway and flipped on the light.

Ross sat on the floor, leaning against a stack of boxes. A trickle of dried blood bisected a large bruise on the side of his face.

"LT," Hardin said, checking him for other injuries. "Are you okay?"

Ross tried to stand but fell back down. "Dizzy."

"Medical's on the way. What happened?"

"Bitch ambushed me."

"Avery Byrne?"

"Last time I do you a favor, Hardin."

"What are you doing here at this storage facility?"

"She claimed she was going to show me where she hid the murder weapon."

"The murder weapon?" Valentine appeared next to Hardin. "We got the murder weapon. Remember?"

"Check your ballistics, detective. The nine mill you found in the backyard was not the murder weapon. Slugs didn't match. Murder weapon was a .45 caliber."

"Same caliber used to shoot one of Byrne's friends in Las Cruces," Hardin said, mostly to himself.

"Why didn't you call?" Valentine asked.

Ross held up his phone. "No signal in this place. Like a damn bunker."

"Sir, with all due respect, why were you interviewing Byrne?" Hardin asked. "I only asked you to pick her up."

Ross glared at him. "Don't tell me how to do my job, Detective. I may not be a detective per se, but I've served in homicide long enough to know how to conduct an interview."

Hardin nodded. "Of course. Sorry."

"I want this Byrne girl found and locked up. Spare no resources. She is an imminent threat to public safety."

"Yes, sir," Valentine replied.

Hardin considered his next question carefully. "Sir, was there a reason why the camera was turned off partway through the interview with Byrne?"

"What are you talking about?"

Hardin caught a glance from Valentine then continued. "After forty-five minutes, you stepped out of the room. The recording ended shortly thereafter."

Ross scoffed. "Software or camera must have glitched. Fucking technology."

"Don't worry, LT. We'll get to the bottom of it," Valentine insisted.

A clanging sound of a gurney approaching caught Hardin's attention. A bevy of medical personnel appeared at the door of the unit.

"You just relax and feel better, sir. These people will take care of you."

Hardin and Valentine stepped outside the unit, away from the cluster of officers.

"He's lying." Valentine sounded dejected.

"Yep."

"Why would he lie? And why interview Byrne? None of this makes any sense."

"I can think of two and a half million reasons why."

"But where the hell'd this money come from? Is Byrne some kind of high-level drug trafficker?"

"No, but I suspect Theodore Bramwell is. And Samantha Ferguson worked for him. My guess is that Ferguson stole the two mill from her boss. It would explain why her killers tortured her and why they've been hell-bent on finding Byrne. She must have gotten the money from her girlfriend."

"Okay, I'll buy that, but how does Ross fit into it?"

"As much as it pains me to say it, I think the lieutenant is working for Bramwell."

"Ross dirty? Bullshit. "

Hardin felt nauseated at the idea. "So far, Byrne's story lines up more than Ross's."

"Gotta be some other explanation," Valentine insisted. "This Byrne chick must've gotten into Ross's head or something. And I'm still not convinced she's innocent. Maybe she tortured her girlfriend for the money and made up this entire story to cover her tracks."

"Why are you so hung up on Byrne as the one who killed her girlfriend?"

Valentine didn't answer right away, but Hardin could see the wheels turning in his head.

"Look, I know it's not politically correct, but these trannies, they're undermining the very fabric of decent society. They can't be trusted."

"Bullshit!" Hardin glowered at his partner.

"Come on, man. Going around pretending to be girls? It's vile and indecent. Hell, whenever I go on a date with a new chick, in the back of my mind, I wonder—"

"Stop. Now you listen up, youngblood, and listen good. Trans women are women. We had a gal working patrol several years back. Jinx Ballou. Good officer. Got jammed up and eventually quit the force because of narrow-minded idiots like you."

"But, Hard "

"Don't 'but Hardin' me. Not saying I understand it all. But every major medical and psychological organization agrees these people are who they say they are. Jinx and the few other trans people I've met have all been solid citizens. It isn't about political correctness. It's about common decency."

"Doesn't make this Avery Byrne innocent."

"Doesn't make her guilty either. We're detectives, Valentine. We follow the evidence, not our prejudices."

Valentine sighed, a hint of concession in his eyes. "Either way, we still have to find Byrne. Guilty or not, she's got answers we need."

"Agreed."

## CHAPTER 40
# THE LATE HOUR

CUERVO LAY in bed after spending the previous day driving back from Las Cruces. What little sleep he'd managed had been haunted by his part in Sam's death and the chaos that had ensued.

What worried him more was what to do about Avery. Bramwell wanted her dead. No loose ends. But the thought sickened him. Doing Sam was bad enough, but she'd had it coming. But Avery was just an innocent kid. And she claimed she had dirt on the organization.

His phone rang. He picked it up off the charger without checking the caller ID. "Yeah?"

"Mr. Santiago will be here at one." Bramwell's tone was terse and threatening. "You got the money?"

Cuervo tried to wipe the sleep from his face. "You gotta stall him, sir. I won't have the cash until two. He's still in Mexico?"

"I understand he was calling from Rocky Point. So yes, at least for the next hour or so"

"I'll call Dante, have him detain Santiago at the border until I have cash in hand."

"See that you do, or we will all be hanging from a bridge

with our guts hanging out. And deal with this threat she made about having dirt on us."

"I'll do my best."

"I don't want your best, Mr. Cuervo. I want it done. Beat her, torture her—hell, seduce this woman if you have to, but see to it she's got nothing on us."

"Yes, sir." Cuervo headed to the door.

"Otherwise, don't bother coming back."

Cuervo hung up and placed a call. "Yo, Dante. It's Julio. How's it going down there?"

"Well, well. Mr. Tequila. Busy. Lotta snowbirds coming through getting their Mexican prescriptions. Wha'sup?"

"There's a Jesus Santiago coming up. I need you to hold on to him for a while. Do not let him through."

"Jesus Santiago? As in the cartel's top enforcer?"

"That's him."

"Guy like that won't be coming through under his own name. Any idea what alias he might use?"

Cuervo tried to think. He'd heard it mentioned when Santiago was there delivering the product. "Leonardo Peña."

"Rings a bell. Hold on a sec." There was a pause before Dante continued. "We had a Leonardo Peña come through last night."

A chill ran down Cuervo's spine. "Shit."

"Maybe it was a different Leonardo Peña. I'll put a flag in the system just in case."

"Thanks, man." Cuervo hung up and debated whether to tell Bramwell. He held off for now.

# CHAPTER 41
# PROTECTION

"YOU'RE LEAVING AGAIN?" Bobby J. asked after Avery explained that Jinx would be by soon to pick them up.

"Just until we get this situation resolved. I want you to come with me."

Bobby shook his head. "No, I'm not going anywhere. I have clients coming in. Some of them are your clients. But I'm glad you've got Jinx to watch out for you. I'll rest a little easier knowing you're safe. Do you have a plan?"

"I've agreed to give the money to Julio Cuervo, Sam's old partner. He works for Bramwell, but I think I can trust him."

"Did you say Julio Cuervo?" A shadow passed over Bobby's face.

"Yeah, why?"

"It's not important, kiddo. Best to give them back their money."

"What aren't you telling me?" Maybe she didn't have this all figured out after all.

"Cuervo was one Bramwell sent every week to Artoo Tattoo to pickup the insurance money."

"Is he the one who hurt you when you couldn't pay?"

"It's not important."

"Yes, it is. Is he the one who put you in the hospital?"

"Him and another guy. A black guy named Luther something."

"Luther Jackson."

"Yes, how did you know?"

"I can't let them get away off scot-free. They've hurt you, Sam, and Chupa. They need to be punished."

"Is this the voice of Avery the Avenger I hear?"

"Appa, if no one stops Bramwell, he'll just keep on hurting people."

"Sweet daughter, I understand you want justice for Sam and Chupa. And while, Bramwell and his thugs deserve to be punished for their many crimes, this is not a job for a beautiful young tattoo artist such as yourself."

"Hey, if Luke Skywalker can blow up the Death Star…"

"Luke had a lot of help."

"I have help. Jinx, her husband, and their bounty-hunting team."

"Also, *Star Wars* is fiction. Too many people have already died trying to bring down Bramwell. I will not lose you over this."

"And what about the innocent people Bramwell hurts every day? Business owners he's shaking down and hurting when they don't pay. Have you forgotten what he did to you?"

"Turn over that backup drive to Hardin. Jinx says you can still trust him."

"The police had their chance. They double-crossed me."

The two sat looking at each other for a while without speaking.

"I don't have an answer for you, kiddo. I'm sorry. You have to do what you feel is best, and I'll be there to love and support you as best as I can. But before you do anything, talk to Jinx and maybe that lawyer Kirsten. They can certainly advise you better than I can."

"I will. I promise. I should have listened to you when you warned me about dating Sam."

"I understand why you didn't. Love is ever optimistic. Melissa's father warned her about dating me."

"But she was killed by a terrorist. Nothing to do with you."

"Perhaps," Bobby said with a sigh. "But maybe if she had married someone else, she wouldn't have been at the rally when the bomb went off."

"Or if you two hadn't taken me in, maybe she wouldn't have been there that day."

Bobby cocked his head. "What does our taking you in have to do with anything?"

"Nothing. That's my point. Who's to say the same thing wouldn't have happened if she'd married someone else? And maybe if you two hadn't married, you wouldn't have taken me in, and I would be still on the streets or dead."

"You are becoming a wise student of the Force. Perhaps the student is becoming the master."

"Oh, please." She managed to laugh a little and elbowed him gently. He feigned injury.

A loud knocking at the back door sent a ripple of panic through Avery.

Bobby stood. "I'll see who it is. But get out of sight, just in case."

Avery slipped into the restroom, leaving the door cracked so she could hear. She straightened her wig so that it looked passable.

The back door creaked opened.

"May I help you?" Bobby asked.

"Jinx Ballou. I'm here to pick up Avery."

"Ave!" Bobby called.

"Coming." She stepped out.

Jinx Ballou was deeply tanned with dark hair pulled into a ponytail. She wore a bulletproof vest, with a Taser on one hip and a gun on the other. A badge hung from a chain around her neck.

A muscular man with coppery curls and freckles stood next to her. He was similarly outfitted with a vest, badge, and weapons. Jinx's husband, Conor Doyle.

"Wow, new look," Jinx said after they hugged.

Avery shrugged. "A wig from a friend of mine."

"Not a bad idea. Cops got a BOLO out on you. Assaulting a cop doesn't go down real well out here."

"That piece of crap Ross kidnapped me and was going to kill me. What else should I have done?"

"I would've done the same. Trust me. But cops go ballistic when someone hurts one of their own. I know. I used to be one."

Conor cleared his throat. "Pleasure to meet ya, Avery. I'm Conor." He had a lyrical brogue.

"Sorry," Jinx said, blushing. "Where are my manners?"

Avery shook Conor's hand. "Nice to meet you, too, finally. I was at your wedding but…"

"Aye, it was a real pisser the way those bloody TERFs wrecked it." He put an arm around Jinx. "Fortunately, Jinx's da pulled through, we're married, and those cheeky bastards are in lockup. That's a happily ever after in my book."

Avery felt a pang of sadness, thinking about Sam again. "I'm happy for the both of you."

"We should get going. Surprised the cops aren't already knocking down the doors of the shop looking for you."

Avery glanced at Bobby J. "Jinx, could you spare someone to watch after Bobby?"

"I'll be fine, kiddo. If the cops or Bramwell's guys show up, I'll just use one of my Jedi mind tricks on them." He wiggled his fingers in the air as if casting a spell.

"Appa…" The thought of losing him terrified her.

"Go before anyone shows up. I'll see you soon."

They grabbed her bags and piled into Jinx's SUV. Avery

climbed into the back and noticed there was a plexiglass barrier between her and the front seats. No doubt to keep the bail jumpers Jinx arrested from attacking her on the way back to jail.

"What if the cops or Bramwell's thugs?show up at your place?" Avery asked.

"Don't ya worry, love," Conor said with a wink. "The Bunker can withstand anything they can dish out. You'll be okay."

Avery wasn't so sure.

# CHAPTER 42
# THE BUNKER

ON THE RIDE OVER, Jinx explained that the exterior walls of their home were composed of cement-filled cinder block. The windows were inch-thick polycarbonate, which meant they were essentially bulletproof. The doors were nearly impenetrable as well.

Avery expected the place to look like some overly armored castle. But the moment she stepped inside, the house felt warm and inviting. It may have been armored like a bunker but something about the energy here made it a home.

A golden retriever appeared and jumped on Avery, nearly knocking her over.

"Diana, down!" Jinx shouted, and the dog obeyed. "You're not afraid or allergic to dogs, are you? I forgot to ask. Sorry."

"No, I like dogs." Avery stroked the dog's shiny fur. She felt safe for the first time since Sam's murder. But she still couldn't help worrying about Bobby J. and everyone at the shop.

"Ya hungry for some breakfast, love?" Conor asked. His Irish brogue was absolutely enchanting. Jinx was so lucky to have him.

"A little." It was nine thirty, and she couldn't remember when she'd had that dessert at Denny's.

Jinx helped get her settled in their guest room, while Conor set to cooking in the kitchen.

"How are you holding up?" Jinx asked.

The two sat next to each other on the guest bed. Diana lay on the other side of Jinx, her tail wagging as Jinx petted her.

"I feel like a dried-out leaf ready to crumble at the slightest touch."

Jinx put an arm around her. "I know how you feel. When I lost Conor, it broke me."

"But at least he's alive," Avery said.

"Yeah, but I didn't know that at the time. And even after I learned he was alive, I knew I couldn't run away with him, always looking over my shoulder. I essentially lost him all over again. Then I started dating Shea. And that was amazing."

"Until Conor came back."

"Yeah, it's been a wild ride."

Neither of them spoke for a while.

"I've lost so many people in my life, Jinx. The Lost Kids. Melissa. And now Sam. I'm cursed."

"You're not cursed. But I get it. I've felt that way sometimes. Any time a member of my team gets hurt. When my father got shot at our wedding."

"How do you go on?"

"Almost didn't." Jinx rubbed Diana's head. But this little angel saved me."

"Saved you how?" Avery asked.

A deeply wounded look crossed Jinx's face. "Before Conor came back, I spiraled the drain for a while. Drinking, smoking weed. Anything to stop feeling the bottomless ache. I got reckless, taking stupid chances when I did parkour. Free-climbing the Papago Buttes. Driving like a maniac in Conor's sports car. Didn't care if I lived or died."

"Sounds familiar."

"I was about to eat a bullet. Literally had the muzzle of the gun in my mouth, finger on the trigger. Then Diana strolled into the room, looking at me with those sad doggy eyes. I knew then I had to live. I couldn't abandon her. She was just a puppy. And I couldn't abandon all my friends and my family. I'd be letting everyone down. Even though I felt that in a lot of ways, I already had."

Jinx heaved a big sigh. "I got back on the horse. Fought back to reclaim my life. Rising strong, as Brené Brown says."

Avery had heard the name but hadn't read any of the woman's books.

"A lot of trans people take their lives," Avery said.

"Or been murdered. All the more reason for us to fight back. If for no other reason than not to let the fuckers win. Nothing drives those bastards crazy so much as us living the best lives we can despite them."

Avery let the words sink in and felt a fire burst to life inside her. "I will not let the fuckers win."

"Knock, knock, ladies." Conor appeared in the door. "Who's up for some Boursin eggs, potatoes, and bacon?"

"Boursin eggs?"

"Scrambled eggs with Boursin cheese," Jinx explained. "It's fucking amazing."

"Sounds good."

The doorbell rang. Avery froze. "Shit."

"Just relax. I'll see who it is. Probably a landscaper looking for work. The shrubs in front of the house have needed a good trimming."

Jinx and Conor walked out, Diana trailing them. Avery strained to listen, but sound didn't carry well in the house. Jinx returned a moment later, carrying a familiar large box with a padded envelope on top.

"I'm guessing this is from you." Jinx set it down in front of the bed, flicked open a black-bladed knife, and sliced open the box. Multiple copies of the books Avery had bought at the OfficeMart lay on top. Jinx picked up a copy.

"*How to Reach Your Target Market.*" Jinx gave her a wink. "You think my business needs better marketing, Ave? Should I start a newsletter for fugitives?"

"Look underneath."

Jinx removed the second layer of books and stared. "Wow. That's a lotta cash."

"Yeah."

"What are you planning to do with it?"

"I'm supposed to give it to Sam's old partner—this guy, Cuervo, who works for Bramwell. We're meeting at Grumpy's at two."

"Probably the best move. Money like that makes people do some crazy shit. I have a duffel bag you can put it in. Make it a little easier to lug around."

"Thanks."

"So, what's in the envelope?" Jinx tore it open.

"It's a backup drive of Bramwell's computer. Sam must've made it when she stole the money. I have a copy and sent one to Kirsten, as well."

"Wow."

"If anything happens to me, send the hard drive to anyone you think might give a damn."

"Let's hope it doesn't come to that, but I got you covered. Well, let's eat before it gets cold."

As she ate, she thought about what Bobby J. had told her about Cuervo. A plan formed in her head. She shot off a text to a phone number she'd found in the emails. It was a long shot, but right now, all she had were long shots. Maybe one of them would land where she intended.

After breakfast, Avery gave Jinx half the money to put in wall safe.

"You sure about this?" Jinx asked warily.

"No, but at this point, it's the only thing that feels right."

The rest of the cash she put in the duffel bag along with her copy of the hard drive.

Jinx's phone rang and she stepped out of the room. When she returned a few moments later, she said, "Hey, I just got a tip on a fugitive we've been pursuing. You going to be okay for a little bit while Conor and I grab him?"

"I'll need to be at Grumpy's at two."

"Don't worry. Should be a problem."

The doorbell rang again, followed by a loud pounding. Definitely not another delivery.

"Conor?" Jinx called down the hall.

"Got it, love."

The front door squeaked open.

"Can I help you, lads?" Conor said from the front door.

"Phoenix PD. We're looking for Avery Byrne."

"Hardin," Jinx whispered. "Grab your stuff and follow me."

Avery grabbed her purse, computer bag, and the money. Jinx led her to the coat closet in the hall and shoved some things on the floor to the side.

"Avery Byrne?" Conor asked. "Afraid you blokes have the wrong house. No one with that name lives here."

"Don't give us your bullshit, Lucky Charms," said another voice. "We got a witness who saw Byrne get into a truck owned by your wife. We got a warrant to search the premises."

To Avery's surprise, Jinx opened a trapdoor in the closet floor. "Go down the ladder. I'll hand you your stuff," she whispered.

Avery did so, her heart pounding. The place might protect against gunfire but not a search warrant. She didn't want Jinx or Conor getting busted on her account.

She shimmied down a metal ladder and found herself in

an echoey, inky blackness. The only light came from above. She took her purse and computer bag from Jinx, followed by the bag of money. It felt heavier than she remembered. Jinx followed her down, shutting the closet door and then the trapdoor behind her, pitching them in absolute darkness.

A moment later, a bare light bulb flickered on, followed by a stream of others leading down a tunnel.

"You have an escape tunnel?"

"Conor had it built before we got together. Something he learned when his father was in the IRA. 'Always have more than one way out, love,'" Jinx said in a comical brogue.

"Where's it lead?"

"You'll see."

"What about Conor?"

"Conor's fine. He'll probably stall them. The man's a master at bullshitting. I think it's an Irish thing."

# CHAPTER 43
# FRENEMIES

HARDIN GLARED through the security door with the search warrant in his hand. "Open the door, Conor, and let us in, or we will open it for you."

He wasn't entirely sure his team could breach the door with the pry bars and battering rams they had. As security doors went, this one looked like it would take the Jaws of Life to force open. But it didn't hurt to make him think they could get through it.

"'Little pig, little pig, let me come in. Not by the hair of me chinny-chin-chin,'" Conor recited, his accent growing thicker. "Only, I suppose, you're the pigs, aren't ya?"

Hardin ignored the slight. It might have been different if he didn't know the man. Hell, he'd attended Jinx and Conor's wedding, as disastrous as it had turned out. "Conor, we're trying to help the girl out."

"Are ya now? Little birdie told me you coppers did your best to kill the poor lass."

"Open the door, asshole, or we'll arrest you for obstruction!" Valentine yelled.

"All right, all right. Don't get your trousers in a twist. I'm sure the key's somewhere around here. Damn dog must've been playing with it. Ever had a dog, detectives?"

"You're trying my patience, sir," Hardin replied.

"Dogs," Doyle said with a chuckle. "Damned beasts think ever'thing's a toy, I tell ya." The man got down on his knees and appeared to be looking underneath the furniture.

"Don't play with me, Mr. Doyle. This is a murder investigation."

"Murder, ya say. How terrible! Who d'ya say got themselves murdered?"

"I didn't."

"Ah, here it is." Doyle returned to the door and unlocked it with a goofy grin. "It was in my pocket the whole time. I must be losing my bloody mind. Probably could use some more coffee. Would you lot care for a cuppa?"

Hardin stepped into the living room. "Where's Avery?"

Valentine directed the uniformed officers to begin a systematic search of the house.

"Don't rightly know. Not really my day to keep track of the lass."

"I'm not fucking around, Conor. This is serious. She attacked my lieutenant."

"Did she now? And why would she 'ave done that, ya suppose?"

Doyle's tone was like a tick burrowing under Hardin's skin. They exchanged a knowing glance.

"Look, I know her and your wife are friends. Believe it or not, I'm trying to help Ms. Byrne."

"Are ya now? 'Cause with all due respect, I heard it kinda differently."

Valentine returned to the room and shook his head. "Tell us where she is, scumbag, or we'll charge you with conspiracy after the fact."

Hardin waved him off. "Conor, I was at your wedding. Me and my men arrested quite a few of those damned bigoted protestors, as you may recall. You owe me. Now do me the courtesy of helping me out on this one."

The joviality in Doyle's face evaporated. "Your bastard of a lieutenant's in the pocket of the Desert Mafia. Was gonna kill poor Avery over a bag of bloody cash."

"Says the man who was wanted by the Irish police for an act of terrorism," Valentine said.

"Shut yer bloody mouth, boyo, or you'll wish ya did."

"All right! Enough! Both of you!" Hardin stepped between them. "Valentine, back off. Conor, let's not escalate this. The best way for Ms. Byrne to clear her name is to come with us."

"Sorry, Hardin. Don't know where she is."

The patrol officers returned to the living room. "No sign of her, detectives."

"If you lads are quite done, I'll appreciated it if ya leave."

When they returned to the SUV, Valentine asked, "You think it's true about the lieutenant? That he's working for Bramwell?"

Hardin cruised down the neighborhood street and pulled onto McDowell before he answered. "I didn't want to think so, but Byrne's story is consistent with the security footage from the storage place. While Ross's…"

"I know, but Ross? The man chews my ass if I leave out so much as a comma on a report. The man's clean as a whistle."

"A few years ago, I would've agreed with you. But last year, he told me he was having financial troubles. Alimony increase. Daughter lost her scholarship to Stanford. But when I asked him about it after holidays, and he said everything was fine now."

"Doesn't mean he's on the take."

"After what happened last night, I'm saying it's worth looking into. Let's pull the LUDs on his phones. Office number, department cell, even his personal."

"Geez, Pierce. You serious? How we going to get a judge to sign off on that?"

"I don't know, but we follow where the leads take us."

"I don't know, man. This is career suicide."

"Trust me, I don't like this any more than you do. I've worked with LT for years. Let him crash on my couch for two weeks when Loretta kicked him out. But I will not be party to a coverup. If that means crossing the blue line, so be it. I'll take my pension and retire."

"Easy for you to say. I got another fifteen years before I'm eligible."

"That's why we cover our bases with the facts before we make any accusations or bring in PSB."

# CHAPTER 44
# MARIPOSA

AVERY SHOULDERED her computer bag and followed Jinx, carrying the money through the tunnel. After a hundred feet, they came to another ladder. Jinx climbed it, unlocked the trapdoor at the top, and went through.

Avery hefted the bag of money up to Jinx, followed by her computer and purse.

"Can ya get the lights?" Jinx asked.

Avery noticed a switch on the wall. She flicked it, and darkness once again swallowed the tunnel.

After climbing the ladder, Avery found herself in a storage room. She recognized the brands on some of the stacked boxes. She knew this place. "Is this Prowling Tiger Tattoo?"

"Give the lady a prize."

They emerged from the storage room into the main part of the tattoo studio. A scruffy-haired man in his forties with a braided beard was inking the back of a young woman who lay with her eyes closed on his padded table. Two other artists were at work in the shop as well.

The scruffy man looked up and said with a smirk, "How many times I gotta tell you, Jinx? No human trafficking through my shop."

"Hey, Weevil," Avery said.

Weevil studied her for a moment. "Well, chew me up and shit me out. Avery Byrne? Didn't recognize you as a blonde. What are *you* doing in my shop?"

Avery stiffened at the mention of her name in front of the other people in the shop. "Long story."

"You two know each other, I take it," Jinx said, taking out her phone.

"Weevil came in second in the Ink Phoenix Convention a few years ago."

Weevil laughed. "And who was it who beat me? Can't quite recall. How you been, Avery?"

"Been better."

Jinx made a call and stepped away.

"Yeah, thought I saw your sexy mug on the TV. You been a naughty girl. Murdered your girlfriend. Attacked a police officer. Kidnapped the Lindberg baby."

"Don't believe everything you hear," Avery said sourly.

"When it comes to cops, I rarely do. You're a good kid. And I know how much you loved that girl of yours. What can I do to help?"

Avery glanced at the others in the shop.

"Don't worry. We all got your back. Clients included."

"I'm just trying to stay outta jail at the moment."

"Aren't we all, darling. Aren't we all?"

Jinx hung up. "Zahara's on her way to pick us up."

"Zahara?"

"Member of my crew. Used to be an MMA fighter."

"Wait, Zahara Washington?"

"Yeah, joined up a little over a year ago after an injury sidelined her."

"I remember that fight," Weevil said. "Lost a hundred bucks on her."

"I'm sure she wasn't thrilled about it either," Jinx said. "But she's made a helluva bounty hunter."

While they waited, Avery's burner rang. "Hello?"

"Señorita Burns?" asked a thickly accented voice.

"You the one I texted?"

"Sí. How you get my number?"

"It's complicated."

"You a cop?"

"No. I'm a tattoo artist."

"It true what you say in your message?"

"Yes."

"Hijo de puta. That cabrón cost me a lot of dolares. You got my money, chica?"

Avery stared down at the bag near her feet. "I have it."

"How you get it?"

"Does it matter? You agree to the terms?"

"With pleasure."

"See you soon."

"Who was that?" Jinx asked.

"One of Bramwell's dissatisfied business associates."

A black Ford Explorer pulled up in front of the shop's plate-glass storefront. Avery instinctively stepped back, her pulse racing. "Shit, they found us."

"No, it's Zahara," Jinx replied. "Let's bounce."

"Good to see you again, Ave," Weevil said. "Give them cops hell."

Avery was too disoriented and shaken by the sudden panic attack to say anything other than "Yeah."

Jinx opened the back seat of the Explorer for her then hopped in the front passenger seat.

Avery shoved the bag of money on the back bench seat first then climbed in after it.

"Zahara, this is Avery. Avery, this is Z. Let's move."

"Caden's got our fugitive pinned down at his dealer's house," Zahara said. "We need to get over there before the guy rabbits on us again."

"Soon as we drop Avery off."

Jinx's phone rang as they drove. "Hey, babe. Yeah? Okay, we'll figure something out."

"That Conor?" Avery asked.

"Yeah. Cops searched of our house and there's now a patrol car sitting on the street out front."

"You won't get in trouble hiding me, will you?" The last thing Avery wanted was more of her friends becoming collateral damage.

"No. But I think we'll drop you off at my other place."

"Other place?"

"You'll see. Z, take us to Mariposa."

Zahara turned onto Central then back into Jinx's neighborhood. They stopped a few streets north of the Bunker. Three vehicles sat in the driveway of a small house. The lawn of Bermuda grass was high and out of control. The shrubs in front of the house covered two-thirds of the windows.

"Welcome to Casa Mariposa," Jinx said.

Avery remembered hearing about this place. Jinx had lived here until she moved in with Conor. Then she'd offered it up as a home for trans people with nowhere to go. Avery could have used a place like this when she was homeless.

Avery grabbed her purse and the money and followed Jinx inside. In the living room, someone was sitting on the couch, reading what looked like a textbook. Music drifted in from a bedroom down the hall.

"Hey, Max," Jinx said. "Meet Avery Byrne."

"Max Fields, they/them. Nice to meet you," Max said, glancing up from their book. "You moving in?"

"Avery Byrne, she/her. And no, just needed a place to crash for a few hours." Avery sat in an overstuffed chair.

"I'll leave you to it, then. Zahara and I will be back in a while to take you to Grumpy's."

"Thanks, Jinx. I don't know what I would've done without you."

"Hey, we're family. Us trans folks gotta stick together. See you soon."

After Jinx left, Avery opened her laptop again. She had another email from Hardin.

*Avery,*

*I believe your story about being kidnapped. We've watched the security feed at the storage place. You need to come in and make a formal statement so we can clear you and start an investigation into Lt. Ross. Please call me. I want to help you.*

She considered it, but until she got rid of the money, she wasn't trusting any cop, no matter who vouched for them.

## CHAPTER 45
# CHOICES AND CONSEQUENCES

AVERY SPENT the next couple of hours watching the clock and playing through likely scenarios. She kept thinking about what Bobby J. had said about vengeance. He'd been right about so many things, even with his corny mishmash of Buddhist wisdom and *Star Wars* quotes. Playing Avery the Avenger had cost the lives of the Lost Kids.

And then she thought about Melissa, who had taught her so much about being a woman and had helped Avery work through so much of her earlier trauma. Until that December day at Wesley Bolin Plaza.

Those racists who had set off the bomb all had records with suspended sentences. Maybe if someone had had the courage to hold them accountable for their earlier crimes and actually put them in prison, Melissa would still be alive.

Bramwell and his organization had to be stopped. And Avery didn't trust the so-called justice system to do it. Bramwell had been running the Desert Mafia for years and never once stood trial. Powerful straight white men like him rarely paid for their crimes. But she would make sure he would. And maybe some kid's mom or dad would be saved as a result.

She was terrified of her upcoming meeting. So many ways it could go badly. At least she would have Jinx and her team seated strategically around the restaurant to protect her.

Still, as the time grew closer, her panic grew.

At one-thirty, Jinx called. "Hey, girl. Bad news. This fugitive gave us the slip. We're closing in, but we're in East Mesa right now."

"East Mesa? Jinx! I need you here."

"I know, but this asshole killed three people in a DUI hit-and-run. And he's a Mexican national. If we don't grab him now, we could lose him forever. I'm so sorry. You think you could postpone this meet?"

She knew she couldn't. "It's fine. I'll figure something out."

She looked around the living room, trying to figure out her next move. Max had left. Avery followed the music coming from down the hall. Someone with a tight Afro haircut sat at a desk, their back to the door. They looked up when Avery knocked on the doorframe.

"Hey, I'm Avery, she/her," she said.

"Hi, I'm Ciara, the house manager. Also she/her."

The woman had a misshaped eye and a scar on her dark-brown cheek—apparently, the result of an injury of some kind.

"You're early," Ciara continued. "No, wait. You said Avery? I was expecting an Abby."

"I don't understand. Jinx dropped me off a couple of hours ago while she chased down one of her fugitives."

Understanding dawned on the woman's face. "Oh, right. Max mentioned someone was here right before they left for work. Did you need something? There's some sodas and left-over pizza in the fridge unless Max snarfed it all."

"I was wondering if you could give me a ride. Jinx was

supposed to pick me back up and take me to Grumpy's at two, but she got held up chasing one of her fugitives."

Ciara made a pained expression. "Normally, I'd be happy to. But I'm expecting a new resident, and I have to get her settled in. Tons of paperwork. Sorry."

"Yeah, okay. Thanks, anyway. I'll call an Uber."

She pulled up the app on her phone and requested a ride. Grumpy's Bar and Grill was only a few miles away. She could have run there but not while carrying the bag of money or her computer. By the time the Uber driver showed up, it was already two o'clock. Her plan to bring down Bramwell was already falling apart.

It was ten after when she walked into the restaurant. A couple in their fifties wearing matching tracksuits sat at the lunch counter, making silly faces at each other and laughing like a couple of teenagers. A scruffy-faced man who looked homeless ate soup in one of the booths. At a freestanding table, a young woman in her thirties was talking on her phone with her laptop open.

No sign of Cuervo or the other person she'd asked to meet her here. "Shit," she muttered.

"Sit anywhere," said a gruff voice. "Be with ya in a minute."

A stocky man in a dirty white apron appeared behind the lunch counter. What little hair he had was snow white. Half an unlit cigar dangled from his lips. Grumpy.

*What's the use?* she asked herself. She considered asking Grumpy if he'd seen any Latino men walk in around two o'clock but decided against it.

She took a seat at a table near the back, facing the front door. No texts or emails on her phone. As she pondered her next move, someone stepped out of the men's room.

Cuervo.

"Was afraid you'd ghosted me." He sat down opposite her. "Again."

This was the first time she'd seen him in normal lighting. For a guy, he was hot. Not that she was into guys. Still, her heart rate accelerated like a race car. Her plan was back in motion, at least partially. But would she survive the encounter without Jinx and crew as backup?

"My original ride bailed on me."

"How are you managing?"

The question surprised Avery. Did he actually care? In a whispered growl, she said, "Let's see, you people murdered my girlfriend then chased me all the way to New Mexico and shot my friend. How the hell do you think I'm doing?"

He actually looked stung by her remarks. "I am truly sorry. I never wanted any of this to happen. Sam was a good person. Impulsive sometimes. But a good person. I don't know what she was thinking by robbing the boss. But believe me, I did not torture or kill her. And I did not shoot your friend. But I eliminated the man who did."

"So you claimed."

"You saw the photo."

"I did."

A female server appeared at the table. "Hi, I'm Marisol. Do you two know what you'd like to order?" Her cheerful tone seemed almost comical considering the discussion at the table.

Avery pasted on a smile. "Could you give us a few minutes?"

"Sure." She scuttled away.

"Why'd you do it? Why kill Luther?" Avery asked.

"Payback for hurting Sam. I felt I owed you that. And to prove that you could trust me. That I have your back."

"But only if I give you the money."

"Personally, I don't care about the money. But my boss does," Cuervo explained. "Half of it belongs to the cartel. And if they don't get paid, everyone in the organization is as good as dead. So yeah, I need the money. That it?" He nodded toward the bag.

"Yeah."

"Looks a little light."

Movement caught Avery's attention. Someone had walked in and was scanning the room, obviously looking for someone.

"It's half."

"Half won't cut it with Mr. Bramwell, I'm afraid."

"I don't care. And this is as close as you're going to get to it."

Cuervo cocked an eyebrow. "What are you saying?"

A slender man with an angular face and fiery eyes sat between them. In a thick accent, he said, "What the lady is saying, cabrón, is this money belongs to me."

For a moment, Avery's pulse was racing so fast, she thought she was having a heart attack. She was sitting at a table with two murderers. Then she remembered killing that pimp when she was fifteen.

*Three murderers walk into a bar and grill…*

"Santiago." Cuervo now looked like he was the one having a heart attack.

Santiago appeared chill and terrifying all at once. His jet-black eyes radiated danger.

"Bramwell's little errand boy," he said then turned to Avery, as if Cuervo were no longer there. "How you get this dinero, chica? ¡Digame!"

She took in a deep breath. "Does it matter?"

"Not to me. It true what you say? Bramwell had my product seized at the border?"

She slowly reached into her purse and pulled her copy of Bramwell's hard drive.

"What's that?"

"Copy of Bramwell's computer. It's how I got your number. It also details how he had your shipments confiscated at the border. A guy named Paco Diaz was feeding him information."

"Paco. Que puto." Santiago's expression didn't change. Maybe he already knew. Maybe he had just had a convincing poker face.

Cuervo glared at Avery. His hands trembled. "Avery, you want to give Santiago what we owe the cartel? Fine. But the rest belongs to Mr. Bramwell. As for this"—he gestured toward the hard drive that Santiago now held—"we had a deal, and this was not part of it."

An emotional alchemy was now taking place inside her —a technique Bobby J. taught her. Fear was energy that could be redirected and channeled. She was now transforming her panic into confidence. "New deal. Santiago gets paid. You get screwed. Consider it karma for all the awful shit you and the mafia have done."

"Avery, please. I risked everything to protect you. I eliminated the man who killed Sam and shot your friend. And now you double-cross me?"

"You used to collect protection money for Bramwell."

"So?" Cuervo looked indignant.

"One of the shops on your route was a tattoo studio on Roosevelt run by Bobby Jeong. A place called Artoo Tattoo."

"That was years ago. What's that got to do with you?"

"Bobby's my dad."

"What? That can't be true. He's Chinese, and you're white."

"He's Korean, you asshole. And he took me in when I was homeless. But you shook him down every week. Didn't leave him enough to pay his lease, much less support his family. And when he refused to pay anymore, you put him in the hospital. You did this. Not Luther. You."

"Look, I'm sorry. That was a long time ago."

"Fuck your sorry. You act like you're so noble trying to

protect me. But at the end of the day, you're just another thug."

Santiago stood and shook Avery's hand. "Pleasure doing business with you, chica." He then pulled Cuervo to his feet. "Come on, ese. We gonna have a nice talk with your boss."

Cuervo pushed him away. "Get off me, bitch."

Santiago's face contorted, and his hand rested on a bulge on his right hip, concealed by his plaid shirt. "You wanna do this here, vato?"

All eyes in the place were on the two men. Avery wasn't sure whether to duck under the table, run, or freeze.

After a long moment, Cuervo marched out the front door with Santiago on his tail. The room released a collective sigh.

"What the hell was that?" Grumpy shouted once the door had shut and the men were gone. He turned to Avery. "I don't allow drug deals in my restaurant, missy. Get the hell out before I throw you out."

"It wasn't a drug deal," Avery asserted, though as she thought about it, technically, she was giving money to a drug dealer, money he was owed as part of a drug deal, though not with her.

"Whatever it was, I don't want it in my shop. Now get the hell out!"

"Can't I at least order some lunch?"

Grumpy pulled the stump of a cigar out of his mouth. "No. And I don't wanna ever see you in here again. Ya got me?"

She stood, her pulse finally slowing. She felt both invigorated and exhausted. For the first time since Sam was killed, she felt free. Hopeful. Let the bad guys kill each other. She was pretty sure who would end up on top and who would end up hanging from a bridge.

It annoyed her she was getting thrown out of Grumpy's. But she was wearing Kimi's blond wig and no makeup.

Maybe he wouldn't recognize her when she came back as herself.

She grabbed her computer bag and her purse. "Can I at least wait inside for an Uber to pick me up? Please? I wasn't dealing drugs. Do I look like a junkie to you?" she said in her most pitiful voice.

Grumpy just harrumphed and walked off. She took that as a yes and sat back down to request a ride from Uber to take her to Seoul Fire.

Twenty minutes later, the front door jingled. Avery looked up to see two men in suits—one Black, one white—striding toward her, accompanied by a swarm of uniformed cops.

"Shit."

"Avery Byrne, Detectives Hardin and Valentine. I'm going to need you to come with us."

# CHAPTER 46
# COMING CLEAN

EN ROUTE TO POLICE HEADQUARTERS, Avery called Kirsten Pasternak, the attorney she'd sent a copy of the backup drive to. Kirsten agreed to meet her and warned her not to say anything until she arrived.

An hour later, the two of them sat in the same interview room where Lieutenant Ross had questioned her the day before. Fortunately, the light on the camera was off while she consulted with her attorney.

Kirsten was tall with a deep voice that often outed her as transgender. Fortunately, this hadn't stopped her from being one of the most successful defense attorneys in the Valley—or one of the more expensive.

*Good thing I got that cash in Jinx's safe,* Avery thought, though she worried whether Kirsten would take cash, especially stolen blood money.

They discussed what had happened over the past week, including some points not to mention to the police unless absolutely necessary. When they were done, Kirsten opened the door and flagged down Hardin. He and Valentine walked in, along with a stern-looking woman, and shut the door. The camera light was on.

"I'm glad we finally have a chance to sit and talk," Hardin began.

"I talked to your fucking lieutenant, and we see how that turned out."

Avery caught a look from Kirsten and remembered her warning to stay civil.

"It is sixteen hundred seventeen hours on May 4, 2022," Hardin said, obviously for the recording. "In the room, we have Detectives Pierce Hardin and Lorenzo Valentine from Homicide and Lieutenant Selena Iglesias from Professional Standards. We're speaking with Avery Byrne, who is represented by Kirsten Pasternak."

Hardin began by going over the same ground as Ross had. Avery explained about Sam's unexpected plans to move to Seattle, her going back to the house for Rainbow the Unicorn, Avery finding her brutalized, and then Bramwell's men showing up and killing her.

"That's when I drove to my friend Kimi's house. She agreed to let me tag along on the band's tour."

Retelling the story brought up all the trauma and feelings. It felt like an oubliette in her soul, a deep dark hole pulling her in where she could be lost and forgotten forever. Horrifying and yet all too familiar after all the trauma she'd endured.

"Let's talk about the money," Lieutenant Iglesias said.

Avery stiffened. "What is it about you lieutenants and money? You all on the take?"

"Ave…" Kirsten cautioned.

"What do you mean by that?" Hardin asked.

"I never brought up any money with Ross."

"Ross mentioned it on the storage facility security feed," Iglesias clarified.

"Did you offer Lieutenant Ross a bribe to drop any charges against you?" Valentine asked.

"Fuck no!" Avery ignored the look from Kirsten. She was tired of being civil.

Iglesias's expression softened. "Did Lieutenant Ross offer to drop the charges if you gave him money?"

"Fuck you people! There were no charges! I've done nothing wrong!"

Kirsten put a hand on her arm. "Avery, why don't you explain about the money?"

"Fine. The money belonged to Theodore Bramwell. Sam..." Her voice caught with the mention of her girlfriend's name. "Sam must've stolen it from him. I guess that's why she wanted to get out of town so bad. I didn't even know about it until I looked in one of Sam's bags when I was in Tucson."

"What did you do with the money?" Hardin asked.

"I gave it to one of Bramwell's business associates. That's who I met at Grumpy's."

"Who specifically did you give it to?"

"I met with a guy named Cuervo. Julio Cuervo. He used to be Sam's partner. They both worked security for Bramwell. He agreed they wouldn't hurt me if I turned the money over to him." That was all technically true, if completely misleading.

"And who told Lieutenant Ross about the money?" Iglesias asked.

"Have to ask him. I never brought it up. Soon as he started asking about it, I knew he was working with Bramwell. He threatened to frame me for Sam's murder and put me in a men's prison if I didn't take him to it."

Iglesias looked confused. "Men's prison? Why would he do that?"

"Hello? I'm trans! That's where you people put trans women when we fuck up. Or when you think we fucked up. Or when you just want to frame us for your dirty shit. And what happens to us when you put us there?"

A heavy, uncomfortable silence filled the room. "I agreed to turn over the money to keep from being raped to death in prison for a murder I didn't commit. And then I realized he wouldn't let me go after all. He was going to kill me. And yet here I am, being grilled over it all over again." She was getting hysterical, but she didn't care.

To her surprise, it was Hardin who reached across the table and put his hand on hers. "I am really sorry for what has happened to you. And if Ross threatened you—"

"If? If? Are you fucking kidding me? Did you watch the security video from the storage place? He was holding me at gunpoint. And you people have the audacity to say, '*if* he threatened me'?"

"Ms. Byrne," Iglesias said in a consoling voice. "I am very sorry that Lieutenant Ross threatened you. I believe you. I saw the recording and heard his threats. It was wrong. More than wrong. It was criminal. That's why I am here. Lieutenant Ross is the one under investigation, not you. You are here merely as a witness, not a suspect. That's why we need you to share with us exactly what happened. To hold Ross accountable for whatever crimes he may have committed. Okay?"

Kirsten put a reassuring arm around Avery's shoulder. "Tell them what they need to know."

"I was in Tucson when I found the money. I wasn't sure what to do with it at first. Didn't even know where it came from."

"So, what did you do with it?" Iglesias continued. "Obviously, you didn't have it with you when Ross picked you up at the train station."

"I held onto it at first. Then after Chupa got shot in Las Cruces…"

"Chupa?" Iglesias looked at Hardin and Valentine.

"The member of the band who was shot in Tucson," Hardin explained. "Legal name is Marco Melendez."

Iglesias looked saddened. "I am sorry that happened to your friend, Avery. Is he okay?"

"Still in the hospital, but I'm told he'll recover."

"After your friend was shot, what did you do with the money?"

"I shipped it back to the Valley."

"To whom did you ship it?" Iglesias pressed.

"Someone I trust." Avery locked eyes with Hardin. "Someone you trust."

"Jinx Ballou," Hardin replied. "Used to be in patrol. I was her FTO."

"You sent Ballou the money?" asked Valentine.

"Yeah."

"And she put it in the storage unit?"

Kirsten whispered in Avery's ear, to which Avery nodded.

"The money was never in the storage unit. When Ross threatened me, I was afraid for my life. I took him to the storage place, hoping I could escape. I acted in self-defense."

"So, you led the lieutenant there to ambush him?" Valentine's questions were nothing but thinly veiled accusations. Was this guy working for Bramwell too?

"I was afraid for my life. I acted in self-defense."

"We understand your motives, Avery," Iglesias said. "Tell us what happened."

"You saw the security tape. You tell me."

"What happened inside the storage unit? There is no video of that."

Again, Kirsten whispered into Avery's ear.

"I defended myself against an armed man who intended to kill me. I locked him inside the unit so he couldn't hurt me or anyone else."

"And you drove away in his car?" Valentine asked.

Avery wondered if Valentine was working for Bramwell, though she hadn't seen his name on the hard drive.

"I escaped, running for my life. I drove the car to a nearby shopping center and left it."

"You stole a vehicle belonging to the Phoenix Police Department."

"My client acted completely in self-defense," Kirsten replied sternly. "She was terrified out of her mind after being threatened by one of your own, a man who wielded great power. This, after suffering the traumatic death of her girlfriend and an aggravated assault on a dear friend.

"Bottom line, the Phoenix Police Department was complicit in a conspiracy involving drug trafficking and murder to protect the head of the Desert Mafia. So don't you dare threaten my client with charges of grand theft auto. No jury would convict her of that."

"Everybody just take a breath," Iglesias said with a calming gesture. She looked at Valentine. "Detectives, as much as it pains me to admit about a fellow lieutenant, Ross clearly crossed a line. He had no business questioning Ms. Byrne, much less doing so for two hours with little recording. And then to force her to take him to that storage unit at gunpoint, where he clearly intended to harm her. We're still trying to get past the whole Black Lives Matter scandal. The press is going to have a field day with this."

Valentine harrumphed, but Iglesias ignored him.

"Is Ross working for Bramwell? I do not yet know, but I intend to dig a lot deeper. I will not fault Ms. Byrne for defending herself. And under the circumstances, I do not recommend charging her with stealing the car. Are we clear?"

"Yes, ma'am," Hardin said.

"Valentine?"

"Whatever."

"Excellent. Ms. Byrne, I appreciate your candor in this matter. And on behalf of the Phoenix Police Department, I deeply apologize for Lieutenant Ross's actions. Is there anything else we should know about what occurred between you and Lieutenant Ross or regarding the tragic death of Ms. Ferguson?"

"I've said all I have to say. Ross is a dirty cop." Avery turned to Kirsten. "You got the hard drive?"

Kirsten produced the backup drive that Avery had mailed to her from Las Cruces. She slid it to Iglesias.

"What's this?" Hardin asked.

"A backup copy of Bramwell's computer. Contains info on a lot of his contacts, including Ross and other cops, people in the county attorney's office, politicians, and our state legislature. You should have a field day with it."

Kirsten stood up. "I think we're done here."

Iglesias extended her hand to Avery. "Thank you, Ms. Byrne, for coming in and talking with us this afternoon."

Avery wanted to respond with sarcasm. But something about the lieutenant reminded her of Melissa, despite the obvious racial differences. Both were petite with short black hair. Same heart-shaped face. And there was something in the cop's voice that evoked memories of her foster mom's nurturing voice.

"Glad I could help," Avery said, shaking the lieutenant's hand.

"You need a ride back to Grumpy's?" Kirsten asked when they walked out of the building.

It was nearly five o'clock. Commuters heading home jammed the downtown streets.

Avery considered Kirsten's question. Her money was at Jinx's, and who the hell knew where she was. She wasn't angry about that. Jinx had already done so much for her. And it wasn't like she had blown Avery off. She was trying to catch a murderer so that someone else didn't have to go to bed without a mother or father.

The Gothmobile was locked up at McCobb's place. The band wasn't scheduled to be back for another few weeks yet.

She could probably pick the lock on the gate and retrieve it, if necessary, but she didn't feel like going to the trouble.

"Drop me off at Seoul Fire Tattoo," she finally said. "And thank you for your help."

"My pleasure."

"Does that mean you won't charge me?" Avery said half-heartedly.

Kirsten shook her head. "Why does everyone always ask me that?"

# CHAPTER 47
# CHILDHOOD HOME

IT TOOK Avery a few minutes to remember where she was when she woke the next morning. A familiar aroma clued her in. Jing Kwan incense. She hadn't smelled it in a while. Not since she moved out and got her open place.

She opened her eyes and recognized her old room at Bobby J.'s. Rainbow the Unicorn sat on her old dresser.

After Kirsten had dropped her off at the tattoo studio, she and Bobby had hugged and cried for what felt like hours. She had filled him in on all the details, including her meeting with Santiago and Cuervo.

Bobby didn't say anything, but she worried he disapproved of how she had handled things. But what else could she have done? She had given the cops a chance.

Avery had then spent the rest of the evening rescheduling client appointments she had missed over the past week. Most were understanding when she briefly explained she'd had a death in the family.

Jinx had called at nine to apologize for not being able to take her to Grumpy's. Avery assured her she understood. They'd agreed she would leave her money in Jinx's safe for the time being.

"Morning, Appa," Avery said when she walked into the

kitchen. The air was rich with the scent of kimchi and coffee. Her mouth watered.

"Morning, kiddo. I'm making your favorite. Kimchi eggs and blueberry pancakes. How'd you sleep?"

"I don't remember," she answered honestly. She poured herself a cup of coffee before sitting at the table. The outside of her mug was printed with "In Goth We Trust."

"That's probably a good sign." He smiled and handed her a small bowl of kimchi eggs over rice. A stack of blueberry pancakes was in the center of the table.

"How are you doing?" He met her eyes, and she knew he meant it earnestly.

"It still feels weird without Sam. Like a big block engine on my chest."

Bobby nodded. "Yes, I know that feeling. It doesn't go away, not completely. But you grow around it. It doesn't hurt as much, but it becomes a part of you, like a scar."

"It still hurts sometimes when I think of Melissa," Avery admitted, getting misty-eyed.

"I know, sweetie. Hurts me too."

"I am glad to be back home. Even if it's not Sam's house."

"Have you thought about the future at all?"

"I'm still a little worried about Bramwell coming after me."

Bobby's expression darkened. "There has been a development."

"Well, spill it, Mysterio!"

"Police found several bodies hanging from a bridge over the I-10 early this morning."

"Was Bramwell one of them?"

Bobby nodded gravely. "And Lieutenant Ross."

"Good," Avery said, taking a bite of eggs.

"I am glad you are no longer in danger from these men," Bobby said. "But do not celebrate their deaths…"

"They had it coming, Appa. And I didn't kill them."

"No, but you played a part."

"You expect me to feel guilty? These people hurt you, killed Sam, shot Chupa, and tried to kill me. I went to the police, and look where that got me. They were criminals who had double-crossed some business associates. I merely informed said associates of their unscrupulous activities and let karma work it out."

Bobby sighed. "No, I do not expect you to feel guilty. And perhaps it would have played out like this eventually without your intervention. But now your karma has also been affected."

"I think I can live with it." When Bobby still looked concerned, Avery added, "All I did was love someone who made some bad choices. And she was trying to make better ones. And when it all went to hell, I did what I had to do, not just to protect myself but to protect Kimi and the guys and even you. Am I any worse than when Luke and Han and the Rebellion blew up all those people on the Death Star?"

To her surprise, Bobby smiled. "Fair point. Sometimes life does not give us good options from which to choose. And you have a kind soul, kiddo. I am proud to be your father."

"Was Julio Cuervo among those hanging from the bridge?"

"His name was not mentioned in the news story I read."

They ate in silence for a while. "I've been thinking about the money I left in Jinx's safe."

Bobby put his fork down and met her eyes. "Yes?"

"I'm going to use part of it to pay Chupa's medical expenses plus a little extra for lost income for the shows they missed."

"That is very generous."

"Seems only fair. They stuck their necks out for me."

"And the rest?"

"I owe Kirsten a wad for representing me during the police interrogation. Though she won't take cash. I'll have to filter it through my tattoo work."

"You mean laundering it?"

"I mean declaring it as income and paying taxes on it. What else can I do? Give it to the cops? What would they do with it? Use it to buy more military-style equipment to attack protestors?"

"You make your choices. And I will love you regardless" was all he said.

"I love you too, Appa." She clasped his hand. "It's great to be home."

"Good to have you home, kiddo."

"I'm thinking eventually I'll buy a house of my own. I notice the old Peterson place down the street is up for sale."

"You would want to live so close to your nerdy old father?"

"Nerdy is good. Better than a hypermacho, transphobic father who kicks his kid out when she's thirteen," she replied.

"Come here, you." They hugged again.

Avery let the tears of gratitude stream down her face. When she released him, she asked, "You still seeing that investment banker?"

"Dana? Actually, yes. For all her straitlaced lifestyle, she has a rebellious side. She even has a couple of tattoos."

"Where?"

Bobby's face turned rosy with embarrassment. "Places you need not know about. And she adores my action figure collection."

"Sounds like love," Avery teased.

"We shall see."

# CHAPTER 48
# A MURDER OF CROWS

A FEW WEEKS LATER, Avery was preparing to work on a sleeve for a new client named Walrus. He was a big man with a bushy mustache that stretched below his chin. She had met him at some of the Sonoran Crows' hot rodder events. He'd been impressed with the work she'd done on the other Crows.

Just after she'd set up her machine and was laying out the ink in little cups, the front door opened. Kimi appeared, followed by Chupa, McCobb and Torch.

Avery jumped up and hugged each one of them. "What're you guys doing here?"

"Just got back into town," Kimi said. "Heard you had a little excitement here."

"Yeah. But I think I got it worked out." Avery turned to Chupa. "How are you feeling?"

"Better, thanks. Still a little sore."

"I'm sorry. You shouldn't have had to take a bullet for me."

He waved it off. "I survived. Now it only hurts when Kimi wants to jump my bones. But hey, a guy's gotta do what a guy's gotta do."

Kimi slapped him playfully. "TMI, honey."

"And you," Avery said to McCobb. "The big hero taking out a crazed gunman."

McCobb shrugged and blushed a deep scarlet. "If there's one thing drummers know how to do, it's hit things."

"Yeah, with my axe," Torch whined. "That guitar cost me nearly two grand."

"How's the tattoo?" she asked him.

"It itched for a while."

"You're using the antibiotic cream and moisturizer I gave you, aren't you? And not scratching it?"

"Yes, yes, and well, maybe a little. Don't worry. It's not red or infected or anything. Feeling better than it did. And Farrah loves it. She cried when she saw it. I think it was happy tears. But with pregnant women, it's hard to tell."

"I wish Murray was here. Never got to thank him for running interference for me in Las Cruces. I hope he doesn't think I was involved with cling-wrapping his car."

At that, Kimi burst out laughing, while McCobb and Torch looked chagrined.

"What?" Avery asked.

Every time Kimi started to speak, she started laughing all over again.

"Murray knows you weren't involved," Chupa said. "And he got back at the ones who were."

"Why? What happened?"

McCobb folded his arms and blushed. "Dude put baby powder in the van's AC vents. When we turned it on…"

"They looked like they'd been dipped in flour," Kimi managed to say. "Pure white from the waist on up."

Avery chuckled as both Torch and McCobb turned a darker shade. "So good you're here. I owe you all my life."

"We're glad you're safe," Kimi said.

Walrus cleared his throat.

"Oh, sorry, guys. Got a client. I'm still trying to catch up on the backlog."

"Call me about getting the Gothmobile," McCobb said. "If I'm not there, my neighbor, Ms. Bronson, has a key. She can let you in the gate."

"Thanks. And tell Murray thanks for me."

"Will do." Kimi hugged her again and gave her a kiss on the cheek.

"Sorry," Avery said as she donned a fresh pair of sterile gloves. "Friends of mine just got back from a tour with their band."

"One of them got shot?"

"My friend Chupa. The guy who killed my girlfriend chased me all the way to Las Cruces. Shot Chupa when he wouldn't tell the asshole where I was."

"Wow. That's fucked up," Walrus said. "Did you hear a couple of the Crows were killed?"

Avery began sketching out the design on Walrus's arm. "Really? Who?"

"Hatchet and Boze."

"Hatchet? He was just in here a month ago. What happened?"

"According to the cops, they died from a drug overdose. Heroin or fentanyl or some shit. But it's a fucking lie. Boze was a goddamn teetotaler, and Hatchet, well, the guy might drink a little too much at a party, but dope? Naw, he wouldn't touch that shit with a ten-foot pole."

Avery let Walrus's words sink in. If Hatchet had been a junkie, surely, she would have noticed the track marks on his arms.

Someone was out there murdering Crows. And the question was, would they stop at just two?

She knew Bobby would tell her to mind her own business and let the police handle it. But she couldn't.

"Tell me more," said Avery the Avenger.

~

## ENJOY A BONUS CHAPTER

Did you enjoy ***A Conspiracy of Ravens***? Would you like to read a free bonus chapter?

No need to subscribe. No strings attached. Just click the link below to read.

https://dharmakelleher.com/pages/a-conspiracy-of-ravens-bonus-content

## ENJOY A FREE BOOK

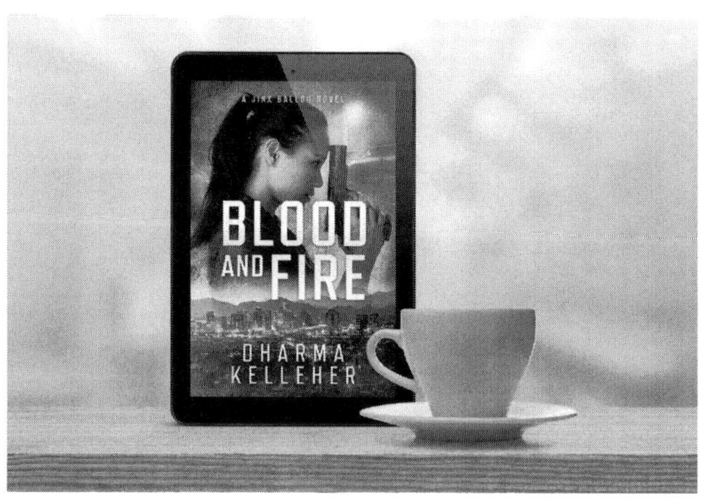


Download a free copy of *Blood and Fire*, a Jinx Ballou crime thriller, by subscribing to Dharma Kelleher's Readers Club at dharmakelleher.com / subscribe.

Join now to receive special offers, exclusive behind-the-scenes details, cover reveals, new release announcements, and to **get your free book**.

# ALSO BY DHARMA KELLEHER

**Shea Stevens Outlaw Biker Series**

Iron Goddess

Snitch

Blood Sisters

Road Rash

**Jinx Ballou Bounty Hunter Series**

Chaser

Extreme Prejudice

A Broken Woman

TERF Wars

Red Market (Coming February 2023)

**Avery Byrne Gothabilly Tattoo Series**

A Conspiracy of Ravens

A Murder of Crows (Coming October 2023)

# ABOUT THE AUTHOR

Dharma Kelleher writes gritty crime thrillers including the Jinx Ballou Bounty Hunter series and the Shea Stevens Outlaw Biker series.

She is one of the only openly transgender authors in the crime fiction genre. Her action-driven thrillers explore the complexities of social and criminal justice in a world where the legal system favors the privileged.

Dharma is a member of Sisters in Crime, the International Thriller Writers, and the Alliance of Independent Authors.

She lives in Arizona with her wife and a black cat named Mouse. Learn more about Dharma and her work at https://dharmakelleher.com.

# ACKNOWLEDGMENTS

As much as I like to keep my author business a solo act because I can be a bit of a control freak, the truth is, it really is a team effort.

Thanks to Electric Linda and the wisdom she shares on her YouTube channel about her experiences as a professional tattoo artist.

Thanks to Erin Wright and the members of the Wide Done Wright mastermind group. Erin is a treasure trove of information on how to get traction when you're an indie author who chooses not to be exclusive with Amazon. The mastermind group she created has helped me reach readers consistently.

I want to thank Lynn McNamee and her team of editors at Red Adept Editing. You make my words look good.

Last, but certainly not least, I want to thank my wife, Eileen, for her diligent support of my writing. I don't know how I lucked out to be with someone like you, but I am grateful beyond words. You are my hero.

I am truly grateful for these amazing people and for what they've contributed to this work and my author journey.

Made in the USA
Middletown, DE
09 June 2024